TU

TULA

Hannah Howe

Goylake Publishing

Goylake Publishing, Iscoed, 16A Meadow Street, North Cornelly, Bridgend, Glamorgan. CF33 4LL

Print ISBN: 978-1-7392877-1-9
EBook ISBN: 978-1-7392877-2-6

Printed and bound in Britain by Imprint Digital, Exeter, EX5 5HY

Hannah's books are available in print, as eBooks and audio books with translations in progress

The Sam Smith Mystery Series

Sam's Song
Love and Bullets
The Big Chill
Ripper
The Hermit of Hisarya
Secrets and Lies
Family Honour
Sins of the Father
Smoke and Mirrors
Stardust
Mind Games
Digging in the Dirt
A Parcel of Rogues
Boston
The Devil and Ms Devlin
Snow in August
Looking for Rosanna Mee
Stormy Weather
Damaged
Sugar Daddy

Stand-alone Novel

Saving Grace

Eve's War

Operation Zigzag
Operation Locksmith
Operation Broadsword
Operation Treasure
Operation Sherlock
Operation Cameo
Operation Rose
Operation Watchmaker
Operation Overlord
Operation Jedburgh
Operation Butterfly
Operation Liberty

Ann's War

Betrayal
Invasion
Blackmail
Escape
Victory

The Olive Tree: A Spanish Civil War Saga

Roots
Branches
Leaves
Fruit
Flowers

To my family, with love

KINGS COUNTY ASYLUM

PATIENT ADMISSION FORM

Patient's Name: Tula Bowman

Title: Miss

Gender: Female

Address: 1, Irvine Avenue, Manhattan Beach, Brooklyn, New York

Age: 24, born July 30, 1905

Height: 5′ 5″

Weight: 110 lbs

Occupation: Actress

Next of Kin: Gregory Powell, actor (fiancé)

Admitted: July 7, 1930

Voluntary: Yes

Criminal Court Order: No

Institution Transfer: No

Principal Cause: Nervous Exhaustion

Secondary Causes: To be determined

Length of Time Patient Has Experienced These Afflictions: Six Months

Previously Certified: N/A

Previously Recovered: N/A

Physical Health: Undernourished, otherwise good

Epileptic: To be determined

Involuntary Fits: To be determined

Women Trouble: No

Suicidal: No

Alcoholism: No

Tuberculosis: No

Egotism: No

Exposure in Military: No

Political Charisma: No

Excessive Novel Reading: Yes

Immoral Living: No

Religious Excitement: No

Superstition: No

Self-Abuse: No

Business Anxiety: No

Abandoned by Husband: No

Brain Injury: To be determined

Opium Habituation: No

Ward Assignment: Ward 2

Attending Physician: Dr R.M. Brooks

Doctor's Notes: This patient admitted herself to our care after collapsing whilst filming a "movie", *The Bridge*. This represents her sixth collapse in as many months. I considered that her menstrual cycle might be a reason for these collapses, but after a physical examination, I dismissed the possibility.

My initial diagnosis is "nervous exhaustion" brought on by over-work, under-nourishment and a general state of hyperactivity.

This patient's grandmother and mother were admitted to this asylum, in 1898 and 1921, respectively. Both the grandmother and mother died in the asylum. Their records suggest that they were troubled by epilepsy and general mania.

Given the family's medical history, there is a likelihood that this patient is suffering from epilepsy. Further tests and observation will be required to determine if she is suffering from epilepsy.

Until the facts of the matter are established, I have prescribed sedatives, to wit: chloral hydrate, plus a course of hydrotherapy and rest.

Signed: Dr R.M. Brooks, Senior Physician, Kings County Asylum

Update, July 14, 1930. After further tests and observation, I have ruled out epilepsy. This patient has been working up to eighteen hours a day on her "movie". Furthermore, her eating habits are poor. Therefore, I am inclined to believe that she is suffering from nervous exhaustion. However, her general manner leads me to suspect that other factors are at play.

Update, July 20, 1930. This patient represents no danger to herself or our other patients. She spends her time quietly – reading and writing. She complained that the chloral hydrate is making her feel physically unwell, so I have suspended that medication. She also complained about the hydrotherapy, but I informed her that we must proceed with that treatment. I am of the opinion that to regain her mind, in the short-term at least, this patient requires a prolonged period of rest.

Update, August 1, 1930. Close observation of this patient has revealed her to be quiet, shy and of a nervous disposition. I am led to believe that these traits are at odds with the roles she plays on the

"Silver Screen".

Update, August 12, 1930. To further understand this patient, I troubled myself to watch four of her "movies" – *Kiss Me Twice*, *The Parisian*, *The Primitive Path* and *The Bee Hive*.

Her performances in these movies are far removed from her natural persona. While on the ward and walking around the grounds, this patient has displayed no signs of schizophrenia. However, given the dramatic dichotomy between her behaviour in this facility and her performances on the "Silver Screen", I feel that we should consider that this patient is suffering from schizophrenia.

Update, August 17, 1930. This patient does not hear voices or experience hallucinations. Therefore, I am confident to assert that she does not suffer from schizophrenia. I hold the opinion that this patient will respond well to psychotherapy, and this is an avenue I feel that we should explore.

Update, August 25, 1930. This patient performed well in the mental agility and intelligence tests. Her schooling was sub-average, but she displays above average intelligence. I have troubled myself to watch four more of her movies – *Slave to Love*, *Four*

Can Play, Vixen and *The Pleasure Seeker*. I believe that these "movies" are classed as "romantic dramas" and that they are very popular with womenfolk these days.

I also sought the opinions of experts in the field of motion pictures. All were eager to inform me that this patient possesses a great natural talent for acting.

Update, August 28, 1930. I feel that we should address the following questions: this patient is a great dramatic actress – is she now acting the part of a psychotic, and for what reason? I can find no satisfactory answer to these questions and, therefore, hold the opinion that her condition is genuine.

Update, September 2, 1930. This patient received a visit from her fiancé. She was pleased to see him and I detected genuine affection between the couple. It is not possible to measure love on a scientific scale. However, I am of the opinion that these two people are in love.

Update, September 4, 1930. This patient wishes to leave our facility. I cautioned that this would not be a good idea on the grounds that she still requires a period of rest and care. With reluctance, she agreed with me.

Update, September 12, 1930. Through rest, this patient continues to make steady progress. In the near future, I believe that she will be strong enough to leave our facility. However, my concern is that unless we identify her underlying issue, or issues, she will be prone to a relapse.

Update, September 22, 1930. This patient continues to complain about the hydrotherapy treatment. Therefore, I have brokered a deal with her. I informed her that I would suspend the hydrotherapy treatment if she would record her daily thoughts in her notebook. She spends many hours writing in her notebooks and I believe that this exercise would represent good therapy. Furthermore, I am now convinced that an underlying factor is the root cause of her nervous nature, and that to strengthen her nerves we need to identify that root cause. This patient agreed to my request. I have supplied her with fresh notebooks and pens, and I will read her notes as they unfold.

My Mother

I had a large number of fantasies as a child. I lived in a dream world, probably to escape the reality of my life in Brooklyn. In my fantasies, my mother was a princess, with royal blood. In reality, her folks arrived from Britain; they landed in New York sometime in the 1830s and settled in Brooklyn. In my fantasies, my mother's folks were related to kings and queens, and that made my mother special.

My mother, Alicia, looked like a princess. She had long flaxen hair, which she wore in a ponytail, piercing blue eyes, a regal nose and perfect skin. She was slender, with not an ounce of spare flesh. She was short, yet her presence dominated a room; everyone stopped and stared at my mother.

Furthermore, my mother used to sit on her chair and stare into the empty space for hours, as though she were in a trance. A princess from Spain used to do that. I read about her in a book, so it was only natural for my ten-year-old mind to associate my mother with the Spanish princess.

My mother was born to have servants. I was her servant. My earliest memories are based on helping my mother, on fetching things for her, on running errands for her. When I was young, my mother didn't tend to me, I tended to her. I loved my mother. I'd do anything for her.

We were living in a brownstone, in bleak, sparsely furnished rooms above a dilapidated Baptist Church. Given our surroundings, some people might consider me silly for fantasising about my mother, for thinking that she was a princess. But I'm not silly. I'm gullible and naive at times, but I'm not silly. Even my teachers said that I was smart. I was bullied at school because I was smart. Sometimes, you can't win.

I've always realised that these fantasies about my mother were just that, fantasies. Although my mother sometimes said that my mind was 'away with the fairies', I could always distinguish between fantasy and reality. I've always had a good grip on reality. Sometimes, to my detriment, that grip has been too strong.

In my fantasies, my mother was a princess, so I suppose that made me a princess too, but I never thought of myself like that. I was just a working girl from Brooklyn, and my mother used to remind me of that fact.

"Ya jest a woikin goil from Brooklyn," she used to say. "Don't put on no airs or graces; you ain't nothing special."

Sometimes, my mother could be mean to me. But that wasn't her fault. She used to have episodes when she'd go all peculiar. She used to sit there, as though frozen, barely breathing. I used to massage her throat, back and chest, to get her to breathe. Then she'd return to me with a gasp.

Sometimes, my mother was violent towards me. But that wasn't her fault. She became violent because of her sickness. I wondered if I'd suffer from the same sickness, but I've never been violent with anyone. If anything, I'm too passive.

My mother used to attack me because of her sickness. I don't think that I have that sickness. I try to be kind to people. I try to do good.

One area where my mother and I did clash was over my love for the movies. I'll explain.

When I was ten, I used to lie on my bed and read my movie magazines, *Photoplay* and *Motion Picture*. I used to read every word in those magazines, and study all the pictures.

One day, I was so engrossed in *Motion Picture* that I didn't hear my mother enter my bedroom. She walked over to my bed, scowled at me and said, "Tula, what are you doing?"

I knew that I was in trouble because my mother had used my name; she always used my name when I was in trouble. Anyway, I tried to hide my movie magazine under my pillow. Then, I turned to her and said, "Nothing; I ain't doing nothing."

"I will be the judge of that," my mother said.

"What have you hidden under your pillow?"

"Nothing," I said.

"Don't lie to me, Tula!"

My mother screamed at me. Her face went red. She could look scary when she was angry. Sometimes, she even scared my father.

"Show me what you hid under your pillow."

My mother held out her hand. I bit my lower lip. I wondered if I could push my movie magazine further, so that it fell behind my bed. However, there were rat droppings behind my bed, and I didn't want my magazine to fall into the goo, so I handed it over to my mother.

My mother snatched my magazine from my outstretched hand. She turned a page and stared at a picture. My mother's eyes looked like two blue ice cubes when she was angry, they looked so cold. In a frenzy, she tore my magazine to shreds and scattered the pages like confetti, all over the wooden floorboards.

"You will not read these sinful magazines," my mother said. "They will turn you into a whore." When she was angry, my mother pronounced the word 'whore' as 'hoor', and she was blazing angry now. "You'll end up like Submarine Lil."

Submarine Lil was one of our neighbours. I understood why the local men called her by that name. I understood why scores of men visited her every day. Everyone knew and understood. It was that sort of neighbourhood.

I'd heard my mother's words before; they didn't disturb me. However, the sight of my movie magazine, torn into little pieces, made me cry.

"You deserve a punishment," my mother said. "How shall I punish you?"

I held out my hand and my mother nodded.

"Follow me into the kitchen," she said.

I followed my mother into the kitchen where she picked up a long wooden spoon. I held out my hand and my mother rapped my knuckles hard, five times. I cried. I cried a lot as a child. I'm easily moved to tears now.

My mother didn't want to beat me. I'm sure it upset her when she beat me, but she was doing it for my own good. I had to learn my lesson. But sometimes I could be stubborn. I could be slow to learn my lessons. I was slow to learn over the movie magazines. I loved the movies so much. Sneak-reading my magazines was worth a knuckle beating.

As a ten-year-old child, I was sure that my mother loved me, even though she never said that she loved me, even though she never used those words.

Now, having written these words, I'm not sure what to make of my mother. I was hoping for clarity. But, in my tired state, I have discovered more confusion. I hope enlightenment will reach me as I make more notes.

My Father

My father was a big man with fine, slicked-back hair, bushy eyebrows, weary eyes, a small chin, and a big nose. I guess he wasn't handsome, but he was my hero.

My father, Stanley, could sing. He had a beautiful voice, which he used to entertain the patrons at the bars, where he worked. On good days, the patrons would flick a dime or two his way, and that money would supplement his meagre wages.

My father had his vices, principally alcohol and cigarettes. Sometimes my mother would scream at him and accuse him of visiting Submarine Lil. I don't know the truth of that because I used to place my hands over my ears whenever they argued.

Work was scarce. Often my father had to travel. He'd be gone for months on end, but would always return to us, usually with a pay-packet, food, or some knick-knacks he'd picked up on his travels. Most of my childhood toys came from my father's travels.

I was lying on my bed, reading the latest issue of *Photoplay*, when I heard a creak in the hall, from the floorboards. My instincts told me to hide my movie magazine, in case my mother had returned home early from her church meeting. However, another creak confirmed that the footsteps were heavy, my father's footsteps, so I relaxed and turned a page.

My father staggered into my bedroom. He was drunk – no surprise there. He steadied himself against the doorframe then adjusted a brown paper parcel, which nestled under his left arm. He offered me a watery smile and said, "Hello, Tula; how's it going?"

"Fine," I said.

"Reading *Photoplay*?"

"Yes," I said.

My father was relaxed about my movie magazines, and my interest in the movies. Indeed, he liked to borrow my magazines after I'd finished reading them. I don't think he read my magazines; he liked to look at the pictures of the glamorous actresses.

"I'd like you to do me a favour," my father said.

"Sure," I said.

"I want you to deliver this parcel to a man on Brooklyn Bridge."

I sat up, closed my magazine and frowned. "How will I recognize him?" I asked.

"He'll be wearing a porkpie hat," my father said, "with a chequered band around the crown.

Also, he's got a beard, a big, heavy, bushy beard. It's white, like pure driven snow."

"Like Father Christmas," I said.

My father laughed. For some reason, he found my comment funny. "Yeah; just like Father Christmas."

I jumped up from my bed and collected the parcel. I shook the parcel, but it made no sound. "What's in it?" I frowned.

"Never you mind that," my father said. "Just deliver the parcel. The man will give you thirty dollars."

"Thirty dollars," I whistled. That was more money than my father earned in a week.

"Yeah," my father smiled. "Thirty dollars. Call at Gadsden's on the way home and buy me a packet of cigarettes."

My father staggered into our living room. He collapsed on to the couch and within minutes was asleep, his snores threatening to disturb our neighbours.

I grabbed the parcel, my tam, and my pea coat. I placed some coins in the pocket of my pea coat, to pay for the tram fair, then set off to meet 'Father Christmas'.

It wasn't snowing on that particular December morning, but it was bitterly cold, so I pulled my pea coat tight around my slender frame and fixed my tam firmly on my head.

At the Brooklyn Bridge, I searched for 'Father Christmas'. The bridge was huge, the longest suspension bridge in the world. Some people said it was 1,500 paces long. I tried to count the paces once, but gave up when I reached 176.

A steamship passed under the bridge, along with three smaller ships; those ships had huge white sails. I turned and looked for a man sporting a big white beard, but couldn't find him.

I couldn't find 'Father Christmas', but I did spy a man with a movie camera. He was filming pedestrians as they walked across the bridge. I had no idea why he was filming them, but it occurred to me that if I walked past his camera, I would be in his movie.

So, I adjusted my tam and parcel, and walked past his camera. I looped around and did this four times. I've no idea why I did this four times, maybe to make sure that I appeared in his movie.

Maybe a big movie producer would see me and invite me to be in his film. My mind ran riot at the possibilities. Today, I was Tula Bowman, a nobody; tomorrow, I could be a star; not that I wanted to be a star; I just wanted to act in movies.

Of course, aged ten I didn't understand how the movie system worked or how unlikely it would be for someone to catapult me overnight into fame.

But walking along the Brooklyn Bridge, I lived that fantasy. In fact, I became so engrossed in the fantasy that I failed to notice when someone snatched my father's parcel from underneath my arm.

At that moment, I caught sight of 'Father Christmas', but I ran away from him. I ran along the length of the bridge, looking for the thief. I wore myself out, looking for the thief. Eventually, I had to concede defeat. Trembling with anxiety, I made my way home.

I had enough money for the tram fare, but not for my father's cigarettes. So, I sneaked into Gadsden's and when old Mr Gadsden wasn't looking, I stole a packet of Chesterfields. I hoped that the Chesterfields would save me from a belt-beating.

At home, I found my father asleep on the couch. My mother wasn't home. I assumed that she was still at her church meeting. She spent hours at the church meetings. She was usually the first to arrive and the last to leave.

Deliberately, I kicked the leg of the couch to disturb my father. If he was going to give me a belt-beating for losing his parcel, I wanted to get it over and done with before my mother arrived home and added her ten cents' worth.

My father yawned. He stretched his arms above his head, then rubbed the sleep from his eyes. He stared at me without really seeing. Eventually, he focused his eyes and offered me a tired smile.

"You got my thirty dollars, Tula?"

"I lost the parcel," I said. "I'm sorry. I deserve a belt-beating."

I'd practiced my words and my look on my way home. I knew that if I apologised it would take some of the sting from my father's anger. Also, I was very good at cute looks; I could pout better than all the leading movie stars.

Despite my apology and pout, my father glared at me. His fingers toyed with his belt buckle. I knew what was coming, so I held out my hand and revealed the packet of Chesterfields.

"I stole these for you," I said, "from Gadsden's."

My father eyed the Chesterfields and, slowly, he smiled. He grabbed the cigarettes, took me into his arms and smoothed my hair.

"Not to worry, princess," he said. "I'll get hold of another parcel. Meanwhile, make me some soup. God knows where your mother is, and I'm hungry. Make me some soup, and tell me what you saw on the bridge."

I made chicken soup for my father; it was nothing special, just a bowl of gruel. While he slurped his soup, I told him about the cameraman and his filming, and the ships that passed under

Brooklyn Bridge.

My father didn't beat me, even though I deserved a beating. My father praised me for cooking the soup. He never mentioned the parcel again.

My father was my hero.

My Teacher

For most of my childhood, I attended the local school. It was a big school in that the main building was huge with lots of classrooms. However, the schoolyard was too small, which meant lots of jostling, and fighting amongst the pupils. The smallest incident could spark a fight.

When the fighting broke out, the children would gather around the two kids brawling and yell, "Fight! Fight! Fight!"

I must admit, I was drawn to these fights, as a spectator; they held a primitive fascination, even though most of the brawls were centred on two boys arguing over who stole whose marbles or conkers.

Davy Coombes was the biggest brawler in the school. He was also the tallest and heaviest pupil. Indeed, he was bigger than all the male members of staff. He was something of a freak in that he was too big for his age. Added to that, he was emotionally young for his age, and easily provoked. As sure as the school bell would ring for home time, you could guarantee that at some point during the day we'd witness a Davy Coombes brawl.

My favourite teacher was Mr Hopkins. He was strict, but fair. Mr Hopkins was a man of medium height. He possessed thinning grey hair, combed back from his forehead, blue rheumy eyes, large ears and a bulbous nose. The lines on his forehead formed intricate patterns, and they used to fascinate me for some reason.

Habitually, Mr Hopkins wore small wire-framed spectacles and a bowtie. He wore a different bowtie every day. Sometimes his bowties were spotted, or they contained a thin pinstripe. They were colour-coded: if it were a Monday, he'd wear a red bowtie, a Tuesday, a blue bowtie, and so on. If ever you were uncertain about which day of the week it was, you would look at Mr Hopkins' bowtie and say, "Green, ah yes, it must be Friday."

Actually, it was a Thursday when this incident occurred. As usual, I was daydreaming in class, thinking about the latest articles I'd read in *Photoplay* and *Silver Screen*. Gallantly, Mr Hopkins was trying to educate our unruly class about angles and cuboids, circumferences and something called pi. I thought a pie was a pastry you baked in an oven and that he was trying to inform us how you divided it up equally.

However, by the time that Mr Hopkins mentioned that pi equalled the circumference divided by the diameter, my mind was dancing with my favourite actress, Mary Pickford.

Eventually, the school bell broke my reverie.

Home time. My classmates gathered up their books and cheered. I was reaching for my books, when I found Mr Hopkins towering over me.

"Not you, Tula," he said. "I want a word with you; you will stay behind."

"She's gonna get a beating," my schoolmates chorused.

"She's gonna get the cane."

"He's gonna give her a sore behind."

For some reason, everyone giggled at that remark, everyone except Mr Hopkins. He removed his spectacles, polished them on a yellow cloth, and stared at me through his blue rheumy eyes.

"Where were you this afternoon?" Mr Hopkins asked.

"I was here," I said, "sitting at my desk."

"You were sitting at your desk," he said. "However, your mind was away with the fairies; tell me, child, which land did you visit today?"

I shuffled uncomfortably on my seat. I didn't want the cane, not today, not after a recent beating; I'd upset my mother, I'm not sure how, but she'd taken the long wooden spoon to my behind. The cheeks of my behind were still sore. I didn't want the cane.

"I was concentrating," I said. "I heard every word you said."

Mr Hopkins eased his spectacles on to the

bridge of his bulbous nose. He peered over the rims of his spectacles and glared at me.

"I will reward the truth," he said. "However, I will punish lies."

Mr Hopkins knew that I was lying, so I decided to tell him the truth.

"I was thinking about Mary Pickford," I said, "and the way she uses her eyes in her movies."

"Tell me more about Miss Pickford and her eyes," Mr Hopkins said. "I am keen to hear your opinion."

"Well," I said, "in *Cinderella*, she conveyed so many emotions through her eyes, and I don't just mean by crying; she managed to smile with her eyes as well, and she used them to alert the audience to danger."

Mr Hopkins nodded. He adjusted a chair and sat beside me. "You are very perceptive," he said, "for an eleven-year-old."

"I study all the leading actresses," I said. "I read about them in the movie magazines."

Once again, Mr Hopkins smiled. He reached across and patted the back of my hand, in paternal fashion. He noticed the bruising on my knuckles, and frowned.

"I fell," I said. "I grazed my knuckles on the yard."

Mr Hopkins knew that I was lying. I think he

knew that my mother always rapped me over my knuckles with her wooden spoon. However, he said nothing; he allowed the moment to pass.

"In my younger days," Mr Hopkins said, "I trod the boards, albeit at an amateur level. I made notes about my observations; I recorded my opinions on acting; I created a blueprint for actors, a plan for how one could refine one's craft. Would you care to read my notes?" he asked.

"I'd love to!" I said. In my excitement, I jumped up. Then, I remembered my place and sat down again.

"Excellent," Mr Hopkins smiled. "I will regale you with my notes tomorrow. You may borrow them, take them home and read them over the weekend."

I was overjoyed, overwhelmed with Mr Hopkins' kindness, his generosity. However, I frowned, stared at my desk and fidgeted with my pencil.

"Is something troubling you, child?" Mr Hopkins asked.

"My mother," I said. "If she discovers your notes, she'll burn them."

Mr Hopkins pursed his lips. He adjusted his spectacles. He offered me a solemn inclination of his head. "I understand," he said. "In that case, I shall set aside a time so that you can read my notes in class."

I thanked Mr Hopkins. Then I made my way home. I walked the two miles as though I were floating on air.

An Episode

Mr Hopkins set aside some classroom time so that I could read his notebook and learn about acting. This caused resentment amongst the other pupils because while I was reading Mr Hopkins' notebook they were ploughing through *The Adventures of Tom Sawyer*. Everyone in my class, it seemed, hated reading; it required too much concentration. Everyone hated reading, except me.

At home time, Mr Hopkins dismissed the class. He pulled up a chair and sat beside me at my desk. "Tell me, Tula," he said, "what did you learn from my notes?"

"Lots of things," I said.

"Be specific," he said. "Details are important, in life and in acting."

I knitted my eyebrows together and summoned up my concentration. I recalled Mr Hopkins' notes and the lines that made an impression on me.

"The eyes," I said, "the eyes are very important in acting."

"Correct," Mr Hopkins said. He removed his spectacles and wiped his eyes with a handkerchief. His eyes always looked sore. I wondered if he was going blind. "My notes mainly refer to stage acting, but many of the skills of the stage are transferable to the movie screen."

"However," Mr Hopkins said, "it's also important to recognise the differences. On the stage, you need to project to the audience, to people sitting in the front seats, and those sitting at the back. You need grand gestures, eye-catching gestures. The movie camera, on the other hand, magnifies everything; just a subtle movement of your eyes can convey a strong mood or emotion; when you act before a movie camera, less is more."

"And facial expressions," I said. "You must remember to express what your character is thinking, and not what you are thinking."

"Correct," Mr Hopkins said. "At all times, you must stay in character. You must understand your character and express her emotions."

"Mary Pickford does that," I said.

"She does," Mr Hopkins agreed. "However, you must not fall into the trap of projecting your character through the lens of a Mary Pickford performance; you must project your character as you see her; do you understand what I mean?"

Once again, I knitted my eyebrows together and summoned up my concentration. "I think so," I said.

"Good girl," Mr Hopkins smiled. "In a few months," he said, "I hope to arrange a play for the class to perform. I would like you to take a lead role in that play."

"Wow!" I said. "Thank you, Mr Hopkins."

"I believe that you will do well," he said. "But first we must get the delights of pi and trigonometry into that head of yours." He leaned forward and offered me a censorious frown. "From now on, you will concentrate in class, won't you, Tula Bowman?"

"For sure," I said.

"Good girl," Mr Hopkins said. "Join me at my desk; I have something to show you."

I stood and followed Mr Hopkins to his desk. There, he produced a satchel and from that satchel, he removed a large collection of movie magazines. All my favourites were there, including *Photoplay*, *Silver Screen*, *Motion Picture*, *Movie Weekly* and *Screenland*.

"I no longer have any use for these magazines," Mr Hopkins said. He removed his spectacles and polished them on a cloth. "My eyes are not what they used to be. I would like you to accept these magazines, as a gift. I believe that you will offer them a better home."

"Wow!" I said. "Thank you, Mr Hopkins."

"But keep them away from your mother," he said. "I don't want to cause any upset in your home."

As Mr Hopkins spoke, we both looked at my

knuckles; the bruises were out now; therefore, I could move my fingers with more freedom.

I stuffed Mr Hopkins' movie magazines into my school bag. Then I made my way home. Once again, I drifted past the smoking industrial chimneys, the railway line and the streetcars, as though I were walking on air.

At home, I found my father in the living room, slumped in a chair. He was sound asleep, snoring. The depths of his snores told me that he was drunk. I wished that he didn't drink so much. However, he worked in a bar, so I suppose drinking was only natural.

I tiptoed past my father and entered the kitchen. There, I found my mother sitting on a straight-backed wooden chair. She was staring at the stove, but nothing was cooking. I recognised her look; she'd drifted into one of her 'episodes'.

I feared that, one day, my mother would drift into an episode and not return to us. Fighting back tears, I dropped my school bag on to the floor, and the movie magazines spilled out. No matter, I could tend to them later. First, I had to bring my mother out of her episode.

Crouching beside my mother, I rubbed her back. I also rubbed her chest and throat. I had no idea what I was doing, no idea if my caresses were offering any medical assistance. I only knew that when I did this in the past, my mother came out of her episodes.

I suppose I should have run for a doctor. However, we couldn't afford the doctor's fees. Anyway, I don't think the doctors understood what caused my mother's episodes.

I continued to rub my mother's back, and mumble words into her ear. With a gasp, she returned to me. This was the normal pattern of events; she always gasped when she regathered her senses.

Slowly, my mother turned her head. She blinked, refocused her eyes and glared at me. "What are you doing, Tula?" she asked.

"Nothing," I said, "I ain't doing nothing."

I always used those words when my mother emerged from an episode; it was far easier to use those words than to explain the events that had just transpired.

"What's them on the floor?" my mother asked, pointing a spindly finger at my movie magazines. Her glare intensified; she looked shocked, as though she'd seen the Devil. "Magazines," she said. "Where did you get them? Get rid of them this instant!"

"Yes, mother," I said. I feared that she'd drift off, into another episode, so I dropped to my knees and gathered up the magazines. "Don't worry, I'll rip them up and burn them; I'll place them on the fire."

"You'll keep them," my father said.

I looked up and found my father standing by the kitchen door. He was leaning against the doorframe, for fear of falling over.

"The child will keep them," my father said, "and I will not hear a word said against it." He walked over to the stove and picked up an empty pan. "Woman," he glared at my mother, "I'm hungry; where's my dinner? Make it," he ordered. "And after dinner, you'll darn my socks."

I glanced at my father's feet and noticed that his big toes were poking through his socks. They looked so funny. I couldn't help myself, I laughed.

My mother glared at my father, then frowned at me. She regarded fun, indeed all forms of pleasure, as sinful.

I knew that my mother wouldn't darn my father's socks and that that task would fall to me.

My father was strict with my mother, but I believed that he loved her. She didn't love him; I knew that for a fact. She didn't love him, and I found that very sad.

Bullying

I tried to keep my clothes clean, but it wasn't easy. My mother washed my clothes every week, but she wasn't the greatest washerwoman. Mrs Jilks, who lived on the next block, was the best washwoman in our corner of Brooklyn. However, we couldn't afford her modest fees.

My clothes were old and frayed. Initially, they belonged to a cousin who was four years older than me. My mother wouldn't touch a darning needle – apparently, when she was younger, she'd pricked her thumb with a needle and developed blood poisoning – so I tried to darn my clothes myself, the best I could, but I wasn't very good.

I saved my 'best' clothes for school but, compared to the other children, I still looked shabby. One day, I was standing inside the school gate when a gang of girls approached me.

Mary-Jane Sinclair tugged at a thread in my cardigan and the garment started to unravel. "Look at that," she said, "Tula wears tramp's clothes. I bet she sleeps with the tramps."

The other girls found that hilarious and started to laugh.

"Tula is a tramp," Lauren Bonetti said, "just like her mother."

"My mother isn't a tramp," I replied with all the indignation I could muster.

"Yes she is," Zelda Walters said. "I know because my father used to visit her when Submarine Lil was busy."

"You're lying!" I yelled, and the girls in the gang started to laugh.

"Tula's a tramp," Mary-Jane Sinclair said, "and her clothes prove it."

"She is a tramp," Zelda Walters said, "but Mr Hopkins treats her like the teacher's pet."

"Yeah," Mary-Jane Sinclair said, "how come you're the teacher's pet?"

"It's because Tula is an ac-tress," Lauren Bonetti said, stretching the word 'actress' over two syllables. "She's gonna be in the movies, ain't you, Tula?"

Before I could reply, everyone laughed again.

"If you're an ac-tress," Mary-Jane Sinclair said, "do some ac-ting for us."

"I can't," I said.

"Why not?" Lauren Bonetti frowned.

"Because I need a script. Actresses take direction from a script, and a director."

"Hark at Little Miss La-De-Da," Zelda Walters said. "Who does she think she is, Mary Pickford?"

"How about this for a script," Mary-Jane Sinclair said, screwing up her freckled face, stamping on my foot with some venom.

"Oh, look," Lauren Bonetti laughed, "Tula's acting; she acting the part of a girl with a broken foot."

Everyone laughed as I hopped around in agony.

"How do I become the teacher's pet?" Mary-Jane Sinclair asked. "Stop hopping around like a flea and tell me."

"I don't know," I said. "Anyway, I'm through talking with you."

"No you're not," Mary-Jane Sinclair said. "I decide when we quit talking."

"We quit talking now," I said. "I'm going into class."

I pushed my way through the gang, but Mary-Jane Sinclair grabbed hold of my shoulder. She spun me around and pushed me on to the yard. Annoyed, I scrambled to my feet and grabbed hold of her hair. Flailing blindly, she tried to slap me, but I dodged her blows.

"Fight! Fight! Fight!" Everyone chanted, and a crowd gathered round.

I grappled with Mary-Jane Sinclair. We kicked each other's shins, grabbed each other's hair and tried to scratch each other's faces. Mary-Jane Sinclair had lice in her hair. However, I refused to let go.

Then, during a clinch, Mary-Jane Sinclair surprised me. She whispered into my ear. "Let me win. Fall to the ground, and I won't hurt you."

I stared at her with some suspicion and continued to tug her hair.

"It's the truth," she said. "I'll spit on it if you'll let me."

I released my grip on Mary-Jane Sinclair's hair and she spat on the ground, pledging her word. I allowed her to push me to the ground. At that point, she wheeled away in triumph.

"I'm the winner!" Mary-Jane Sinclair said.

"Yeah," Zelda Walters said, "you beat that tramp good and proper."

"Her dirty clothes are all covered in dust," Lauren Bonetti said, and everyone peeled away, the schoolyard reverberating with their laugher.

As the crowd dispersed, I stood and dusted myself down. I was still brushing the dirt from my cardigan when a boy approached. Around my age, he was tall and lean, with shaggy fair hair. He had a squint in his right eye, which gave the impression that he was staring at his nose.

"Are you all right?" he asked.

"Yeah," I said. "I fell on purpose. I let her win. I could have licked her, if I'd wanted."

"Sure," the boy grinned. "I'm Finn O'Malley."

"I'm Tula," I said. I glanced at a book that

nestled under his left arm. "What you got there?"

"*The Adventures of Huckleberry Finn*," he said. "My father named me after this book, so I always carry it around."

"That's a strange thing to do," I frowned.

"Not really," Finn said. "Not when a book has your name on it."

"Have you read the book?" I asked.

"I've read the cover," Finn smiled.

"Yeah," I said, "but have you read the pages."

"You don't need to read the pages if you've read the cover," Finn said. "If you've read the cover that counts as reading the book."

"You're not making any sense," I said. "Has someone bashed you on the head? Or do you have a fever?"

"I'm fine," Finn said. "But you have a graze on your head. Let me take a look."

Finn parted my hair and prodded my abrasion.

"Ouch!" I yelled. "You're worse that Mary-Jane Sinclair."

"Sorry," Finn said. "I was only trying to help."

"That's okay," I said. "And don't you worry about my graze. I bruise easily and heal real quick."

We walked on, towards the school building. On a grey day like today, the large building offered a foreboding air.

On the concrete steps, Finn said, "Mary-Jane

Sinclair is a bully."

"Yeah," I sighed. "And don't I know it."

"She bullies me too," Finn said.

I gazed at his face, and understood the reason. "Because of your eye," I said.

"Yeah," Finn said. "I was born with a cack eye." He stared at me with his good eye, searched my face for my true feelings. "Do you think I look weird?" he asked.

"I think you look cute," I said.

Finn smiled. "Maybe we could be friends."

I smiled back. "Maybe we could," I said.

The bullying at school, over my appearance, my ambitions to become an actress, and my status as the 'teacher's pet', continued to the point where I developed a stammer; whenever I spoke, I stuttered over the first letter of the first word. Of course, my classmates noticed this and bullied me over my stammer as well.

I sat on the stoop and thought about bunking off school, but if I did that then I'd get my father into trouble. And I didn't want to get my father into trouble. Also, he'd have to pay a fine, and I knew that money was tight.

As I walked through the school gates on a cold and frosty morning, Mary-Jane Sinclair's gang approached me. To my horror, Davy Coombes accompanied them as well.

"Oh look," Mary-Jane Sinclair said, "it's T-T-T-Tula Bowman."

"S-S-S-Shove off," I said.

"S-S-S-Shove off," the gang mocked in unison, before falling over themselves in fits of laughter.

"Why should we s-s-s-shove off?" Mary-Jane Sinclair asked. "This is our school as much as yours."

If I replied, I knew that they'd mock me, so I

decided to hold my tongue.

"Answer me," Mary-Jane Sinclair said. "Why should we s-s-s-shove off?"

"Leave her alone," Finn O'Malley said.

I glanced over my shoulder and noticed that Finn had joined us. As ever, he carried a copy of *The Adventures of Huckleberry Finn* tucked under his left arm.

"Oh look," Zelda Walters said, "it's the Cyclops, Tula's boyfriend."

"H-H-H-He's not my boyfriend," I said. "H-H-H-He's just a friend."

"That's easy for you to say," Lauren Bonetti said, and all the girls in the gang laughed.

"Leave her alone," Finn repeated.

"Why should they?" Davy Coombes asked.

Finn and Davy stepped forward. They squared-up to each other. They were going to fight. Davy was three times the size of Finn; he'd kill him; I had to stop the fight.

"N-N-N-No," I said to Finn. "D-D-D-Don't do this."

Finn thrust his copy of *The Adventures of Huckleberry Finn* into my hands, but I returned the book. I pushed Finn aside and squared-up to Davy Coombes.

"T-T-T-This is my fight," I said. "G-G-G-Go on, put 'em up; hit me."

Davy Coombes frowned. He looked confused. Nevertheless, he was a fighter by instinct, a boy who brawled every day, so he raised his fists and offered me a mean look.

I'm only small, but I don't back down for anyone. I raised my dukes and prepared to punch Davy in the groin. I'd seen bar brawls on nights when I'd met up with my father. I knew what caused boys and men pain – rabbit punches and blows to the groin.

Davy Coombes swung a huge fist at me, and missed.

"Hey, stop that," Zelda Walters said. "A man can't hit a woman. A boy can't hit a girl. That's not allowed."

"Why not?" Mary-Jane Sinclair scowled. "My father always bashes my mother. And he bashes me."

"Yeah," Lauren Bonetti said. "My father always bashes my mother too. My mother likes it. After she's received a good bashing, she always takes my father into their bedroom. She gives me a quarter and tells me not to come back for half-an-hour."

"Why is that?" Zelda Walters asked.

"I dunno," Lauren Bonetti said and everyone – except me – stood around in silence, looking confused.

The gang departed. They left to pick on

someone else. Davy Coombes went with them. However, Finn O'Malley stayed with me. He didn't look best pleased.

"You shouldn't have done that," Finn said. "You shouldn't have made me look small in front of the girls."

"H-H-H-He would have killed you."

"Better that," Finn said, "than to lose honour."

"Y-Y-Y-You're silly," I said. "I-I-I-I don't want to talk with you."

My stammer was getting me down. I didn't want to talk with anyone, so I made my way into the classroom and sat by myself.

At the end of the lesson, another excruciating hour spent studying the meaning and uses of pi, Mr Hopkins dismissed the class and approached me.

I suppose we should have been grateful that Mr Hopkins was a progressive thinker and that he taught us subjects that other teachers shied away from, but I digress.

Mr Hopkins pulled up a chair and sat beside me. He offered me a bundle of papers, tied up with string. "I want you to study this script," he said. "I've cast you as Hermia in *A Midsummer Night's Dream*."

"T-T-T-Thank you," I said. "B-B-B-But I can't speak proper."

"Study the script," Mr Hopkins said. "Speak

the parts, all of them, in front of a mirror. Do this for two weeks, then we'll discuss the play again."

"O-O-O-Okay," I said. "T-T-T-Thank you."

I returned home with the script for *A Midsummer Night's Dream* hidden in my school bag. I knew that if my mother should discover it, she'd kill me.

I waited until my mother went out, until she went to the market, the drug store or the local church meetings, then I removed the script from my school bag and rehearsed the lines in front of my bedroom mirror.

My bedroom mirror had a crack in it, which ran from the top to the bottom, along a diagonal. My mother had cracked the mirror when she'd thrown a boot at me, and missed.

The mirror distorted my reflection. It made me look like a freak from an asylum. That thought disturbed me, so I didn't dwell on it. Instead, I learned the script for *A Midsummer Night's Dream* by heart, speaking all the lines, playing all the parts. The process came naturally to me; it wasn't a struggle.

Two weeks later, I met Mr Hopkins after class. He smiled and said, "What do you make of the play, Tula?"

"I think it's good," I said. "I think I'll enjoy playing Hermia; I understand her character."

"I knew you would," Mr Hopkins said. "We have a lot to learn this term, but as soon as I can find a gap in the curriculum, we will begin rehearsals, so keep the play fresh in your mind, and keep rehearsing in front of your mirror."

"I will," I said. "And thank you, Mr Hopkins."

Ten minutes later, while walking home, I realised why Mr Hopkins had given me the script early, and asked me to practice in front of my bedroom mirror. Speaking the lines had removed my stammer. That burden had gone.

My Birthday

For my twelfth birthday, I received a book from my father, *The Wonderful Wizard of Oz* by L. Frank Baum. On an inside page I noticed a stamp: 'Property of the Library of Brooklyn'. I suspected that my father had stolen the book from the library. However, he seemed pleased with himself when he handed me the gift, so I didn't mention the stamp.

My mother didn't offer me a gift on this occasion. She did join us at the dining table though where we ate rabbit stew and lemon cake.

I also received a gift from my Aunt Tula, my mother's older sister. My mother named me after Aunt Tula. My aunt gave me a gingham dress that had belonged to her daughter, Tamara. The dress was knee-length and patterned with blue and white checks.

I measured the dress against my slender frame and my mother nodded her approval. "Very nice," she said. "You must thank Aunt Tula."

"I will," I said.

"Put it on," my mother said. "I want to see you in the dress."

I retired to my bedroom and swapped my school dress for my birthday dress. By the time I returned to the dining table, my father was asleep in his armchair; with his rabbit stew, he'd consumed a lot of whiskey, straight from the bottle, and that whiskey had knocked him out.

"Give me a twirl," my mother said.

I smiled, held the dress by its hem and pirouetted.

"Very nice," my mother said. "You must thank Aunt Tula."

"You've already said that," I said.

My mother scowled at me. "Thanks are no hardship," she said. "And they are worth a reminder."

"I won't forget," I said.

"You've been trouble since the day you were born," my mother said. "You came out the wrong way round, a breech birth. You've been trouble ever since."

I'd heard this story a million times before, so I made my excuses. "I'm going out," I said. "I promised to meet my friends."

Before my mother could reply, I skipped down the wooden steps and ran into the street. In a local park, I met up with Finn O'Malley.

"Wow," Finn said. "That's a cool dress."

"It's a birthday present," I said. "From my Aunt Tula."

I offered Finn a twirl and he grinned.

"I can see your knickers when you do that," he

said.

I scowled, straightened my dress and reminded myself not to twirl in it again.

Finn led me to a park bench. We sat on the bench, under an oak tree. There, he placed his copy of *The Adventures of Huckleberry Finn* on the wooden slats and removed a package from the lining of his jacket.

"I have a birthday present for you too," he said.

Finn handed me the package, wrapped in brown paper and tied with string. I untied the string and ripped open the paper. Inside, I discovered a bundle of movie magazines: *Photoplay, Silver Screen, Screenland* and *Motion Picture*.

"Wow," I said. "Thank you, Finn."

"It's okay," he replied somewhat bashfully. "I saw them and reckoned you'd like them."

"They're wonderful," I said. "Where did you find them?"

Finn glanced away. He shuffled his feet. The sole on his right shoe flapped when he shuffled his feet. The gap in the stitching revealed his socks, which were dirty from the street dust.

"I stole the magazines," Finn said. "From Gadsden's. They're hot right now, so don't try to swap them. Just keep them to yourself."

"You shouldn't steal for me, Finn," I scowled. "You'll get into trouble."

"I don't mind stealing for you," Finn said. He gazed into my eyes with his good eye. "I'd do anything for you."

A month later, I met a gang of boys in the park. We met to swap magazines.

"What you got?" I asked.

"I got *Photoplay* and *Movie Weekly*," Rex Staines said – everyone teased him because of his surname, so we had teasing and movies in common. "What you got?"

"*Screenland, Motion Picture* and *Silver Screen*," I said.

"I'll swap you *Movie Weekly* for *Screenland*," he said.

"That ain't a fair swap," I said. "*Screenland's* got more pages than *Movie Weekly*."

"But this is the latest edition," Rex Staines said.

"Fair enough," I said, "but *Screenland's* got Mary Pickford in it."

"Lemmie see," Rex Staines said.

"No," I said, pulling my magazines away from him. "You keep your grubby mitts off them until we've made the deal."

Rex Staines' friends looked on with boredom etched on their dirty faces. All the boys in the gang were older than me, aged around fourteen or fifteen. One of the boys was bouncing a basketball. It was clear that he wanted to run off and play.

"I'll swap you two *Movie Weekly's* for one *Motion Picture*," Rex Staines said.

"That ain't a good deal," I said. "*Motion Picture's* got more pictures in it than *Movie Weekly*."

I knew what Rex Staines, and boys in general, wanted – pictures. I liked looking at the pictures, but I also enjoyed the words; I learned more from the words, and I was keen to educate myself about all aspects of the movies.

"Okay," Rex Staines said, "I'll give you three copies of *Movie Weekly* for one of *Motion Picture*."

"Make it four," I said.

"Give her the magazines," the boy with the basketball said. "Jeez, we'll be here all day. Give her the magazines; come on, let's play."

Rex Staines scowled at me. He scowled at his mates. His mates passed the basketball from one to the other. They started to drift away.

"Okay," Rex Staines said, "four for one. But you ain't fair, Tula Bowman, you don't cut a fair deal. I'll tell the other swappers that."

We made the swap, and Rex Staines ran through the park, in pursuit of his mates. I had two more swaps lined up, two more boys. By the end of the day, I'd have more magazines than I could carry.

I knew how to do good swap deals; hiding my magazines was a problem. But I'd worked on a solution to that too. When standing on a stool, I was tall enough now to reach the top of my wardrobe. My wardrobe had a strip of wood running across the front and that strip hid the top from view. My mother never looked up there because she'd have to stand on the stool too, and her legs were none too steady. So, I hid my magazines on top of my wardrobe.

I was twelve. I wasn't the smartest, but I reckoned that I was learning something new every day.

Finn's Birthday

When I was twelve, I earned a few nickels from babysitting. Nancy Wheeler was sixteen and she had a baby. Nancy wasn't married. Nancy had her baby out of wedlock, which meant that she was a harlot. At least, my mother reckoned that she was a harlot. A lot of women in our neighbourhood had babies out of wedlock. My mother regarded all of them as harlots. Some of the men joked that we lived in Harlot City.

Nancy had a job at the bread factory, cutting rolls. It was a part-time job, so she needed a babysitter. When I was available, that is when I wasn't at school or tending my mother, for a few nickels, I offered to babysit.

Babysitting was no problem. I liked the baby, Nita. She was quiet and docile, at least most of the time. I think Nancy gave Nita a rag to suck on to make her docile. I think she soaked the rag in opium because there was a funny smell in her house.

I gathered my babysitting nickels and offered to treat Finn O'Malley. For his thirteenth birthday, I offered to take him to a movie palace. I also offered to buy him an ice cream. The last of the big spenders, me.

Finn O'Malley had been kind to me, so I thought it was only fair to return his kindness. He wasn't dead keen on the movies, but he did have a passing interest. *20,000 Leagues Under the Sea* was showing this week, and I reckoned that he'd enjoy the movie. I'd seen it before and reckoned that it was cool.

I met Finn outside his house, a three-storey wooden affair located in a rough neighbourhood. The house was ramshackle, on the point of falling down. Our brownstone wasn't great, but at least it had stones in it. Finn's house looked no better than a cardboard box.

I wondered how Finn coped, how he managed to live in such a dilapidated building. I guess the rent for this building was all his parents could afford. I liked Finn, but I didn't like the idea of him living in this building; the thought of it made me shiver for some reason.

"You should get out," I said, "your home's a death trap."

"We will," Finn said, "when my father gets out of prison."

"He's in prison?" I frowned.

"Yeah," Finn smiled. For many men in this neighbourhood, a spell in prison was a badge of honour, a sentence to serve with pride.

"What's he in for?" I asked.

"Brawling," Finn shrugged.

For brawling, you usually received a fine, so I reckoned that this wasn't a first offence; either that or Finn's family couldn't afford the fine.

We walked down the street and I continued to shiver. The street reminded me of a frontier town I'd seen in a cowboy movie. Like a frontier town, I imagined that brawling, drunkenness and gambling were common in Finn's street. Come to think of it, brawling, drunkenness and gambling were common in my street too.

"We've got to get out of this place," I said; "we've got to better ourselves."

Finn shrugged. He appeared content with his lot. I couldn't work out if his attitude was good or bad.

We caught a tram into central Brooklyn. There, we made our way to a movie palace with its colourful posters out-front and plush velvet curtains in front of the silver screen.

We paid our nickels and found our seats. Finn wanted to sit in the back row, for some reason. I preferred to sit in the front row, so that I could take in every detail of the movie. However, this picture was Finn's treat, so I agreed to sit in the back row.

Finn sat on his book, which I found amusing. I didn't laugh at him though because I thought that would upset him, and far too many people already caused him distress.

The velvet curtains parted and the small orchestra played their opening notes.

The scary parts of movies never really scared me – I reckoned that real life was far more frightening, so 'terror' scenes didn't drag me to the edge of my seat.

Instead, I was more interested in how the director had filmed the underwater sequences. If you mixed electricity with water, you'd end up electrocuting someone, so I wondered how he'd managed to achieve the underwater effects. Maybe 'it was all done with mirrors'; I'd read that phrase in my movie magazines.

When I visited the movie palaces, I liked to study the actresses. Through instinct, I reckoned that I could tell good acting from bad. The cast of *20,000 Leagues Under the Sea* was mainly male with only two prominent roles for actresses. 'A Child of Nature' was the main female character and Jane Gail performed that role.

I studied Jane Gail closely, her gestures, facial expressions and hand movements. I would remember every detail and, in front of my bedroom mirror, relive the part.

Halfway through the movie, a reel broke and the film ground to a halt. Everyone in the theatre groaned. The lights went up and I noticed that the theatre was about two-thirds full, a good attendance for a re-run. *The Innocent Lie* was billed for next week, and I reckoned that the theatre would be packed for that showing.

While the projectionist fixed the reel, I fantasised about appearing on the silver screen. Would people pack the movie palaces to watch me? Would I receive 'fan' mail? Did I want 'fan' mail? Why did I want to appear in the movies? At this stage, I couldn't really answer my questions. All I knew was, everything about the movies filled me with excitement.

The lights dimmed again, the movie flickered on the screen and the audience cheered. Edna Pendleton appeared. She played 'Aronnax's Daughter'. Without wishing to sound boastful, I reckoned that I could play that part.

At one point in the movie, I glanced at Finn and discovered that he was staring at me, and not at the screen.

"What are you doing?" I whispered.

"Huh?" he frowned.

"Watch the movie," I said.

Finn grinned. I'd swear that his cheeks turned red when he said, "I'd rather watch you."

Boys are so weird.

At the end of the movie, as promised, I bought Finn an ice cream. He managed to spill some of his ice cream down his shirt. I hoped that his mother would not get angry. At home, I tended to get the blame for everything, so with Finn's stained shirt I hoped that his mother would not blame me.

While riding home on the tram, I smiled and said, "Before I get much older, I'm going to appear on the silver screen."

I turned to Finn for his reaction to my bold statement and discovered that the tram had rocked him to sleep.

An Argument

Over the next week, every evening, I re-enacted the roles of 'A Child of Nature' and 'Aronnax's Daughter'. I imagined Mary Pickford playing those roles, and how she would interpret them. Then Mr Hopkins' words came to mind: I should not copy Mary Pickford, I should not copy any actress; I should filter each role through the lens of myself.

With Mr Hopkins' words in mind, I revisited the parts. To help me get into character, I applied make-up to my lips. My mother would not allow me to use make-up. However, I'd discovered a neat trick.

The wallpaper in my bedroom had a decided tinge of red colouring. I discovered that the colouring would come off quite easily, so I dampened my finger, removed the colouring from the wallpaper and applied it to my lips.

I'd done this before, and my mother had discovered me with red lips. On those occasions, she'd demanded to know where I'd acquired the make-up. I told her that my lips were sore and that the colouring was natural. Of course, she didn't believe me for a second. Instead, she went storming through my bedroom, looking for the make-up but, much to her chagrin, she didn't find it.

I didn't like deceiving my mother, but she was so inflexible, sometimes it was necessary.

I was practicing my looks and gestures in my cracked bedroom mirror when I heard a scream from my parents' bedroom. It was my mother.

"You're drunk, again," she said. "That's the eighth day this week."

"There are only seven days in a week," my father said. "See, I know which day of the week it is; I'm sober."

"You're drunk!" my mother yelled.

"I'm sober," my father said.

"You're drunk!"

I heard something clatter against the bedroom wall and, instinctively, I ducked. It was my mother throwing an object at my father, probably her hairbrush. My mother liked to sit for hours combing her hair; I think the action of running a brush through her hair soothed her.

"I had one drink at the bar," my father said. "I had to, to be sociable."

"You've had ten drinks or more," my mother said.

"I can't drink like that anymore," my father said. "I get a pain in my lower back if I drink too much. I only had the one drink."

"You're a liar," my mother said.

"Maybe Charlie Stratton bought me a drink as

well," my father said. "He asked me to sing. I sang 'Danny Boy'; that's Charlie's favourite. I got a good round of applause for that. And everyone in the bar tipped money into my hat."

"Where is that money?" my mother asked.

"I dunno," my father said.

"Where is it?" my mother insisted.

"I dunno," my father said. "Oh, yeah, I remember now; I repaid Harry Fowler for the loan."

"We repaid Harry Fowler last month," my mother said. "You're lying!"

My mother threw something again and it clattered against the wall. I think she threw one of my father's boots this time. When my parents argued, it upset me, so I placed my hands over my ears, to block out the noise. However, they yelled so loud, I could still hear them.

"You used the money for drink," my mother said.

"I've got this pain in my back," my father said; "maybe I should visit the doctor."

"We ain't got no money for no doctor," my mother said, "and you ain't got no pain in your back."

"It's hurting," my father said.

"Laziness is what you're suffering from," my mother said. "You should go out there and get a proper job."

"Maybe you could earn us a few dollars," my father said.

"What are you suggesting?" my mother asked.

"Like when we first met," my father said.

"Don't you dare call me no hoor!" my mother yelled. I heard a slap. She'd slapped him, hard, across the face. I bit my lower lip and started to cry. "I ain't no hoor!" my mother screamed.

"I never said you was," my father said. "Don't yell; you know how much it upsets Tula; you know how sensitive she is. Come here, give us a kiss."

"Keep your hands off me!" my mother yelled. "Keep away from me! You're disgusting! All men are disgusting!"

My mother threw something again; probably my father's other boot. It thudded against the wall and made my picture of Douglas Fairbanks wobble. I placed my head under my pillow and pulled it tight around my ears.

"You never kiss me," my father complained. "You never show me any affection."

"A real man doesn't need affection," my mother said. "I real man goes out there, works hard, and returns home exhausted. You don't work hard, that's your problem; you got too much energy, that's your problem, even when you're drunk."

"Give us a kiss," my father said.

"Your breath reeks of whiskey," my mother

said. "Get away from me!"

I heard another bang against the bedroom wall, my father's head this time.

"You shouldn't push someone like that," my father said. "You could kill them."

"Killing would be too good for you," my mother said. "This whole family would be better off dead."

"If you're thinking like that," my father said, "I'm going to leave you."

"Leave us!" my mother yelled. "See if we care!"

"Where's my suitcase?" my father asked.

"You pawned it," my mother said.

"In that case," my father said, "I'll pack a bag."

"Pack a bag and be off," my mother said. "Go spend your time with Submarine Lil."

"I don't spend no time with Submarine Lil," my father said.

"You're lying again," my mother said. "You were with her last night."

My father didn't dispute my mother's words. An eerie silence descended on the house. I could hear the rats scurrying under the floorboards, and the air rattling in the water pipes. Then I heard my father's heavy footsteps as he tramped down the stairs, followed by the slamming of the front door.

I lifted my pillow from my head – as a soundproofing device, it was useless anyway. I sighed, wiped away my tears and sat up on my bed. My father had left us. I was alone with my mother.

My Sisters

Six weeks passed. It was winter. Our house was icy cold. My mother and I were existing on bowls of thin soup and stale bread. Our rent was a month overdue. Our landlord was threatening to evict us.

At school, I pretended to eat from my lunchbox because I didn't want to show the other children that we couldn't afford any food. I'm slim, I've always been slim, and maybe it has something to do with those days.

I was very good, pretending to eat from my lunchbox; I convinced the other children that I was really eating. In that bleak moment, I realised that I was a good actress. Maybe you could call that a silver lining – finding some light in a moment of darkness.

At night, my mother and I would huddle together for warmth. Before we drifted off to sleep, my mother would start talking. Usually, she rambled; most times, she talked utter nonsense. However, on this particular night she was strangely lucid.

"I could have married any one of five men," my mother said. "All the eligible bachelors in the neighbourhood were chasing after me. I chose your father, or rather, he chose me. My mother protested;

she reckoned that he wasn't good enough for me. My mother was right. But she went into the asylum. She didn't return. We didn't have any money. Your father said he would secure a contract. He said he would sing on Broadway. He said he would make big money. Your father lied."

"I carried you for nine months," my mother said. "You were a burden. You made my back ache. You made me sick. The doctor said I was wrong to get pregnant. He said I wasn't strong enough to carry a baby. But your father had other ideas. Men always have other ideas..."

"The day you were born," my mother said, "we had a heatwave; the temperature was well over a hundred degrees; people were collapsing with exhaustion; they were dying like flies."

My mother adjusted our blanket and stared into the middle distance. "I was weak; you were weak; the doctors said we would not make it through the day. I nodded at them, and smiled. You were not supposed to make it through that day. You were supposed to die, like your sisters."

"My sisters?" I frowned.

"Yes," my mother said. "You were supposed to die like your sisters."

"I never knew that I had any sisters," I said. "You never talked about them. No one in the family ever mentioned them. How many sisters? What were their names?"

"Two," my mother said. "Emmeline and Florence. Emmeline was stillborn. Florence died after twelve hours. You were supposed to die, like your sisters." My mother glared at me; I detected a look of accusation in her eyes. "Instead, you survived."

Outside our bedroom window, the fire bell rang. A neighbour had sought to fight away the bitter cold, but instead they'd been too bold and set fire to their house. I could smell the wood smoke as it drifted in through the gaps in the window frame, I could see it on the breeze as it disturbed the net curtains.

I could smell and see the smoke. However, my mother did not appear to notice. She stared into the middle distance as though in a trance.

"You have no future, Tula; you'll become a hoor, like Submarine Lil. I ain't allowing no daughter of mine to become a hoor." My mother glared at me then offered a peculiar smile. "I'm gonna kill ya."

"No!" I yelled. "No!"

I reached for my mother, to pull her back. However, despite her frail appearance, she was strong; she grabbed hold of my shoulders and hurled me to the floor.

By the time that I recovered my senses, I found

my mother standing over me with a large carving knife in her hand. We fought for the knife. I wrapped my tiny hands around her slender wrist. I kicked out, tried to push her away with my legs. I screamed for help, but my cries were lost amongst the ringing of the fire bell.

My mother thrust the carving knife. I shrieked and rolled along the floor. I glanced over my shoulder and discovered that my mother had embedded the knife deep into the floorboards and was struggling to pull it free.

While my mother struggled with the knife, I tried to push her away. The net curtains continued to billow in the breeze. The fire bell continued to ring. The smoke continued to drift into our room.

The smoke made my mother cough. The smoke settled on my mother's lungs and affected her breathing, sapped her strength; she tugged at the haft, but couldn't free the blade from the floorboards.

Eventually, my mother abandoned the carving knife. Coughing, she staggered over to the window, leaned out and gulped in some air. The air was stale, smoke-stained, and it made her cough even more.

I took hold of my mother and guided her into my bedroom. The smoke affected this room too but, because my bedroom looked away from the fire, not to the same extent.

My mother found some relief, leaning out of my bedroom window. I tried to offer her comfort, but she pushed me away and I went sprawling again, across the bedroom floor.

I was wondering what to do next when I saw my father framed in my bedroom door. At first, I thought he was an apparition. Then, I realised that it was really him; he'd returned, after six weeks away.

My father held the carving knife in his hand; obviously, he'd freed it from the floorboards. My mother turned and stared at him. I wondered what would happen next; I wondered if there'd be bloodshed.

Then, my father opened his coat and revealed a leg of mutton. At that time, it was the largest leg of mutton I'd ever seen. Blood from the meat had stained my father's coat, but he didn't seem to care. He'd shaved. He looked sober. I couldn't smell any alcohol on his breath or clothing.

"Where did you get that mutton?" my mother frowned.

"Never you mind," my father said. "Throw it into a pot; prepare it; tonight we'll have a feast."

My father handed the mutton and the carving knife to my mother, and she made her way into the kitchen.

That evening, we dined on mutton. We didn't mention my father's absence. Indeed, my mother and father talked in a manner that suggested he'd not been away. No mention was made of my father finding the carving knife embedded in the floorboards.

Over dinner, my mother and father talked with each other, talked with me as though it had been another regular day.

The School Play

Mr Hopkins cast me as Hermia in *A Midsummer Night's Dream*, our school play. It was a simplified version of the play, one the performers and audience could easily understand.

For months, I rehearsed in front of my cracked bedroom mirror. Throughout the rehearsals, I came to understand every nuance of my character, and the other characters in the play.

I also learned to appreciate that it was important to listen to the other actors and act, with appropriate words and gestures, accordingly. I learned to appreciate that sometimes the actors didn't follow every line in the script, and that these diversions, these ad-libs, could be more effective than the original screenplay.

I learned how to embrace my character, how to live the part. Equally, I learned how to release the character and become myself again at the end of each rehearsal. Under Mr Hopkins' tuition and guidance, I felt like a 'proper' actress. I felt ready for the silver screen, and stage.

In life situations, quite often I allowed my nerves to betray me. However, when acting I felt totally confident, completely free, in command. True, I did experience some nerves, but I channelled those nerves into my performance. I'd rehearsed well. I was ready for the big day.

Mr Hopkins had also cast Finn in the play, as Snug, a joiner. Finn was a poor actor; that wasn't his fault because he wasn't really interested in acting. He'd only volunteered to participate in the play because he wanted to be close to me.

I sensed that Finn wanted to be my boyfriend. I was thirteen, he was fourteen; I felt that we were too young. I liked Finn, I thought he was cute, but I regarded him as my friend, not my boyfriend. I envisaged the day when his feelings would come to the surface and I'd have to break his heart.

It sounds conceited to say that I could break anyone's heart, but that's how I felt about the situation simply because of the way Finn behaved towards me. He offered me gifts on a regular basis, usually flowers. I knew that he stole those flowers, from gardens, or from Gadsden's. Nevertheless, it was kind of him to think of me.

I arrived at school for the performance. I changed into my stage clothes then peered through the curtain, at the audience. Most of the parents were in the audience. My father couldn't attend because he'd secured a job, helping to paint the Brooklyn Bridge. I noticed my mother in the audience. I was surprised that she'd decided to attend because she hated everything about acting.

Nevertheless, it offered my heart a lift to see her sitting with the other parents.

"All set?" Mr Hopkins asked. He glanced around the cast and smiled at me.

"All set," I said.

"Splendid," Mr Hopkins enthused. "If you require the rest room, use it now; five minutes until curtain up."

Finn, and three other children, required the rest room, but I felt at ease. I was rehearsing my lines, running them through my head when, to my surprise, I found my mother standing beside me. I assumed that she was going to wish me good luck. However, she scowled and said, "Tula, get your coat; we're going home."

"But..." I hesitated and searched for the right words. "We haven't completed the performance; we haven't started, yet."

Mr Hopkins appeared. He removed his spectacles and polished them on a small cloth. Returning his spectacles to the bridge of his nose, he stared at my mother and asked, "Is there a problem?"

"Tula's leaving," my mother said. "I'm taking her out of school."

"For the afternoon?" Mr Hopkins frowned.

"For good," my mother said. "She's needed at home. She's needed to look after me, and she's needed at the bakery; I've secured a job for her."

"What about her schooling?" Mr Hopkins asked. "What about her education?"

"Tula has learned enough," my mother said. "It's time she earned a living and made her way in the world."

"Tula is a bright pupil," Mr Hopkins said. "I'm sure that if she completes her education, the knowledge gained will hold her in good stead for the future."

"Tula is leaving," my mother insisted. "Get your coat, Tula; we're leaving now."

I glanced at Mr Hopkins. I glanced at my mother. I was torn. I didn't know what to do. I wanted to stay; I wanted to take part in the play, but I realised that I had to obey my mother.

"One moment," Mr Hopkins said. He placed a paternal hand on my shoulder and halted my retreat. "At least allow Tula to stay and participate in the play."

"She will do no such thing," my mother said. "Plays are the work of the Devil."

"Why do you say such things?" Mr Hopkins asked.

"Performers are harlots," my mother said. "And no daughter of mine is gonna become a harlot."

"With respect," Mr Hopkins said, "performers

are not harlots; they are talented, creative people."

My mother produced a walking stick from underneath her coat and waved it at Mr Hopkins. I'd seen her beat men with that walking stick; I had no doubt that she would use it on him.

"Maybe I should leave," I said to my teacher. "Maybe you could take my part."

Mr Hopkins adjusted his spectacles and offered me a wan smile. "That would save the play. However, I do not look or sound anything like Hermia."

"Please," I begged my mother, "allow me to perform in the play."

My mother raised her walking stick and slapped me across my knuckles. I rung my hand and cried out in pain.

At that point, Finn returned from the rest room. He noticed my tears and glared at my mother. "Hey," he said, "what's going on?"

"It's none of your business, Finn O'Malley," my mother said. "Get out of our way; Tula's going home."

"For you to beat her with that stick?" Finn wrestled with my mother for possession of the walking stick. "No way, Mrs Bowman, no way."

"Mr Hopkins," my mother complained, "control your pupils. And you, Finn O'Malley, you are not to visit Tula again."

"Finn," Mr Hopkins said, "return to class."

"But..." Finn moaned.

"Return to class!" Mr Hopkins ordered. "I will deal with you there."

"Come on, Tula." My mother retrieved her walking stick, which had fallen to the floor, and grabbed me by my shoulder. "This school is a bad influence on you; you're leaving, today."

My mother dragged me home. At home, she collapsed into an armchair, exhausted. Her exhaustion saved me from a beating. However, my schooldays were over, and so were my chances of appearing in Mr Hopkins' plays.

The Doctor's Office

Over the following months, I worked in a variety of jobs. All were mundane. None challenged my intellect or stimulated my mind. To get by, I daydreamed. I pictured myself in motion pictures, usually as the lead actress in the latest movie screened at our local theatre. I imagined how I would play the part, what changes I would make to the original performance, what technical changes I would make to improve the look of the movie.

Maybe other actresses and would-be actresses thought in the same way. Maybe, in terms of acting, I was advanced for my age. I had no one to compare with, or consult with, so I had no real idea if my thoughts were standard, or somewhat unusual. My thoughts seemed normal to me; they resonated with the person, with the adult, I wanted to become.

I worked in a bakery, part-time. My job was to slice the buns in half. One day, I got careless with the knife and cut my finger. My finger bled over the bread. The baker was very unhappy about that and docked me a week's wages. Losing the profits from one roll did not amount to a week's wages, so I felt that he was abusing his position. However, I was not in a position to argue, so I soldiered on.

After the bakery, I got a job as a messenger girl.

I enjoyed that job more because I had a bicycle to ride, and I spent a lot of time out in the fresh air. I delivered messages to various businesses and, on occasion, small parcels. Of course, I never read the messages, or looked in the parcels.

That job was going well, until I crashed my bicycle and damaged the frame. The accident was my fault – I was daydreaming again, thinking about Enid Markey in *Tarzan of the Apes*. After that accident, the messenger company dismissed me and I didn't work for the best part of a month.

My father secured my next job, as a secretary in a doctor's office. My task was straightforward: I answered the telephone and made a note of the appointments.

The doctor, Dr Crichton, was a short, lean man with fine grey hair, which he combed over his balding head. He wore a waistcoat, a bowtie, and trousers that were two inches too long. I had no idea why his wife did not adjust his trousers. In all truth, I had no idea if he had a wife.

Dr Crichton also wore a gold pocket watch, which he checked every five minutes; he would shake the watch and glare at its face; he appeared captivated by the watch, as though hypnotised. I guess, for him, checking the watch had become an obsession.

Another strange aspect of Dr Crichton practice

was his patients: they were all pregnant women. Some were heavily pregnant, others just showing. They would enter by the front door, step into Dr Crichton's surgery then, half an hour later, leave by the back door. I never saw the women leave; in fact, I never saw them again.

One day, Mrs Stanton, a large woman with a mono-eyebrow, entered Dr Crichton's practice. I confirmed her appointment, and she waddled into the doctor's surgery.

While Mrs Stanton was with Dr Crichton, I took a phone call and made an appointment note on a piece of paper. Dr Crichton did not keep an appointment ledger; I made all the appointment notes on scraps of paper, which he destroyed after the women had visited his surgery. I considered this unusual, but recognised that I was not in a position to query his work routine.

The day that Mrs Stanton entered Dr Crichton's surgery was the day that I had one of the biggest shocks of my life.

I was making an appointment note on a scrap of paper when Dr Crichton rushed past me. He opened the front door and ran out into the street. His hands and waistcoat were covered in blood. Indeed, he was covered in so much blood that some of it dripped from his pocket watch.

Curiosity got the better of me. I wandered over

to the door and peered inside Dr Crichton's surgery. The sight before me took my breath away. Mrs Stanton was sitting back in a large chair, her legs in the air, her skirt pulled up to her waist. A purple cord dangled between her legs along with what appeared to be a tiny, tiny baby. Both Mrs Stanton and the baby were dead. A neighbour had died when I was ten, so I knew how to recognise a dead body.

At first, I panicked; a million thoughts ran through my mind; the thought that scared me most was what if Dr Crichton accused me of murdering Mrs Stanton? And what if the police believed him?

I walked over to Mrs Stanton and confirmed that she was, indeed, dead; I checked the pulse on her left wrist – I'd seen a doctor do this in a movie. Mrs Stanton was dead, of that I had no doubt.

I considered Dr Crichton's dash into the street and tried to fathom his actions. I reasoned that he was looking for help, not to save his patient because she was beyond saving, but to move her body.

I decided that I did not want any part of this, so I left by the back door. At first, I walked along the sidewalk. Then, after turning a corner, I ran three miles home.

At home, I found my mother sitting in her armchair, staring into the empty fireplace. At first, I thought she was enduring an episode, but when I entered the living room, she turned and stared at me.

"What are you doing home?" she frowned. "You're supposed to remain at Dr Crichton's practice until six o'clock every evening."

"She's dead," I said.

"Who's dead?"

"Mrs Stanton. Dr Crichton murdered her."

My mother placed her arms on her armchair and leaned towards me. She glared at me, offered me one of her icy stares. "You're talking gibberish, child; enough; talk sense."

"He killed her," I said. While swallowing hard and pausing to catch my breath, I recalled the scene at Dr Crichton's surgery.

"I see," my mother said. She sat back in her armchair and gathered her thoughts. "Obviously, you cannot return there. You've lost another job, a full-time job, with good pay. You keep finding ways to lose jobs, Tula; you keep disappointing me, and your father." My mother stood and led me into the kitchen. "Bend over that chair; raise your skirt and lower your knickers."

"No," I said. "I will not do that."

My mother yelled at me. "Are you disobeying an order?"

"I can't do that," I said. "I can't do that anymore."

"Why not?" my mother frowned.

"Because I'm a woman now."

As realisation dawned, my mother nodded. "I see," she said. "In that case, hold out your hand; let me see your knuckles."

I held out my hand and received a knuckle beating. I didn't fully understand why my mother administered this beating; I guess it was because I'd lost another job.

Six weeks later, my father found me new employment, this time in a tin factory. It was a noisy, dirty place and my job was mainly to sweep the floors. The pay was poor, but at least I earned enough to finance regular trips to the movies, and to buy my movie magazines.

I told myself not to despair: I would not work in this factory forever; one day, I would abandon the tin for the silver of the movie screen.

The Fire

I established a routine. For ten hours a day, I worked in the tin factory. At the end of the week, I offered my wages to my mother, and she granted me an allowance, a fifth of my wages. I used that money to finance trips to the movie theatres, and to buy my movie magazines. I also put aside some money to buy new clothes.

Occasionally, my father asked me for a 'loan'. He never repaid this money, but whenever he asked, I gave him the 'loan' simply because he was my father. He used the money to gamble, and to buy alcohol.

Finn couldn't afford regular trips to the movie theatre, so I bought most of his tickets. Our 'relationship' had developed. He regarded me as his girlfriend, whereas I considered him to be a friend, albeit my closest friend. I didn't have the heart to tell him that I didn't 'fancy' him. I assumed that over time he'd get the message, become bored and move on. Maybe I was being cruel, stringing him along. I didn't want to hurt his feelings but, in retrospect, maybe I was behaving like a coward.

One evening, after my shift at the tin factory, I took a detour and walked through Finn's neighbourhood. I don't know why, on that particular evening, I decided to take that detour. I had to walk an extra mile to reach Finn's neighbourhood, so it didn't make any sense to take the detour. Nevertheless, I did it.

As a child, I didn't believe in fairies, or ghosts, or anything mystical; I didn't even believe in God – I'd seen too much suffering in my neighbourhood to believe that any benevolent deity could possibly exist. I didn't believe in the supernatural, but I reasoned that sometimes forces we didn't understand guided us and compelled us to take certain actions. And maybe a guiding force placed a hand on my shoulder that evening and led me through Finn's neighbourhood.

The smell of wood smoke alerted my senses to a source of potential trouble. A building was on fire, a common occurrence in Finn's neighbourhood. As I walked along the street, past people running for the fire buckets, I realised that Finn's house was on fire. Without thinking, I ran up the wooden steps into the burning building.

"Finn! Finn!" I yelled his name. Smoke gripped my throat and lungs, and made me cough. "Finn! Finn!" I yelled again, but received no answer.

Finn's father was in prison; but where was his mother? I had no idea. Maybe Finn was not even in the building. Then I saw his book, *The Adventures of Huckleberry Finn*, its pages burning. That book never left Finn's side. He was in the building.

"Finn! Finn!"

I fought my way through the smoke, and held my hands up, to protect my face from the heat. The stench of burnt hair assaulted my nostrils. To my dismay, I realised that that stench stemmed from my hair.

"Finn! Finn!"

My cries were becoming ever more desperate, my movements laboured. I lost my bearings; I wasn't sure where I was in the house, or where I'd find Finn.

I passed out, only for a few seconds. The flames engulfed the wood. The building crackled and groaned, as though in pain.

I passed out again.

When I came to, I realised that the flames had encircled me. I tried to run through the flames, but the heat was too intense. I began to cry. However, my tears evaporated before they could reach my cheeks.

The roof collapsed. It fell past me and burned its way through the floorboards. I ran to a window and cried for help.

A man appeared in the street, a total stranger. He waved a hand and encouraged me to jump. Another man appeared and between them, the two men held a blanket. They encouraged me to jump into that blanket. It seemed a long way down, from the second storey, a long way to jump.

I glanced over my shoulder. The flames were approaching. I had no option, no choice – I had to jump.

I closed my eyes, took a step back, and ran on to the balcony. I was about to launch myself into the air when the balcony collapsed and I went crashing to the ground.

When I came to, I found my father standing over me. "She's alive," someone said. Someone else said, "Thank God."

My father took me in his arms and caressed my singed hair. My hair stank to high heaven. I stank. My skin was covered in soot and dust, my clothes charred.

"It's okay," my father said, "it's all over; you're safe; you'll be fine now."

I could smell the whiskey on his breath; I could see the tears in his eyes. My father never cried; the men in our neighbourhood were not allowed that emotion.

My mind was still in a fog, a smoke fog; it remained fuzzy, confused. Could smoke enter the brain? At that moment, I would have said, yes, it could.

Slowly, I came to my senses. I realised that the fire truck had arrived and that men were dousing the flames. I realised that the women had gathered in the street and that they were talking together, in a tight knot. I realised that someone lay beside me – Finn.

I reached over to nudge Finn, but he did not respond. I nudged him again. Then my father grabbed my wrist and held my hand.

"No," he said. "Finn's dead."

I didn't believe my father. I didn't want to believe him, so I broke his grip and nudged Finn again. He didn't move. His body remained unblemished, his clothes in better condition than mine, yet he would not, could not, move.

"Finn's dead," my father said. "He's dead."

I stared at my father through startled eyes. How could this be so? How could this happen? How could Finn die? He'd never harmed a single living soul.

"Smoke," my father said. "The smoke engulfed his lungs."

"Any sign of his mother?" someone asked.

My father glanced along the street to a body wrapped in blankets. He offered a sad shake of his head and said, "She's dead too."

The undertaker carried Mrs O'Malley away. Water ran along the street, through the gutter. It washed away the litter. It carried blobs of chewing gum.

My father helped me to my feet. He dusted me down and wrapped his jacket around my shoulders. The undertaker walked over to us. He stooped and gathered Finn into his arms.

"Wait!" I cried.

Startled, the undertaker stared at my father. At first, my father looked confused, then he nodded at the undertaker. I'd cried "wait" because I'd noticed something from the corner of my eye.

I walked over to the remains of Finn's book and brushed away the damaged pages. I handed *The Adventures of Huckleberry Finn* to the undertaker and said, "Make sure you bury this book with him."

A few days later, I attended Finn's funeral. I cried. Maybe I'd loved him after all. Too late now. I should have said so at the time.

It was a bitter lesson learned. I promised myself that I would not repeat that mistake, should love enter my life again.

The Nightmares

I grew fearful of the dark. For several months after the fire, I had difficulty sleeping. Whenever I closed my eyes, I pictured the flames.

I tried to keep myself awake, by reading. It was dark, so I used a candle. Sometimes, I fell asleep with the candle burning. That made me realise that I was being stupid: the flames were only in my nightmares, in my subconscious; by sleeping with a naked flame, I risked a real fire. So, I abandoned the candles and tried to sleep.

I was fourteen, too old for night terrors. I admonished myself for being such a coward, for being so stupid. Over time, about a month, I drifted off to sleep soon after my head hit my pillow. The nightmares still arrived, mingled with some pleasant dreams.

A recurring nightmare featured my mother and father arguing. Since the fire, they'd argued a lot, almost every day. I sensed that my father loved my mother and that she did not reciprocate his love. My mother banned my father from their bedroom on a number of occasions and he slept on the couch.

In my nightmares, my mother gave my father a knuckle beating; she'd never done this in real life, that I must say. Recently, my mother had stopped beating my knuckles. Her episodes were becoming more frequent and, physically, she was deteriorating; she no longer had the strength to punish me with any force.

That said, when my mother drifted into an episode, she appeared possessed with super-human strength. Maybe some 'thing' did possess her when she behaved in that way. At times, my mother could be kind and gentle, but she always caught herself when she acted in such a fashion. It was as though displaying kindness towards me upset her in some way.

I wondered if the deaths of my sisters, on the days they were born, affected my mother's attitude towards me. I sensed that she'd expected me to die, as a baby, and that her mind had never adjusted to the fact that I'd survived my first day, that I was in her life to stay.

My dreams centred on the movies, of course. Often, I was in a movie theatre, watching my performance on the silver screen. I felt no sense of pride or, conversely, embarrassment, when viewing my performance because that person on the silver screen was not me; she was the character I was portraying.

I did have a recurring nightmare, which centred on acting. A casting director was allocating parts and, for some reason that he never fully explained, he always overlooked me.

A variation on that nightmare involved the casting director selecting me for a bit part in a motion picture. He would tell me to visit the costume department, and change into my costume. After that, either I couldn't find the costume department, or it took me an age to change into my acting clothes. I found these nightmares most distressing. They suggested to me that I'd failed.

One night, I was dreaming about Mary Pickford. She wanted me to appear alongside her in her latest motion picture. For some reason, I was being stubborn, and I refused. I felt like shaking myself and giving myself a good talking to, all within the context of the dream.

Then I realised that someone was shaking me – my mother. She was standing over me, the carving knife in her hand, the look of madness in her eyes. She smiled and said, "I'm gonna kill ya, Tula." She spoke calmly, her tone matter-of-fact.

At first, I was confused. At first, I thought it was a nightmare. Then, when my mother thrust the carving knife past my head into my pillow, I realised that this scene was all too real.

My mother retrieved the knife from my pillow and feathers flew everywhere. She lunged for me again and this time embedded the knife in my wardrobe door.

It took my mother a minute to pull the knife from my wardrobe door. In that minute, I ran from my bedroom, into the corridor. I entered my parents' bedroom, in search of my father, but he wasn't there.

My mother approached me again. I knew from experience that, when gripped by an episode, there was no point in trying to reason with my mother; she was not 'with us' when she drifted into these episodes, she was 'somewhere else'; or maybe she was 'someone else'.

I couldn't reason with my mother, so I went in search of my father. I looked for him on the couch, but he wasn't there.

I ran out, into the street. It was dark. The Moon was high, the stars bright and numerous. The sidewalk was slippery, coated with a thin layer of ice. I slipped, and regained my footing. My mother ran after me. She slipped, and fell.

The street was deserted; all our neighbours were in bed. I thought, maybe, I'd see someone as they wandered home from the nightshift, but the blackness of the sky told me that it was too early for that.

For some reason, I ran towards Submarine Lil's house. Men were forever wandering in and out of her house, so maybe my subconscious had suggested that I was sure to find someone there, someone to rescue me from my mother.

I needed rescuing from my mother; I didn't understand the mental process, but I knew that that was not right; mothers should love and nurture; they should not intimidate and threaten to kill.

I hammered on Submarine Lil's door and screamed for help. It seemed to take hours, but in reality, it was only seconds before someone opened the door and stepped into the street. That someone was my father, wrapped in a blanket.

My father seemed surprised to see me. However, I was not shocked to see him. I had no proof, I sought no proof, but I'd sensed for some time that my father was one of Submarine Lil's 'clients', one of her 'johns', as the men in the bars were wont to say.

My father glanced at me. Then he stared down the street to my mother. She was sitting on the kerbside, the carving knife glinting in the moonlight, nestling in her hand. However, now she looked confused, bewildered.

Submarine Lil appeared. She was naked. She didn't care who saw her unclothed. "You're still on the clock," she said to my father. He nodded, went inside and searched for his wallet. He dressed, handed Submarine Lil a handful of coins, then joined me in the street.

Submarine Lil shrugged, closed the door and

returned to her bed. She always ate alone, but rarely slept alone. I reckoned that that was no way to live.

I guess I should have felt ashamed of my father, ashamed for my father, but I didn't. The reality was this was how men behaved in our neighbourhood.

My father helped my mother to her feet. He prised the carving knife from her fingers and slipped it into his belt. We returned home.

Needless to say, my nightmares intensified over the following week.

The Contest

My father had a problem – he was an alcoholic. He'd always 'enjoyed' a drink, but now he was drinking to excess. He was spending all his money on drink. He was 'tapping me up' for 'loans'. And when I told him that I didn't have any money, he'd steal it from my bedside drawer.

My mother was slipping away; mentally and physically, she was deteriorating; I didn't want to lose my father as well. I wanted to help him, wanted him to quit drinking, but I didn't know what to do. I was sixteen 'going on thirty'. I was a confusion of experience and inexperience. I was an adult who'd lost her childhood. More importantly, I was in need of money to buy this month's movie magazines.

I couldn't wait until payday; I had to have the latest issue of *Motion Picture* simply because Lillian Gish featured on the cover. She was the star of this year's hot movie, *Way Down East*. I concocted a plan, a risky plan, but one that would satisfy my need.

I entered Gadsden's and wandered around. Old Mr Gadsden ran a small store that sold a bit of everything. I guess you'd call it an all-purpose store, or a general store.

Mr Gadsden was always in a bad mood. At

least, that's how he appeared to me. He was a short man with bow legs and a barrel chest. He wheezed from time to time. Maybe poor health was responsible for his bad mood. He always wore a spotted bowtie, pinstriped trousers and a plaid waistcoat. He looked like a man who'd dressed in the dark.

Mr Gadsden liked to gossip with his customers. I waited until he was suitably engaged, then I slipped a copy of *Motion Picture* under my pea coat. I glanced around the crowded store, my face a picture of innocence. I smiled at my fellow customers and made my way to the store door.

At the door, I felt a hand on my shoulder. "Wait there, Tula Bowman," Mr Gadsden said. "You owe me twenty-five cents for that magazine."

"What magazine?" I asked, feigning innocence.

"That magazine," Mr Gadsden said. He pulled open my pea coat and my copy of *Motion Picture* fell to the floor.

The people in the store turned and stared at me. Most scowled. Some muttered that I was evil, like my mother. Their words about my mother upset me; she was not evil, she was sick; people offered sympathy if you injured your body, but they called you wicked names if you injured your mind.

"You owe me twenty-five cents," Mr Gadsden said. He stood beside me, his hairy hand on the wooden doorframe, his brown brogues tapping the stone floor.

"Do we have a problem here?" a woman asked. She was elderly with a head of beautifully styled grey hair, and a large mole on her chin. Her smile touched her eyes; her face was soft and gentle. In her shopping bag, I noticed a novel by Charles Dickens, and a copy of a music magazine.

"Tula Bowman is a thief," Mr Gadsden said. "I have a good mind to ban her from my store."

"I am not a thief," I said.

"I caught you in the act of stealing that magazine; and I've seen you filch items before."

"Only once before," I said. "My father needed cigarettes and I didn't have any money."

"How would you like to earn some money?" the elderly woman said.

I frowned. "You want me to run an errand?"

"I will pay for your magazine," the woman said, "if you will grant me a small favour." She turned to Mr Gadsden and smiled. "Is that acceptable to you?"

Mr Gadsden turned and scowled at me. Then, reluctantly, he nodded towards the woman. "That'll be twenty-five cents," he said.

The elderly woman paid Mr Gadsden the twenty-five cents and, with my copy of *Motion Picture* in my hands, I walked from the store.

On the sidewalk, the elderly woman caught up with me. "That was very naughty," she said. "You should never steal."

"I'm sorry," I said, "but I was desperate to read this magazine."

"Why?" the woman asked. "What's so special about that magazine?"

"It contains a feature on Lillian Gish," I said. "I've studied her acting; I want to be like her."

The elderly woman smiled. Whenever I said that I wanted to become an actress, people tended to laugh, they tended to mock me. However, this woman's smile was warm, genuine.

"That's a fine ambition," the woman said. "It reminds me of my youth."

I frowned. "Did you dream of becoming an actress?"

"Not an actress," the woman said. "I dreamed of becoming an opera singer. However," she sighed, "I could never reach the high notes."

We walked on, towards a pleasant side of town. As we walked, we chatted for a good fifteen minutes. Then it occurred to me that I owed this woman a favour; I wondered what she'd ask of me.

"I must repay you for your kindness," I said. "What would you like me to do?"

"You've already repaid me," the woman smiled.

"Repaid you?" I frowned. "I'm sorry, I don't understand."

"You've offered me your company," the woman said. "You've offered me your time. You've talked with me as I've walked home. I live alone. My friends, family, have all gone, gone to meet their Maker. My time on this Earth is short, yet the hours seem to drag. It is good to share a moment with someone, especially someone as interesting as you."

"I could call on you again," I said. Then I bit my tongue; maybe I'd spoken out of turn; maybe my words were an imposition.

"I'm sure we'll meet again," the woman said, "in Gadsden's. And, maybe, on those occasions you can walk me home."

Kindness, I thought; kindness is the way to make progress in this world.

The elderly woman entered her fine house. I walked on, reading my magazine. I reached page three and my jaw dropped. The publishers were running a competition. The first prize was an evening gown and a bit part in a movie. A bit part in a movie! I had to enter that competition. I had to win that prize.

I tripped over the kerb as I read the details, but that didn't bother me. Entry was simple: I had to complete a form and submit two photographs. The form was easy, but the photographs were expensive, especially with my father stealing all my money.

I had to find the money for those photographs; I had to find it from somewhere.

I walked home feeling as light as air, with my head full of dreams, with my feet dancing on clouds.

At home, I searched for my father, to share my exciting news. However, I found him looking morose.

"What's the matter?" I asked. I stared at my mother's armchair and discovered that she wasn't there. "Where's mother?"

"She had another episode," my father said. "A really bad episode. I had to take her to the doctor. We had to place her in the asylum."

My Aunt

I went to the asylum to visit my mother, but she refused to see me. That upset me. It made me cry.

"She blames you," my father said. "It's all your fault."

"How can it be my fault?" I asked. "How am I to blame?"

"Your mother is sick," my father said. "Don't try to make sense of her thoughts or words."

My mother's illness wasn't my fault; I knew that it wasn't my fault, yet a nagging doubt remained. I felt guilty, as though I'd disappointed her, as though I'd sinned.

My father sat back in his armchair and slugged whiskey from a bottle. "It's just the two of us now," he said. "Just you and me, kid; your mother will never leave that asylum."

"We'll get by," I said. "We'll cope."

"I ain't got no work at the moment," my father said, "so we'll need to get by on your wages."

"We will," I said. "My wages will cover the rent, and food."

"And whiskey," my father grinned, holding up his empty bottle.

"That too," I said.

"Good," my father said. He closed his eyes and

allowed his empty bottle to fall to the floor. "My back's playing me up," he moaned. "I won't be able to cook or clean."

"I'll do that for us," I said.

"Good," my father said. "You're the woman of the house now, Tula; you'll perform your mother's duties."

"I will," I said. "We'll get by. But, from now on, you must control your drinking."

I'd felt apprehensive saying those words and, now that I'd expressed them, I glanced at my father. His chest was rising and falling, slowly; he was snoring; he was sleeping. My words had reached the wall; they had not permeated his ears.

My father and I established a routine. I laboured ten hours a day at the tin factory while he visited the bar, 'looking for work'. I cleaned the house and cooked for us. By bedtime, I was exhausted. Indeed, I could barely open my eyes to read my movie magazines.

My goal to enter the acting competition remained pertinent. However, we were drifting into debt; raising the funds for the entry photographs was proving a problem.

I considered a solution: my Aunt Tula. My mother had named me after Aunt Tula, her sister. Aunt Tula was a good ten years, or more, older than my mother – she never let on about her true age.

Aunt Tula lived in a smart corner of Brooklyn, in a townhouse. She was a widow, with one daughter, Tamara. Her late husband had earned a lot of money. Some of my relatives reckoned that he'd won big at a casino. Others reckoned that he'd made his fortune smuggling liquor, while my father said that he'd robbed the money from a bank.

Whatever the source of my aunt's money, it was hers to spend now. I hoped that she'd show me some benevolence, and grant me a loan so that I could pay for the photographs.

I walked the five miles to my aunt's townhouse and arrived carrying a bunch of flowers. I must confess that I stole the flowers from gardens as I walked past. I was becoming 'light-fingered' and that troubled me.

Breaking into the movies had become an obsession. I wondered if I'd reach a limit, or if I'd do literally anything to achieve my aim. The whole venture was a trial, a trial of my character. And, already, it had revealed my weaknesses, exposed my flaws. I was not perfect, far from it. To survive in our neighbourhood, you had to be something of a scamp, something of a scoundrel; living on your wits was the only way to get by.

I offered the flowers – a mixture of roses, carnations and orchids – to Aunt Tula then joined her in her drawing room.

The walls were a mixture of deep purple and light lilac. Pictures crowded those walls, mainly family photographs. I noticed one picture of me as a baby; I looked frightened, for some reason.

Aunt Tula owned a piano; she could play. She could also sing, and paint. She was very artistic, very creative. A short woman, she possessed wavy grey hair, close-set brown eyes, pinched cheeks and high cheekbones. She always wore a pearl necklace, and a number of gold bracelets around her left wrist. She had a penchant for sherry. Indeed, a decanter sat on a small table, beside her favourite armchair.

"How is your mother?" Aunt Tula asked.

"She won't allow me to see her," I said. "But my father says there's no improvement."

"Your mother has always been a bit...peculiar," Aunt Tula said. "She was blessed with great beauty, but cursed with a troubled mind; she was always with us, but never really there."

"I know what you mean," I said.

"How is your father?" Aunt Tula asked.

"He's well," I said. "Except, he can't find work at the moment; his back is playing him up."

"And he's drinking," Aunt Tula said.

"That too," I said.

"I don't wish to be mean," Aunt Tula frowned, "but your father is a wastrel. Even with her troubled mind, my sister could have found someone better than him."

"I love him," I said.

"He's your father," Aunt Tula said. "Of course you love him. Nevertheless, he's a wastrel; loving a person like him is not easy; I admire your loyalty."

Aunt Tula reached for her decanter and poured herself a thimble of sherry. She sipped the sherry, then ran a finger around the rim of the glass. She did this repeatedly. My mother had similar habits. Maybe they were family traits.

"What can I do for you, child?" Aunt Tula asked.

I produced my copy of *Motion Picture* and explained the nature of my visit. "I would like to enter this competition," I said. "The first prize is a bit part in a movie. I need two photographs to submit with the entry form. I was wondering...if...er...you could loan me some money for the...er...photographs."

Aunt Tula frowned. She canted her head to her right. "I thought you were working in the tin factory."

"I am," I said.

Aunt Tula took another sip of her sherry. Slowly, she smiled and nodded. "But your father claims your wages and spends them on sin."

"He buys food as well," I said.

"He's a wastrel," Aunt Tula said. She drank her sherry then poured herself another glass.

Aunt Tula's sherry glasses, and the decanter, were decorated with an interlacing pattern, a series of criss-crossing red lines, which made the glasses easier to grip.

It was said that Aunt Tula drank sherry with every meal, plus a glass mid-morning and another mid-afternoon. At the end of the day, she would retire with her bottle of sherry and pour herself a nightcap.

"I have thought about your request," Aunt Tula said, "and decided to reject it: motion pictures are just a passing fad; they will fade in no time. If you wish to borrow money for a sound purpose, my door will remain open to you. But I will not see you fritter away my money on a passing fad."

"I think..."

"It doesn't matter what you think, child; my mind is made up; now, you must excuse me; I'm meeting my lady friends for a hand of bridge. I lost twelve dollars last week; today, I'm hoping to win that money back."

Twelve dollars was more than enough to pay for my photographs, I thought. However, I didn't dare say those words to Aunt Tula.

I left my aunt's house and meandered home, pausing beside a park. I saw children playing, children around my age. They seemed happy. Probably, their dreams centred on playing on the slides and swings, and not on appearing on the silver screen.

I wondered if I should quit my movie ambitions and be more like those children, more humble, more in tune with my surroundings. Then I decided, no, the parks were not for me; a devil possessed my mother, and a different devil possessed me; my devil insisted that I had to appear in the movies. Somehow – I didn't know how – I would appease that devil; I would appear on the silver screen.

The Offer

I struggled to find a – legitimate – way to make the money for my photographs. I tried hiding my wages from my father, but somehow he always found them. The competition entry deadline was fast approaching – I only had two more weeks to find five dollars.

At moments like these, I missed Finn. He'd never been good at coming up with solutions, but he'd always been a good listener; in the past, I could always talk with him.

At the end of my shift in the tin factory, I fell into step with some of my old school 'friends'. Or, rather, they decided to follow me down the alley.

"Oh, look," Mary-Jane Sinclair said, "it's Tula Bowman."

"She stinks," Zelda Walters said. "Go on, sniff her; she smells of old socks."

"It's dirty in the tin factory," I said. "I'm going home now, to have a bath."

"We heard your mother's in the asylum," Lauren Bonetti said. "We heard she's mad."

"My mother is not mad," I said. "She's sick; she'll be better soon."

The truth was, my mother was not getting any better. Indeed, my father reported that she was getting worse. She'd requested to see me. When the doctor asked her why, she'd replied that she wanted to kill me. My mother said that she was dying and that she wanted me to go with her.

It upset me to think of my mother being ill. It upset me because I couldn't visit her. I struggled with those thoughts. I wondered if I could find a way to connect with her, and if I could connect with her, maybe that would make her feel better.

"We've heard that you've been begging for money," Zelda Walters said.

"I haven't been begging for money," I said. "But I do need five dollars to enter this competition."

I showed the gang a copy of *Motion Picture*, which had become my habitual companion. Until I sent off the entry form and my photographs, I vowed that this magazine would never leave my side.

Davy Coombes joined the gang, and showed an interest in the magazine. A man wandered over to join us. He was tall and lean with greasy hair and a weedy moustache. I didn't like the look of him. He seemed kinda creepy.

"Show me your knickers," Mary-Jane Sinclair said, "and I'll give you five dollars."

"I'm not showing anyone my knickers," I said, holding my skirt tight to my thighs. "Besides, girls shouldn't want to see each other's knickers."

"Mary-Jane's a dyke, aren't you, love?" Zelda Walters laughed. "She's in love with girls."

"Shut up," Mary-Jane Sinclair scowled, "or I'll smash your face in."

"There's nothing wrong with being a dyke," Lauren Bonetti said, her voice soft, her eyes cast down to the ground.

"Give Davy Coombes a kiss," Zelda Walters said. "Let us watch, and we'll all give you a dollar."

"I'm not kissing Davy Coombes," I said. "I'm not kissing anyone. Go away; leave me alone."

I increased my pace and left the gang laughing on a corner. However, by the time I reached the end of the alley, the greasy man with the thin moustache had caught up with me.

"I hear you're looking for money," he said.

I frowned. "What's it to you?"

He caressed the corners of his moustache and grinned. "I might be able to help you."

"How?" I scowled.

"Come with me," he said. "And I'll show you. Come on. Don't be shy. By the way, my name's Aaron."

I followed Aaron into another alley. This was a really dingy place, even worse than our abode. We climbed a rickety wooden staircase and entered an attic.

"This is my garret," Aaron said, waving a grubby hand around, indicating his clutter with some pride. "Cool, innit? Make yourself at home."

I looked around Aaron's garret. There was nowhere to sit, at least, nowhere clean. However, he did own a camera, perched on a tripod, and a background screen. The screen, originally white, had faded to cream.

"You're Tula Bowman," Aaron said.

I nodded. "I know who I am."

"Your mother's in the asylum."

"I know that too," I said.

Aaron sat on a scruffy armchair. He picked up a bottle of beer, removed the cap with his thumb, then placed the neck of the bottle to his lips. He drank thirstily. I watched with a mixture of curiosity and revulsion as Aaron's Adam's apple bobbed up and down, in time with each swallow.

Aaron drew the back of his hand across his lips and wiped away the excess beer. He offered me a toothy grin. His teeth were uneven. Many were missing. Those that remained were brown.

"Your mother was a whore," Aaron said.

"People keep saying that," I scowled, "but it's not true."

"She was a whore before you were born," Aaron said.

"Liar!" I screamed.

Aaron laughed. "Everyone in Brooklyn, certainly everyone in this neighbourhood, knows about your mother, so why don't you relax and accept the fact."

With a pout, I held my ground. With tears clouding my eyes, I stared at the threadbare carpet.

"Everyone in this neighbourhood knows that you wanna be an actress," Aaron said.

"So?" I shrugged.

"I'll take your picture for free, if you'll perform like your mother."

"I ain't no whore," I said. "And I ain't whoring to break into the movies."

Maybe I'd discovered my limits. Maybe I'd identified a line that I wouldn't cross. If so, I felt mildly proud of myself.

"Come on," Aaron encouraged, "just the once."

"I'm leaving," I said.

"Wait!"

Displaying surprising agility, Aaron leapt up and ran to the door. There, he blocked my exit.

"Okay," Aaron said, "no whoring. But pose for me, allow me to take some personal pictures, and I'll take the pictures for your magazine."

"No way," I said. "I'm leaving."

I made to push past Aaron, but he grabbed my shoulders and held me tight. He adjusted his grip, pinned me to the wall, by my neck, and produced a knife. He held the knife, a switchblade, against my cheek.

Aaron could have killed me, but that thought did not produce any fear. I trembled because if he scarred my face, I would never break into the movies – no one wanted a heroine with a scarred face.

"Pose for me," Aaron said, his stale breath assaulting my nose and ear. "Let me take your picture."

"Okay," I said. "But let me go; you're hurting me."

Aaron relaxed his grip. His whole body relaxed. I seized my chance, drew my leg back and kneed him in the groin. He dropped his knife, sank to his knees and, moaning, cupped his groin.

I thought about kicking him in the ass. However, instead I ran down the rickety staircase and escaped into the alley.

The Gamble

For the following week, I was in a foul mood. Maybe I was depressed. My chance was slipping away. If I failed to enter the competition, it would be a regret I'd carry with me for the rest of my life.

One evening, my father arrived home from a heavy drinking session. He was drunk; yet even in his inebriated state, he identified my mood – that's how low I'd sunk.

"What's the matter, princess?" my father asked.

"Nothing," I said.

"Don't give me no nothing," he said. "Don't be like your mother; tell me what's wrong."

"It's the competition," I said. "I can't get the money together for the photographs."

"Maybe you could put in some overtime at the tin factory," my father suggested.

"There ain't no overtime going. In fact, there's talk of lay-offs."

"Never mind," my father sighed. "I'm sure you'll find another job."

"I want to be an actress," I said. "I want that to be my job. I earn enough money at the tin factory to pay for the photographs, but you take it all, and spend it all on whiskey and cigarettes."

"Are you accusing me?" my father scowled.

"Well," I said, "it's true."

My father hit me, slapped me hard across my face. We stared at each other in stunned silence. Then I started to cry.

"I'm sorry, princess," my father said. He wrapped his arms around me and held me close. "I'm sorry. I don't know what came over me. I'll make it up to you."

"How?" I sobbed.

My father patted my back. Then he held me at arm's length and looked me in the eyes. "It costs money to travel and visit your mother," he said. "That's where all your wages goes."

We both knew that that was a pathetic lie, so I repeated my question. "How are you going to make it up to me?"

My father thought for a long minute. He wasn't the quickest thinker, even when sober. When drunk, it could take him an age to gather his thoughts.

Eventually, my father walked around the room sporting a smile. "Tomorrow evening," he said, "you'll come with me. We'll get the money for your photographs."

The following evening, I accompanied my father to a basement in an extremely rough part of our neighbourhood. We found four men sitting in the basement, around a heavily scarred circular table. The men were drinking whiskey and playing poker. A large number of empty bottles and the stale atmosphere suggested that they were all drunk.

"Sorry," my father said, "but I had to bring Tula. A bit of trouble in our block. Talk of a rapist. I didn't want to leave her alone."

My father took his seat at the table. On our way over, he'd coached me. I knew what I had to do – I was going to help him cheat.

"Five-card draw," the dealer said, shuffling the cards. "Aces high."

The dealer was a lean man sporting a porkpie hat and a heavily stained waistcoat. A scar ran down his right cheek and met with his lips.

The dealer chewed on a cheroot and eyed me with some suspicion. Nevertheless, he dealt the cards. He also poured four fingers of whiskey into five dirty glasses. It saddened me to see my father in such company. It saddened me further to realise that this was his life.

My task was to wander around the basement and, surreptitiously, look at the playing cards. If I saw a red picture card, I had to caress my left eyebrow; for a red ace, I had to rub the left-hand side of my nose.

Before arriving in the basement, my father had told me that I had to repeat that pattern on the right-hand side of my face, for the black picture cards and aces. He assured me that, with my information, he could work out how to play each hand and, more often than not, win. All I had to do was play my part.

And that's how I viewed the situation – I was playing a part.

Despite the dealer's suspicions, I managed to relay the information to my father. Even so, he proceeded to lose the opening hands. I wondered if the losses were a deliberate tactic on his part, of if he was dreadful at poker. I must confess, I suspected the latter.

In the long run, the early losses worked in our favour because the dealer relaxed; he focused on his cards and the whiskey; he dragged his gaze away from me.

Of course, I had to look natural and not show any obvious interest in the game. I had to look like a bored sixteen-year-old, a role I could play 'in my sleep'.

I walked around the basement and stared at the walls. In truth, there was nothing to see, only cracks and mildew. Actually, there was one item of note in the basement – a broken mirror. The mirror angled towards a stout man with a harelip. He was the best poker player in the room. In the mirror, surreptitiously, I studied his cards and relayed the information to my father.

As the evening wore on, my father started to win, not a huge amount, but enough to pay for my photographs. I wanted him to quit while he was ahead. However, riding his luck, my father played on.

After losing the largest pot of the evening, the dealer sat back with a sigh. While my father counted his winnings, and the other players sought solace in the whiskey, the dealer turned to me and said, "I hear you're gonna be an actress."

"That's right," I said.

"And a dancer?"

I shrugged. "Maybe."

"Dance for us then," the dealer insisted. "Go on, put on a show."

I wasn't a natural dancer. Nonetheless, I did my best. While I danced, I noticed that the man with the harelip was marking the cards – everyone in this room was a cheat.

At the conclusion of my impromptu dance, the dealer offered me a round of applause. He rolled his cheroot across his lips, from one corner of his mouth to the other then, with a patting gesture, invited me to sit on his lap.

"No," my father said, holding up his hand, "my Tula don't do any of that."

"None of it?" the dealer frowned.

"None of it," my father said. "She's gonna

concentrate on her career. She won't have no time for men."

At that moment, I didn't fully appreciate what my father was saying. It sounded like he had no wish for me to find a husband.

The men around the card table played their final hand. It boiled down to a showdown between my father and the man with the harelip, the two best cheaters in the room. My photographs, and future career, depended upon who could cheat best.

Having folded his hand, the dealer could concentrate on me, so it was doubly difficult to relay the information to my father. Nevertheless, I came up with an obvious plan. I hitched up my skirt, just a little, so that the dealer would focus on my bare thighs. While he stared at my thighs, I tapped the left-hand side of my nose.

My father and I walked home in the dark, under a star-blessed sky. He handed me five dollars, smiled and looked up at the sky.

"There you are, Tula," my father said. "Go on and get your photographs. Go on and become a star."

The Photographer

The following day, I caught a tram and made my way into the centre of Brooklyn. I'd seen an advertisement in *Photoplay* – 'Star portraits taken, two for only five dollars. Satisfaction guaranteed, or your money back.'

Before setting off, I styled my hair so that I had curls, like Mary Pickford. I applied rouge to my lips and blusher to my cheeks. I also slipped into my mother's sequined dress because that dress was the best in the house.

On the tram, I attracted a number of looks. In the main, the women scowled at me, as though I were a tramp, while the men smiled. One man gave me a quarter. He also gave me his business card – he was a banker in Brooklyn.

I read his address and telephone number. Did he expect me to phone him? Did he expect me to call on him? I wished that I could talk about such things with my mother, but she was still in the asylum, and still refusing to see me.

I found the photographer's studio in an alley off Church Avenue. I entered his premises and looked around.

The photographer was a stout man with a bald head surrounded by a neatly-trimmed corona. His eyebrows were bushy. He also sported a bushy moustache.

The sign above the studio door suggested that the photographer was Mr Hargreaves. His studio looked very professional, at least to my untrained eye.

Glancing around, I noticed a number of painted backgrounds. These backgrounds, in the main, depicted seascapes. I also noticed a number of powerful lights, an uncomfortable-looking chair for the model, and a large camera perched on a tripod. The camera seemed too big for the tripod's legs and I feared that the whole contraption would topple to the ground.

On the way to the studio, I'd imagined all kinds of disasters, from the tram breaking down to an earthquake, from someone robbing us to the photographer, indeed the whole of Brooklyn, running out of film.

This part of the process was out of my control, hence my heightened state of anxiety. I felt that I would calm down, once I had my portrait photographs safely in my hands.

With a frown and nervous steps, I approached Mr Hargreaves. He stared at me and scowled. "What can I do you for?" he asked.

I didn't understand why he'd placed his words in that particular order, so I continued to frown.

Mr Hargreaves canted his head to the right. He wore a leather apron, a chequered waistcoat and a plain bowtie. "Are you all right, miss?" he asked.

"Yes," I said, "yes, I'm fine." I offered him my dog-eared copy of *Motion Picture*. "I'd like you to take my photograph."

"Got five dollars?" he asked.

I opened my hand and revealed the money. I'd held the money tight in my hand throughout my journey. I didn't dare to let it go. I didn't dare to place it in my purse in case I lost it.

"Okay," Mr Hargreaves said, "sit on that chair; I'll get you sorted, shortly."

I sat on the wooden chair and confirmed that it was uncomfortable. Indeed, it wobbled. That cast a doubt in my mind. Maybe Mr Hargreaves wasn't so professional after all. I mean, surely a professional photographer would place his subject on a firm chair.

"Okay," Mr Hargreaves said, before I could raise any complaint, "you want the standard mug shots?"

"Mug shots?" I frowned.

"Yeah," Mr Hargreaves said, "like the police do with the criminals: front and side views."

"Oh," I said. "Okay, I'll have the mug shots."

Mr Hargreaves took two photographs. The flash was very bright and it made me blink. I hoped that the pictures would not display me with closed eyes.

"Right," Mr Hargreaves said, "come back tomorrow and I'll have your photos ready."

"Tomorrow?" I frowned.

"Yes," he said. "I need to develop the film. It's a very tricky process." For some reason, he tapped the side of his nose. "That's why you need an expert like me."

I didn't sleep that night. I was on tenterhooks, wondering what my pictures would reveal. Would I look as glamorous as Lillian Gish, as stylish as Florence Lawrence? I could only hope.

The following day, I caught the tram again and returned to the centre of Brooklyn. I was tempted to run, but somehow I composed myself as I made my way to Mr Hargreaves' studio.

In the studio, I discovered that Mr Hargreaves was taking photographs of a young woman around my age. I wondered if she was entering the competition too. She held a particularly striking pose. I hadn't thought to do that. Instead, I'd just stared at the camera.

The young woman departed and Mr Hargreaves turned his attention to me. He stared at me, as though I were unfamiliar.

"Tula Bowman," I said. "You took my photograph yesterday."

"Oh, yes," Mr Hargreaves said. "Wait there. I'll get your pictures for you in a moment."

While I waited, I tapped my foot on the parquet floor. I was so impatient. I took a deep breath to calm myself down.

Mr Hargreaves returned with a large brown envelope. I ripped open the envelope and stared at the pictures. My heart sank. I didn't recognise the young woman in the photographs; was she really me?

"These are terrible," I said.

"They are top quality prints," Mr Hargreaves said. "The best Brooklyn money can buy."

"But...but...," I stuttered, "I look terrible."

Mr Hargreaves merely shrugged. He left his shop counter and walked over to his tripod. "I just take the pictures," he said, "I'm not responsible for their content. All I can guarantee is, that's you in those pictures, and the camera doesn't lie."

"But...but...," I said, "I look fat and ugly."

Mr Hargreaves shrugged again. "The camera doesn't lie."

"But...but...I'm not fat and ugly."

Mr Hargreaves merely stared at me, a look that filled me with doubt.

"I'm not fat and ugly, am I?"

"Thank you for your custom," Mr Hargreaves said. "I hope to see you again soon."

I placed my photographs in the brown envelope and walked towards the studio door. Then I remembered Mr Hargreaves' advertisement – 'Satisfaction guaranteed, or your money back.'

At the studio door, I turned and glared at Mr Hargreaves. "I'm not satisfied," I said. "I want my money back."

"Get outta here!" Mr Hargreaves said, waving a dismissive hand. "Clear off, or I'll call the police."

I didn't want any trouble, so I made my way to the trams.

On my way home, I stared at my photographs. They were appalling; I had little chance of winning the contest. I thought about ripping my photographs to pieces. However, I had no money or time to take another set of pictures – the deadline was tomorrow.

I thought about ripping up my photographs, but I didn't. They were appalling, but they were my only hope.

The Agent

I didn't have time to post my photographs. Besides, I didn't trust the postal service. So, I caught the tram again and made my third journey into the centre of Brooklyn in three days.

I wish that I could recall that journey in detail, but in all truth I didn't 'see' a thing; my mind was all-consumed with the competition and the agent's reaction – what would he make of my photographs and me?

I made my way into the agent's office and announced the purpose of my visit. The agent's name was Mr Trevors. His secretary performed the introductions.

Mr Trevors was a young man, in his late twenties or early thirties. His hair was very thin – he'd be bald by forty – and he sported a thin moustache. Tall and lean, his clothes – a standard shirt, tie and business suit – appeared at least two sizes too big for him. I also noticed that he suffered from some kind of eczema and that red blotches blighted his otherwise pale skin.

I feared that the agent would be an imposing, intimidating man. However, Mr Trevors appeared friendly, someone I could talk with. When I entered offices or talked with businessmen, I always put on an act – I acted confident or, at least, I tried to. With Mr Trevors, I felt that I could be myself.

"Take a seat, Miss Bowman," Mr Trevors said, "I'll be with you in a minute."

Mr Trevors talked with his secretary. I tried to eavesdrop, but they talked in whispers. I felt that they were talking about me. Or maybe my paranoia was due to my heightened sense of anxiety.

While Mr Trevors talked with his secretary, I glanced around his office. I noticed a calendar, a telephone, an ink blotter, a fountain pen, an official-looking letter, and pictures of my 'rivals'. All the women in these pictures were older than me. All were beautiful. However, could they act?

"Sorry to keep you waiting, Miss Bowman," Mr Trevors said as he settled behind his desk. He leaned forward and smiled. "How may I help you?"

I produced the brown envelope and my atrocious pictures. "I'd like to enter the acting competition," I said. "I've filled in the form, and here are my pictures."

Mr Trevors accepted my entry form and my pictures. He studied the form and nodded. Then he studied my pictures. From time to time, he glanced from the pictures to me.

"These pictures do not do you justice," he said.

"Thank you for your kind words," I said.

"In fact," he sighed, "they're dreadful."

"I know," I said. "Couldn't we somehow arrange replacements?"

"There's no time," Mr Trevors said, glancing at his calendar. "Today is the deadline."

Of course, I was aware of that fact. Also, I'd used all of my spare money on tram fares; I couldn't afford another set of pictures.

Clutching at straws, I stood and made a suggestion. "I'd like to act a scene for you," I said.

Mr Trevors picked up his fountain pen and tapped it on his blotter. "This isn't an audition," he said.

"I know," I said. "But I'd like to act a scene for you anyway."

Mr Trevors sat back. His chair creaked. His secretary eyed me with some suspicion. Mr Trevors glanced at her as she fed paper into a typewriter. She tapped the keys. They made a rhythmic sound. A fly settled on the telephone. Mr Trevors waved a hand and the fly flew away.

"Okay," Mr Trevors sighed. "Here's a scene the judges always request. Pick up the telephone. Listen to some upsetting news. Cry for me."

The fly settled on the secretary's typewriter. She tapped a key and the fly flew away. I watched the fly, then imagined the sound of a telephone ringing. With a smile on my face, I picked up the receiver. Then I listened to the sad news. Tears, real tears, rolled down my cheeks. It was so easy to cry in this scene – all I had to do was think of my mother.

The secretary stopped typing. She stared at me. She exchanged glances with Mr Trevors. I had no idea what they were thinking. Maybe they reckoned that I was an odd person. I didn't care about that. I never felt self-conscious when I was acting.

"All right," Mr Trevors said, "you can stop now."

I replaced the receiver, accepted a tissue from Mr Trevors and dried my eyes. The secretary resumed her typing.

Mr Trevors picked up my photographs and studied them again. He glanced at me and shook his head. I tried to gauge what he was thinking. I was still trying to read his mind when he said, "Could you cry for me again?"

The secretary stopped typing. I had an audience. Inwardly, I smiled. I'd captured their attention. I was ready to perform.

This time I thought of Finn, of his life cut short. Tears bubbled up in my eyes and rolled down my cheeks. I didn't offer any melodramatic gestures. Instead, I allowed the emotion, the raw emotion, to speak for itself.

"Okay," Mr Trevors said. "Thank you. You can stop now."

I dried my eyes and glanced at the secretary. She was staring at me with her eyebrows raised. Mr Trevors offered her a polite cough and she returned to her work. I felt sure that I'd impressed the secretary. However, she was not a judge in this competition.

Mr Trevors studied my photographs for the umpteenth time. "These are dreadful," he said.

"I know," I said.

"You are beautiful."

"Thank you," I said.

"The judges are looking for beauty. They're also looking for talent."

"A chance to appear in the finals," I said, "that's all I want."

Mr Trevors nodded. He picked up his fountain pen and scribbled a note on my photographs. I craned my neck and read his words.

Called in person. Ignore this image. Very pretty. Can act.

"I've made a note on your pictures," Mr Trevors said.

"Thank you," I said.

"Good luck in the competition."

"Thank you," I said.

"If you're successful," he said, "you'll receive a letter."

"Thank you," I said.

Mr Trevors smiled. "You don't have to thank me every time."

"Thank you," I said. I was embarrassing myself, so I prepared to leave.

"If it were my decision," Mr Trevors said, "you'd win."

"Thank you," I said.

"But it's not my decision."

"I know," I said.

I left my photographs with Mr Trevors and walked towards the door.

"Miss Bowman," Mr Trevors called out. "Before you go, please sign this."

I returned to Mr Trevors' desk and accepted his fountain pen. "What's this?" I frowned. "Some kind of form?"

"No," Mr Trevors said. "I want your autograph. I reckon you'll become famous, a real star."

The Audition

I lost my job at the tin factory. I didn't enjoy the work, but we needed the money, so I was disappointed to lose my job. Twenty other people lost their jobs too. Apparently, we were entering some kind of recession.

At home, I counted my wages. I set aside money for the rent, food and household expenses. Usually, my father claimed the rest, to spend on cigarettes and alcohol.

I tried to figure out a plan, so that I could keep some of the money for myself. Of course, I would have to search for a new job. I preferred office work to factory work, so I hoped that I could find a suitable vacancy in an office.

I was pondering our uncertain future when a letter arrived, addressed to me. Normally, most of our mail was addressed to my father. I opened the letter and discovered that it was an invitation to an audition. Despite my terrible photographs, I'd made it through to the next round.

I felt like screaming with joy. However, I held my tongue and forced myself to think straight. I needed a plan.

My clothes were too dowdy. For the audition, I needed a new dress. To buy a new dress, I needed money. I looked at my wages and decided that my father would not claim his share, this week.

I spent my first day off work scouring the employment advertisements and the fashion stores. I found a job that I considered suitable, in an herbal store, and sent off my application.

The dresses in the fashion stores, at least the dresses I liked, were all too expensive. However, I did find a dress that matched my budget. It was a long, off-the-shoulder, red dress. I reckoned that I would stand out in that dress, that I would grab the attention of the judges.

At home, I hid my red dress. I also hid news of the audition from my father. I didn't want anyone to know, in case I flopped, in case I was a major failure.

Thankfully, on audition day, my father had to see 'a man about a dog'. I'd grown to realise that that meant my father was meeting someone for a nefarious purpose. I didn't pry into these meetings. I reckoned that, to control my anxiety, it was best not to know.

For 'special occasions' I had the habit of applying too much make-up. I knew this was a bad habit, and that it didn't enhance my appearance. All the same, I couldn't help myself: for the audition, I applied generous amounts of rouge and lipstick.

The producers held the audition in an old

church hall. Three producers sat behind a trestle table. One was elderly with a bald head and a bushy moustache. A middle-aged woman, offering the appearance of a strict school teacher, sat to his right. The man to his left looked friendly. He was younger, in his early thirties, at a guess. A large scar snaked across his forehead. The scar looked like a shrapnel wound. I wondered if he'd served in the Great War.

Eleven other women attended the audition. All were older than me. We sat against the wall, on wooden chairs, and waited our turn to be called.

The producers called the women by age; at least that's how it appeared to me. This meant that I would go last.

I watched each budding actress as she responded to the producers' directions. All the budding actresses performed like Mary Pickford; they filtered their scenes through Mary Pickford's gestures and facial expressions. Needless to say, they were not as good as Mary Pickford.

The producers called me and I stepped into the centre of the hall. The bald-headed man with the bushy moustache looked bored; undoubtedly, he'd presided over many similar auditions.

The strict woman scowled at me; I sensed that she didn't like my red dress; more to the point, I sensed that she didn't like my naked shoulders;

maybe the choice of this dress had been too daring.

The younger man with the scarred forehead offered me a smile of encouragement. I recognised that he was not favouring me because he'd smiled at all the budding actresses.

"You've received good news," the bald-headed producer said. "How would you react?"

I considered how Mary Pickford would react, then dismissed that thought. Instead, I pictured myself as the strict woman and acted accordingly. I walked around in a haughty manner and offered myself a self-satisfied smile. Her scowl suggested that the woman producer was not impressed. However, the male producers nodded as though satisfied.

"You've received sad news," the bald-headed producer said. "How would you react?"

For me, this was easy: I thought of my mother and cried.

As I dried my eyes, I glanced at the judges. They offered no reaction, not even a scowl or a frown.

"Thank you," the bald-headed producer said. "We will contact the finalists."

On my way home, I wondered if I should have followed the crowd and acted like Mary Pickford.

At home, I found my father waiting for me. He appeared angry. Apparently, his meeting had not gone as planned.

"Where have you been?" my father asked.

"To an audition," I said.

"Audition?" he frowned.

"Yes," I said. "I won through the first round of the *Motion Picture* contest."

"Why didn't you tell me?" my father asked.

"I don't know," I shrugged.

My father circled me. He stared at my dress, eyed it up and down. "Where did you get that dress?" he scowled.

"I bought it," I said, "out of my wages."

"You spent all your wages, on a dress?"

"Only the spare money," I said.

My father brought his hand down hard on the dresser. The slap made a frightful sound. "Pawn the dress," he said.

"Pawn it?" I frowned.

"Yes," he said. "We need to eat."

"And drink," I said, *sotto voce*.

My father understood my meaning all too well. He knew that I was referring to his drinking habits. His cheeks flushed red and he raised his hand, as though to strike me.

"I'm sorry," I said, raising my hands to protect myself. "Please, don't hit me."

My father caught himself in time. He lowered his hand and puffed out his cheeks. "I wasn't going to hit you, princess," he said. "I would never do anything to hurt you."

"I'll pawn the dress," I said.

"Yes," he said, "you do that. And we'll have stew for dinner. You make a wonderful stew."

"Thank you," I said.

"Hurry up," my father said, "I'm hungry."

"I'll be back soon," I said.

The Final

I made it through to the final. Tula Bowman of Brownsville, Brooklyn had made it through to the final of the 'Motion Picture Actress Contest'. I was beside myself with joy. I wanted to run around my neighbourhood, spreading the news. However, I told no one, not even my father.

I didn't tell my father, but he discovered my letter; I think he was looking for my money.

"This is wonderful news," my father said. "You must buy a new dress for the occasion."

Over recent days, my father had earned some money singing in the local bars. This had placed him in a happier mood.

My father loaned me the money and I bought another dress. That meant two new dresses inside a month. I'd never been so extravagant with my money. This time, I bought a green dress. It was far more modest than my red dress, quite plain in fact, but it looked clean and smart, and I felt sure that it would impress the producers.

Once again, we met at the church hall. Once again, the three producers sat behind a trestle table. My rival arrived before me. She was blue-eyed, blonde and lean, quite beautiful. I couldn't compete with her in terms of looks, but maybe I could outshine her with my performance.

While the producers organised the final audition, I sat with my rival and we chatted.

"Hi," I said.

"Hello," she said.

"What's your name?"

"Kathryn. What's yours?"

"Tula," I said.

Kathryn leaned forward and stared at me. "How old are you?" she asked.

"Sixteen," I said. "How old are you?"

"Twenty-two. Have you done any acting before?"

"Not really," I said. "Just a little bit in school. How about you?"

"I've been on the stage," Kathryn said. "I had a small part in *Romeo and Juliet*."

"Wow," I said, rolling my eyes.

"I want to win this," Kathryn said. "I want to be a big star in Hollywood."

"I just want to act," I said. "I want to act for a living."

"You got any money?" Kathryn asked.

"Money?" I frowned.

"Yeah," she said. "Does your family have any money?"

"We pay the rent," I said.

Kathryn laughed. She placed a hand over her

mouth when she laughed. I considered that a childish gesture. Indeed, in our previous audition I considered that all her gestures and mannerisms had been childish. Maybe the producers were looking for an actress who could act in a childish manner; maybe they were looking for an ingénue; after all, I was quite young and Kathryn had made it through to the final.

"I'm not talking about rent money," Kathryn said, "I'm talking about real money."

"We haven't got much money," I said. "We're quite poor."

"Oh," Kathryn said. She leaned forward again and stared at me.

I glanced at the producers. They were reading their notes, probably the comments they'd made at our previous audition. For now, they didn't offer us any attention. Doubtless, that would come later.

Kathryn picked at a thread in her dress. She wore a luxurious dress of transparent chiffon. Her forearms and collarbones were clearly visible, as were her bodice and slip. I glanced at my green dress. My earlier optimism about my green dress faded. Compared to Kathryn's dress, it looked dowdy.

"Would you like some money?" Kathryn asked.

"How much?" I frowned.

"Say, a thousand dollars."

"A thousand dollars!" I rolled my eyes again. Indeed, they threatened to roll out of their sockets. "You have that much money?"

"Yeah," Kathryn said, "of course. My family's loaded. I could give you a thousand dollars, no problem."

"That's very kind of you," I said, "but I couldn't accept your money."

Kathryn leaned close and whispered into my ear. "I could give you a thousand dollars," she said, "if you let me win this contest."

I chewed on my lower lip. We could certainly do with the money. However, this was my big chance, my big chance to break into motion pictures. The money was important, but so are dreams. I shook my head, as though to clear it of all doubts.

"I don't know about that," I said.

"Think of what you could do with a thousand dollars," Kathryn said.

I could buy a new wardrobe. My father could buy new clothes. We could decorate our apartment. Maybe we could move to a new apartment. We could pay a doctor to treat my mother. Surely, that was more important than any acting competition.

"If I win this contest," I said, "I might earn more than a thousand dollars."

"That's true," Kathryn said. "But it's a gamble.

I'm offering you a thousand dollars, guaranteed."
She nudged me with a pointy elbow. "What do you
say, Tula; would you like a thousand dollars?"

"Thank you for your offer," I said, "but I must
decline."

"You're turning me down?" Kathryn frowned.

"Yes," I said. "I want to win this contest. And if
I win this contest I will earn enough money to pay
for my mother's treatment."

Kathryn scowled. She looked ugly when she
scowled. "You're a selfish bitch, aren't you, Tula
Bowman."

"I'm not selfish," I said.

"You'll be sorry," Kathryn said.

The producers called me and I stood for my
audition. However, as I stood, Kathryn trod on the
hem of my dress. She tore my dress, smiled then
said, "Sorry."

Our auditions were familiar to me now – act
happy at good news, act sad at bad news. For
happy, I thought of the time we'd visited the
fairground as a family. For sad, of course, I thought
of my mother. I acted natural in both roles; I didn't
try to imitate Mary Pickford. In all truth, I struggled
with my audition because I had to keep one hand
on my torn dress.

Kathryn threw her heart and soul into her
audition. I thought she was melodramatic in her

performance, overemotional, theatrical. Indeed, I reckoned that her performance was more suited to the wide vistas of the stage than the tight focus of a camera lens. However, that was only my opinion. In a few days, the producers would decide.

Outside the church hall, I found my father waiting for me.

"What are you doing here?" I asked.

"I've been to see your mother."

"How is she?"

My father shook his head. He offered me a sad frown. "Not well. Not well at all."

"Can I see her?" I asked.

"No," my father said. "Your mother reckons that she doesn't have a daughter. She reckons that you died at birth."

I fought back tears and tied a knot in my torn dress.

Kathryn Stewart skipped down the church hall steps and walked past me. She offered a regal wave and a confident smile.

My father hugged me, placed an arm around my shoulders, and we walked along the sidewalk. "How did you get on?" he asked.

"All right," I said. "The producers will write to me, if I've won."

"You'll win," my father said.

"Do you think so?" I frowned.

My father squeezed my shoulder and offered me a generous smile. "You'll win," he said. "You're a Bowman, and Bowmans are the best."

The Turning Point

Three days later, a letter arrived. The letter was from the herbal store. I'd secured employment as an assistant. I should have felt great joy; this was a steady job with decent wages. However, I felt disappointment because I'd hoped for a letter from the producers.

Two days after the herbal store letter, another letter arrived. I read it twelve times.

Dear Miss Bowman,

We are pleased to inform you that you have won the 'Motion Picture Actress Contest, 1921'. We, the judges, were most impressed with your auditions. We considered that your performances were totally natural and highly original. We were also taken by your appearance and beauty. We feel that the combination of your acting skills and youthful good looks will translate well on to the silver screen.

Your prizes: you will receive an evening gown from the Abraham and Straus store and, in the near future, an invitation from a leading movie producer to appear in a motion picture. Your role will be that of a 'bit' player, a part in support of the main players.

We would like to take this opportunity to thank you for entering the 'Motion Picture Actress Contest, 1921', and to wish you every success in your future acting career.

Yours sincerely,

Jeremiah Staniforth
Margaret Leachman
Joshua Trimble

I fantasised about my bit part. Maybe Lillian Gish would be a member of the cast. Maybe I'd meet Mary Pickford. The director would probably ask me to play an ingénue. I'd been practicing such roles; I could easily play that part.

I placed the letter in my keepsake box and locked it with a key. Then, I went to the pawnbroker's and reclaimed my red dress. After that, I visited the butcher and bought two cuts of the finest beef. I would make a stew for my father and we would celebrate.

I paid for my dress and the beef with money I'd discovered in a pot, under the kitchen sink. My mother must have hoarded that money for 'a rainy day'. The problem was, it always rained on the Bowmans. However, the two letters in recent days had provided a rainbow.

I was chopping up the beef when my father

walked in. I turned to him, excited, but he looked away. Indeed, he looked sad.

"What's the matter?" I asked.

"She's gone," my father said. "She's dead. Your mother's dead."

I hugged my father and he sobbed, uncontrollably, on my shoulder. I sobbed too. Between us, we produced enough tears to flood Brooklyn.

When our tears subsided, I asked, "What happened?"

My father pulled away and walked to the kitchen sink. There, he splashed water over his face.

"I'm not sure," he said. "The doctors suggested it was some kind of fever. Your mother was too weak in her body and mind to fight the disease. She was weak the day I married her, but I didn't care about that because I loved her. Now, she's gone and I don't know what to do."

That evening, we picked our way through our dinner, then retired to our beds. In bed, I reflected on my mother and father's relationship.

My father had truly loved my mother, with all his heart. Her death had broken his heart. However, my mother had damaged my father's heart before with her reluctance to return his love.

I wondered why my mother had been so cold towards my father. Maybe she'd never really loved him. Maybe she'd married out of need.

I reasoned that my mother's illness had a lot to do with her coldness, her coldness towards my father, and me.

I thought about the factors that had triggered my mother's illness. Maybe her illness had something to do with a gene that she'd inherited from her mother. Maybe it had something to do with a bad fall she'd suffered as a teenager, a fall that had cracked open her head.

I'd heard that some sexual diseases caused the mind to fester, but in relation to my mother, I didn't want to dwell upon that.

The deaths of my sisters at birth must also have been a factor. Maybe my mother's mental troubles stemmed from a combination of all these factors. She'd been through a lot; she'd suffered plenty, and carried the mental scars.

My mother had resented my ambitions to become an actress. I considered writing to the producers to tell them that I could not accept the evening gown or the bit part. I'd secured a good job at the herbal store. Maybe now was the moment to concentrate on my work, and allow my acting ambitions to go, to fade like the morning mist.

My mind was in turmoil, overburdened with so many thoughts. I realised that I should not make any life changing decisions until after my mother's funeral.

I sobbed into my pillow, then looked up when my father stepped into my bedroom. He was drunk. He was also carrying a bottle of whiskey.

"I don't want to drink alone," my father said. "Drink with me, down to the label."

"All right," I said. In all truth, I didn't want to be alone either.

Throughout the night, I drank whiskey with my father. We drank well past the label. We finished the bottle, and more. I'd tasted whiskey before, but in moderation. That night I drank so much, it went completely to my head.

The following morning, I woke up in my bed, fully clothed. I had no idea how I got there; my father must have carried me. I ached from head to toe, and shivered as though I had the ague. My body was covered in cuts and bruises. I must have stumbled and fell. I must have been drunk. I'd never been drunk before. My memories were hazy, but I realised that I didn't like the sensation.

My pillow was stained with tears. I noticed blood on my bedding. I'd cut my knee; that would account for the blood.

I learned a valuable lesson that night – whiskey did not agree with me. Alcohol did not agree with me. My father needed alcohol to survive. However, I resolved never to touch a drop of the stuff, ever again.

The Funeral

My mother's death deeply affected my father. It deeply affected my relationship with my father. We no longer talked with each other, we no longer communicated. We just got by with the essentials. When my mother was alive, my father liked to joke with me. Now, the humour had gone.

My father was in mourning, I told myself; I was in mourning. Maybe our relationship would return to a sound footing after the funeral.

I made the funeral arrangements; my father was too drunk to cope with the details. My mother had been a member of the local church, so it was natural that the local churchyard would become her final resting place.

I also started work in the herbal store, the day before my mother's funeral. I needed time off, of course, and the owner, Mr Penhaligon, was kind enough to grant me that time.

My personality changed over the three days that led up to my mother's funeral. In retrospect, I can see that I endured some sort of mental breakdown.

My mother's death had triggered that breakdown, of course, along with the estrangement from my father and the stress of learning a new job.

I always liked to please people, to do my very best, and, when under stress, that additional strain could be mind-breaking.

I hid my feelings from my father; at least I hid them until the day of the funeral. Then, all my emotions poured out.

I can recall the day we buried my mother in great detail, in too much detail. Over the years, I've tried to lose those thoughts, but they keep whirling around, like a movie in my mind.

Aunt Tula arrived at the church in all her finery. A symphony in black, she wore a pillbox hat, a veil, a lace-trimmed dress, pearls and a heavy overcoat. Her attire suited her. She looked natural dressed in black, made for funerals.

My father sobered up for the occasion. He even managed to knot his black tie, although it did rest at a drunken angle against his white shirt.

I dressed in black too. In a trance-like state, I buttoned my blouse and skirt. I felt as though I was not there. I felt as though I were an observer. Maybe that's why the memories of that day remain so vivid.

We gathered around the graveside, Vicar Symonds, my father, Aunt Tula, my mother's church friends, and relatives I only ever saw at weddings, occasionally, and funerals, more often.

Vicar Symonds conducted the service. He

spoke well of my mother, reminded everyone how generous she'd been to the church.

I didn't fully understand Vicar Symonds' words because we'd never had any money to donate to the church. Furthermore, when alive my mother saw the church as a social outlet. The religious aspects bored her. She believed in God, but only when it suited her.

Maybe Vicar Symonds spoke out of kindness. After all, you'd only speak harsh words about someone as you laid them to rest if they'd been a true devil. The Devil had possessed my mother on occasions, especially those moments when she'd attacked me with a knife. But at heart she'd been a good person, a bit wicked maybe, but not evil.

The heavens opened as Vicar Symonds concluded the service. Mud slid into the poorly cut grave and landed on my mother's coffin. That upset me. I jumped into the grave to remove the mud.

Of course, this was a ridiculous thing to do because the grave diggers were poised to cover my mother's coffin in mud. However, by that stage, I'd quite literally lost my mind. My thoughts and behaviour were no longer rational. I sat on my mother's coffin and refused to climb out of the grave.

"Tula," my father said, offering his hand, "get out of there; you're making me look stupid."

"I'm not moving," I said. "I want to stay with my mother."

"You can't," my father said. "Get out of there, now!"

"I'm staying," I said.

"She's her mother's daughter, all right," Aunt Tula said, sighing, fingering her black pearls. "The apple hasn't fallen far from the tree."

"You've no right to talk!" I yelled at Aunt Tula. "You never visited my mother when she was ill. You never offered her your support."

Aunt Tula's jaw dropped. Her eyes opened wide. She clutched her pearls, as though for protection, and glared at me.

"You are sick, child, but even a sick child has no right to talk to her aunt like that." Aunt Tula turned to my father and demanded an apology. "Tell her to say sorry. I insist. I will remain at this graveside until I receive an apology."

The grave diggers glanced at Vicar Symonds. The vicar mopped the rain from his balding pate and looked on, somewhat embarrassed. Lightning flashed and thunder rolled across the sky.

Between us, Aunt Tula and I were turning my mother's funeral into a Shakespearian drama, maybe Macbeth, his darkest play.

"Get out of there," my father said, "or I'll jump in and get you."

"I'm staying," I said. "I'm staying with my mother."

The rain continued to pour down. The mourners started to drift away.

"I want an apology," Aunt Tula said. "I'm not moving until I've received an apology."

"Climb out of there and apologise," my father said. "We've got to get to the bar; we've got to make sure everything is right for the wake."

"Say sorry," Aunt Tula said. "Say sorry, now."

"No!" I screamed at everyone, at the world in general. "No!"

Vicar Symonds glanced at the grave diggers. He nodded and they reached into the grave. They grabbed hold of my arms and dragged me through the mud. As they dragged me, I continued to kick and scream.

I was still screaming when the grave diggers handed me over to my father and he slapped my face. The rain mingled with my tears and poured down my face. I'd lost my mother and, in terms of our relationship, I'd lost my father. No wonder I'd also lost my mind.

Literally, my father dragged me to the bar for the wake. I attended in my mud-stained clothes. Aunt Tula refused to attend because I'd refused to apologise.

Naturally, my father got drunk at the wake. By

the end of the evening, he was singing songs, albeit sad and melancholy tunes.

The following day, I resumed my duties at Mr Penhaligon's herbal store as though nothing had happened. But something had happened. When you break a leg, a doctor will set it, tend it, and make it better. Something had broken in my mind, yet my father did not consider that I should visit a doctor. In fairness to him, I did not consider it either. I just got on with my life; I struggled on with a broken mind.

The Incident

My photograph appeared in *Motion Picture* alongside an article that announced me as the winner of the 'Motion Picture Actress Contest'. I should have felt proud of this achievement and, deep down, I did feel some pride. However, I also felt despondent, over my mother's death, and the fractured relationship with my father.

I wasn't sure what to do next. I had enough on my plate, running our family home and coping with the work demands placed upon me by Mr Penhaligon. In fairness, Mr Penhaligon was a kind employer, although he did insist that you earned your wage. With these challenges in my life, I had no time to act or even think about acting. I would have allowed the contest to drift by, except for an incident that occurred after work one evening.

I was adjusting my tam, walking along the sidewalk when, literally, I bumped into Mary-Jane Sinclair, Zelda Walters and Lauren Bonetti. They were smoking cigarettes, hanging out, looking cool.

"Oh look," Mary-Jane Sinclair laughed, "it's grave girl, Tula Bowman."

Of course, bowing to peer-pressure, Zelda Walters and Lauren Bonetti laughed too.

"Tula's gonna be in the movies," Lauren

Bonetti said. "Look, it says so here in *Motion Picture*."

Lauren Bonetti produced a copy of the magazine and Mary-Jane Sinclair and Zelda Walters crowded around to stare.

"Look at Tula Bowman posing," Mary-Jane Sinclair said. "Who does she think she is, Lillian Gish?"

"A tart in a dish, more like," Zelda Walters said, and Lauren Bonetti tittered at the weak joke.

Mary-Jane Sinclair was determined to wind me up. However, my eyes were drawn to a young boy, who was standing on the street corner. My eyes were drawn to him because I'd seen him in Mr Penhaligon's herbal store. Furthermore, now he was clutching a copy of *Motion Picture*.

"Look at this," Mary-Jane Sinclair said. "Watch me; watch what I can do to Tula Bowman."

Mary-Jane Sinclair tore my picture from Lauren Bonetti's magazine and ripped it to pieces. As those pieces fell like confetti, she offered me a self-satisfied smirk. However, I didn't rise to her bait. I merely walked on.

I walked past the young boy who fell into step behind me. I turned and frowned at him. In turn, he held up his copy of *Motion Picture* and smiled.

"Please, miss," he said, "can I have your autograph?"

I didn't have a pen, so I actually signed my name with a lipstick, a brand made at Mr Penhaligon's herbal store. Mr Penhaligon made a lot of medicines and cosmetics. He was a very talented man.

My young admirer skipped away with a spring in his step. By signing my name, I'd made someone happy. I told myself that this was an amazing gift. I liked the idea of making people happy. And that's why I resolved to call on Mr Shuman, an agent, and ask him about my prize, the promised bit part.

Mr Shuman's office was on the fourth floor of an office block in central Brooklyn. It was an expensive-looking building. However, I must add that Mr Shuman ran his agency from one of the cheaper offices, a boxroom that contained little more than a telephone, a typewriter and a desk.

I found Mr Shuman sitting behind his desk. He was a portly man whose belly strained against his waistcoat. A silver watch dangled from his waistcoat, on a chain. Balding, he'd combed his hair from the side, to hide his receding hairline. I regarded his balding head as ironic because his features displayed a dark five o'clock shadow. He was chewing on a cigar and studying a letter. He didn't bother to look up at me.

I offered a polite cough, to gain Mr Shuman's attention, then said, "I'm calling about the competition, run by *Motion Picture*. I won a bit part in a movie. I understand that you are the agent who is going to arrange the bit part."

"What's your name, darlin'?" Mr Shuman asked. He spoke while chewing on his cigar. His lips moved, but his teeth remained clamped to the cigar.

"Bowman," I said, "Tula Bowman."

"Oh, yeah," Mr Shuman said, "I remember now. Your pictures don't do you justice; you're a good looking broad."

"Thank you, sir," I said. Should I thank a man for calling me a 'broad'? I had no idea about the protocol, but it seemed the right thing to do, on this occasion.

Mr Shuman dropped the letter on to his desk and leaned back in his chair. The chair creaked alarmingly and I feared that it was going to crack and splinter. I remained standing simply because there was nowhere for me to sit.

"I'm sorry, darlin'," Mr Shuman said, "but there's nothing doing; call back next week."

"I'm willing to do anything," I said, "anything within reason; I'm not fussy about the part."

Mr Shuman rolled his cigar from one corner of his mouth to the other. He placed his hands behind his head and rocked back in his creaky chair. His posture revealed sweat stains under his armpits. I also noticed a film of sweat on his upper lip and brow.

"You'll do anything," Mr Shuman said, running his beady eyes over my slender form.

"Anything," I said, "anything within reason."

"Okay," he said, scratching the back of his neck. "Let me make a phone call."

Mr Shuman picked up his telephone and dialled a number. I paid no attention to that. Instead, I tried to read his letter. It was a solicitor's letter, requesting alimony for Mr Shuman's ex-wife.

"Hey, Milt, it's Manny." Mr Shuman smiled as he spoke into the telephone. All the while, his cigar remained clamped between his teeth. "How you doing? Great, that's great. Me, I'm muddling along, muddling along."

"Listen, I've got a broad in my office, a Tula Bowman. That's right, the broad who won the *Motion Picture* contest. You ain't got a bit part you can toss my way, have ya?"

"What's she like? She's good looking. With the right make-up, she'd certainly catch your eye. Can she do wistful? I'll ask her." Mr Shuman placed a hand over the mouthpiece and turned to me. "Milt wants to know if you can do wistful."

"Sure," I said, "I can do anything."

By way of a demonstration, I offered Mr Shuman a wistful expression. On recent trips to the movie palaces, I'd seen Lillian Gish, so wistful came readily to me.

"She can do wistful," Mr Shuman said to his friend, Milt. "In fact, she's very good, very convincing."

"Can she do anger? I'll ask her." Mr Shuman turned to me and said, "Milt wants to know if you can do anger."

I pictured Mary-Jane Sinclair tearing up my magazine picture and stared across the tiny office with daggers in my eyes.

"Yeah," Mr Shuman said, "she can do anger; she has looks that can kill. Can she cry? I'll ask her."

Before Mr Shuman could pose that question, I thought of my mother and tears poured down my cheeks.

"Yeah," Mr Shuman said, "she can cry. In fact, she can cry buckets. So, what do you reckon? Have you got something for me? That sounds good. Yeah. Yeah. That sounds great. I'll tell her."

Mr Shuman closed the telephone. He chewed on his cigar and smiled at me. "Be at the Navy Yard, six o'clock tomorrow morning. Milt might have something for ya."

Delilah

That night, I wrestled with a dilemma. If I arrived at the Navy Yard for the potential bit part, I could not arrive for work at Mr Penhaligon's herbal store. I considered lying to Mr Penhaligon, considered telling him that I was sick. However, such a lie did not sit comfortably with me.

There was no guarantee that I would get the bit part. And, even if I did, more parts might not follow. I wanted this role. Yet, I could not afford to sacrifice my job at the herbal store.

I knew that Mr Penhaligon worked late at the herbal store, until ten o'clock, six nights a week. I decided to walk to the store and talk with him. I explained my situation and requested a day off work. Mr Penhaligon granted me that day, with a loss of two days' wages for the inconvenience. I considered his terms fair. Our conversation concluded in a matter of minutes. It was as simple as that. It was another reminder that honesty was the best policy.

I returned home and climbed into my bed. I tried to sleep, but couldn't – I was too excited.

In the morning, I walked the three miles from my home to the Navy Yard, along Fulton Street and Carlton Avenue. Dawn was yet to break and, as I strolled past a park, I noticed birds nesting in the trees.

I walked with light steps, as though I were walking on air. That was partly due to my lack of sleep, but mainly due to my excitement.

On Flushing Avenue, I walked past another park. Dawn was breaking now and the birds were singing in the trees. I felt like joining the chorus. I wanted to sing. I wanted to sing so that the world could hear my joy, so that people could share in my delight.

Of course, because of the technical complexities, sound was not a feature in our motion pictures. I would act with my eyes, my physical gestures, my facial expressions – I would act to my strengths.

The Navy Yard was a shipyard and an industrial complex located in northwest Brooklyn. I was searching for a storage area situated on the East River in Wallabout Bay, a semicircular bend in the river adjacent to Corlears Hook in Manhattan.

I glanced at the street names: Navy Street to the west, Flushing Avenue to the south, Kent Avenue to the east, plus the East River to the north. Once I'd identified the landmarks, I knew that I was in the right place.

The movie makers had secured a warehouse to serve as the base for their production, *The*

Smugglers. This was a location shoot, not a studio set, which suggested to me that the movie had a generous budget. I would receive expenses for my part, but not a fee. That didn't bother me. I was just delighted to be involved in motion pictures.

In the warehouse, I met the director, Milt Greenberg. He was a tall lean man with an agitated air and a habit of forever fingering his small wire-framed spectacles.

I introduced myself and Mr Greenberg said, "Go over there; find your costume; apply your make-up. You'll play Delilah. I'll offer you details of your part when you're ready."

Clearly, Mr Greenberg was a very busy man. Therefore, he didn't have much time for me. I understood and accepted that. All the same, I did look around the warehouse with a sense of wonder, a sense of wonder mingled with confusion.

In all truth, the warehouse was cold, dirty and not at all glamorous. However, it represented motion pictures and that fact alone took the chill from my bones.

From the wardrobe mistress, I collected Delilah's dress, a simple black smock, similar to a smock that hung in my wardrobe. I noticed two young women, around my age; they were sitting in front of a bank of mirrors, applying their make-up. I joined them and stared at the pots of greasepaint. I felt uncertain, unsure what to do.

I'd applied make-up at home, but this was a completely different ball game. Riddled with self-doubt, I turned to a fellow actress and asked for advice. "How much should I apply?"

"Figure it out for yourself," the actress said with a scowl. She rose from the makeshift dressing table and, with a colleague, walked towards Mr Greenberg.

I picked up a pot of greasepaint and scooped out a large measure with my index finger. I applied the greasepaint to my face. In fact, I applied the whole contents of the pot to my face. Then, I went in search of Mr Greenberg.

When I located the director, he glared at me and growled, "What are you playing at? What have you done to your face? You look like a clown. Get that paint off and apply it properly. You're wasting my time. You're costing us money. Bloody amateurs!"

Mr Greenberg waved a hand in my general direction and stormed off, in search of his cameraman.

I returned to the makeshift dressing table and removed my make-up. As I applied a fresh, lighter layer, I reflected on two lessons already learned. One: my fellow actresses could be selfish and bitchy. Two: a movie set was no place for amateurs.

I wanted to be a professional. I wanted the people in motion pictures to regard me as a professional. Therefore, although Mr Greenberg's criticism stung, I hid my feelings and approached him one more time.

"Okay," Mr Greenberg said, "that's better. In half an hour, we'll shoot your scene. Here's your part. Your name's Delilah. Your boyfriend has gone to sea. You'll look wistfully out to sea, hoping he'll return. You'll look down and see his kitbag. You'll open his kitbag and find a picture of a beautiful older woman. Your boyfriend has cheated on you. You'll stare at the picture. You'll become angry. You'll cry. Got that?"

"Sure thing, Mr Greenberg," I said.

"Good," he said. "Now, rehearse. I'll call you in half an hour. First, I must talk with the cameraman and the stunt guy."

I didn't know if the stunt guy featured in my scene, or where he slotted into the picture. In terms of the picture, I didn't understand the plot. But that was the lot of the bit-part player – you just walked in front of the camera, followed the director's instructions and performed your role.

In a quiet corner of the warehouse, I rehearsed my scene. I rehearsed it thoroughly, except for the moment when I had to cry; in rehearsal, I didn't want to ruin my make-up.

A junior member of the film crew called me and I joined Mr Greenberg and his cameraman on the dockside. The sun shone bright now. Seagulls swooped through the air. Ships pulled into the docks. The natural background was all set; the camera was ready; everyone was waiting for me to perform.

A clanging of metal assaulted my ears; the smell of fresh fish drifted past my nostrils; the sun hurt my eyes. However, I ignored all the distractions; I listened to Mr Greenberg and performed my part.

Mr Greenberg captured my performance in one take. He removed his spectacles and blinked. He looked surprised. Then, he talked with the two actresses who'd been cold towards me.

Although Mr Greenberg no longer needed me, I hung around the docks for the rest of the day, watching the film crew. The two actresses performed their parts, together; their scene required five takes.

I returned home, exhausted. My father had left a note: he was in the bar. We were communicating through notes these days. I no longer liked my father. Nevertheless, our estrangement would not ruin the memory of a magical day.

The Smugglers

I had to wait five months before *The Smugglers* appeared at our local movie palace, the Albemarle Theatre. During that time, I worked hard at Mr Penhaligon's herbal store, and managed to save some money. My icy relationship with my father also thawed, to some degree.

Although I tried to avoid Mary-Jane Sinclair and Zelda Walters, occasionally I bumped into them. Lauren Bonetti no longer hung out with them. A rumour circulating the neighbourhood suggested that Lauren had found herself a boyfriend. If the other rumours about her were true, then this was a surprising development.

Of course, word also circulated about my performance in *The Smugglers*. I was the local 'movie queen'. Some people in the neighbourhood offered me more respect, while others were clearly jealous. Most continued to ignore me; for them, I'd always be "Tula Bowman, daughter of Stanley Bowman, 'the singer'".

My father was still singing in bars, earning a few bucks, occasionally. He'd given up looking for work on account of his bad back. Instead, he relied on his bar money and an allowance from me.

I was standing on a street corner, watching as a

man posted an advertisement for *The Smugglers* on a billboard. It was a colourful poster, depicting a dramatic scene from the movie.

Mary-Jane Sinclair and Zelda Walters joined me. They stared up at the poster, their expressions thoughtful.

"That's your movie," Zelda Walters said.

"Yes, it is," I replied with pride.

"If it's your movie," Mary-Jane Sinclair said, "how come your name isn't on the poster?"

"That's simple," I sighed. "I had a bit part in the movie. Posters only name the stars."

"I bet you're not even in the movie," Mary-Jane Sinclair said. "I bet you're telling lies."

"How much do you wanna bet?" I asked.

"A dollar."

"Okay," I said, "you're on."

Zelda Walters continued to stare at the poster. She tugged at her pigtails and frowned. "How are we gonna prove that you're in the movie?"

"You can see it," I said. "It's showing in the Albemarle next week."

"It costs money to get into the Albemarle," Mary-Jane Sinclair said.

"Only a nickel," I said.

"We ain't got a nickel," Mary-Jane Sinclair said. "We're broke."

"Okay," I said. "I'll pay for your tickets. I'll

make my money back, and more, with my winnings."

I bought cinema tickets for Mary-Jane Sinclair, Zelda Walters and myself for the Brooklyn première of *The Smugglers*. I bought a ticket for my father too. I just wished that my mother were alive so that she could witness my silver screen début. That said, if she were alive she'd probably refuse to attend.

We settled in our seats and waited for the lights to dim and the red velvet curtain to open. Mary-Jane Sinclair chewed on popcorn. She offered some to Zelda Walters. However, she didn't offer any to me.

My father settled into his seat too. He'd been drinking and was feeling sleepy. I watched as he slipped down into his seat, closed his eyes and began to snore.

A woman in front of me wore a large hat, so I had to lean to my left to watch the movie. The images flickered on the screen, an intertitle went up and my chest swelled with pride.

Okay, so as Delilah I only had a small part in this movie. But I'd been Delilah – this was my movie.

We watched the story unfold. As the title suggested, the plot centred on smugglers. From what I could gather, Delilah was just one of many girls Harry, the 'hero', had in various ports.

I wondered when my scene would appear. Probably somewhere in the middle of the movie, but that was just a guess.

Harry was involved in a realistic fight scene, and that excited the audience. His opponent was probably the stuntman Mr Greenberg had spoken with at the docks. I surmised this because Harry's opponent took a number of falls, included his final scene when he tumbled into the water.

The story held my attention. Zelda Walters too appeared engrossed. Mary-Jane Sinclair, however, kept making eyes at a man sitting beside her. He was much older than her, around my father's age.

My father slept through the entire movie. He was sleeping a lot these days. I worried that he wasn't well. I feared that he'd drift into poor health, like my mother.

The movie ran for sixty-two minutes. I knew this because I'd read the previews and advertisements in the movie magazines. Of course, I didn't feature in any of those previews or advertisements. I accepted that. After all, I was just a bit player making my way in motion pictures.

The Smugglers reached its halfway point and still my scene had not appeared. Zelda Walters remained engrossed. However, Mary-Jane Sinclair was now necking with the man sitting next to her.

With five minutes left to run in the movie, an

intertitle announced a wedding scene. At this point, I had not appeared.

Mary-Jane Sinclair straightened her dress and glanced at the screen. She leaned forward and shared a whispered conversation with Zelda Walters. Presumably, they were discussing my non-appearance, to date.

I failed to understand how my scene would make any sense in the last five minutes of the movie, but reasoned that the director, Mr Greenberg, would have worked it in, somehow.

Harry kissed his bride and the screen went black. 'The End' appeared and shortly after that, the house lights went up.

Mary-Jane Sinclair's face was a mess, all smudged with lipstick. Her face also contained a satisfied smirk – she'd won her bet; I had not appeared in the motion picture.

Outside the movie palace, Mary-Jane Sinclair said, "Pay up, liar."

Of course, I honoured my bet and paid Mary-Jane Sinclair and Zelda Walters.

Mary-Jane Sinclair placed her winnings in her purse. She laughed at me then said, "You're just a liar, Tula Bowman, a fantasist; you didn't appear in that movie. You made it all up."

"I did shoot a scene," I said. "I was Delilah."

"No Delilah appeared in that movie," Zelda

Walters said, "and I should know; I watched it all the way through."

"You're a sad case, you are," Mary-Jane Sinclair said. "You just make up stories about yourself to make yourself sound important. But you ain't important. You're a nobody."

With Mary-Jane Sinclair's words ringing in my ears, I went scurrying along the sidewalk. I'd found a new reason to cry, and the tears poured down my cheeks.

I ran along the cobblestones. I wanted to get home. I wanted to place my head in the gas oven. I wanted to die. However, while avoiding a cart, I tripped and fell; I went sprawling across the cobblestones.

Before I could pick myself up, my father appeared. He was real but, through my tears, he seemed like an apparition. He reached down, offered a hand and I accepted it. He placed an arm around my shoulders and guided me home.

Seven Months Later

In time, I learned the truth about *The Smugglers*. Although satisfied with my scene, Mr Greenberg had decided to cut my part. On reflection, he felt that Delilah was one girl too many for Harry, and that the scenes already shot conveyed Harry's character as a womaniser.

This came as some comfort to me because it meant that Mr Greenberg had not rejected my performance. However, I'd used up my prize; I could no longer look forward to featuring in motion pictures, not even in a bit part.

I resolved to place my disappointment behind me. My work at Mr Penhaligon's herbal store was satisfying and, on occasions, he even allowed me to mix some potions. Also, young men were starting to attract my attention and I considered a future well away from motion pictures, as a housewife raising a family.

Of course, my movie dreams didn't disappear altogether and, sometimes, while mixing paste for Mr Penhaligon, I found myself dreaming of a producer making a dramatic phone call.

"Miss Bowman...is that you? It is? Excellent. I'm looking for a young lady to play an ingénue in my latest motion picture, and I feel sure that you are ideally suited

to play the part..."

I laughed at myself for indulging in such fantasies. Then, on a bright spring morning while tidying Mr Penhaligon's herbal jars, his phone rang. Mr Penhaligon answered the phone, frowned and handed the receiver to me.

"It's for you," he said. "Be minded, Miss Bowman, I do not allow personal calls at work."

I wondered who was phoning me. My first thought was bad news about my father – he'd endured a serious bout of the flu over the winter months and was struggling with his health. Then I wondered if it could be Jackson Faron. Jackson lived in our neighbourhood. He'd been pestering me lately, asking for a date.

"Hello," I said, holding the telephone as though it were a bomb ready to explode, speaking as though I had a frog stuck in my throat.

"Miss Bowman?"

"Yes."

"My name is James Macintyre. I'm a motion picture producer. I'm looking for a young lady to play an ingénue in my latest motion picture, and I feel sure that you would be perfect for the part."

This was my fantasy made real. I pinched myself to make sure that I wasn't dreaming.

"Miss Bowman...are you still there?"

"Yes...sorry...yes...why...why me?"

"I read an article about you in *Motion Picture*, celebrating your achievement of winning the budding actress competition. I met Joshua Trimble, and he spoke very highly of you."

I remembered Mr Trimble. He'd been a judge at the *Motion Picture* contest. I remembered his look of encouragement as I'd auditioned.

"How did you find me?" I asked.

"Mr Trimble offered me your address. I called and spoke with your father. He suggested that I should telephone Penhaligon's."

Of course, Mr Trimble had my address on my entry form. And my father had had the presence of mind to remember Mr Penhaligon's telephone number. I glanced at Mr Penhaligon. He was tapping his pocket watch and staring at me.

"Miss Bowman, are you still there?"

"I'm still here," I said.

"Would you care to audition for me?"

"When?"

"The day after tomorrow. You'll find me on 11th Avenue."

My eyes rolled as Mr Macintyre offered me his full address. Was this really happening to me? I pinched myself again. It hurt. This was real.

"I'll be there," I said.

I handed the telephone to Mr Penhaligon and he offered me a grunt. The stars were aligning – in two days time, I'd enjoy a day off work; I could attend the audition without causing further friction with Mr Penhaligon.

Mr Macintyre's office overlooked Prospect Park. From his fifth storey window, I could see the lake, Lookout Hill, the Quaker graveyard and the Maryland Monument. It was a wonderful view. Furthermore, Mr Macintyre's office was plush with mahogany furniture and rich leather armchairs.

Mr Macintyre was in his early forties. He possessed straw-coloured hair, blue eyes, a handsome face and a lean body. Dressed in plus fours and a chequered waistcoat, he was bending over a golf club, addressing a putt when I entered his office.

"Ah, Miss Bowman," Mr Macintyre said, his gaze fixed on his golf ball, "good of you to call; I'll be with you in a moment."

Mr Macintyre offered his golf club a gentle swing. His golf ball rolled across the thick pile of the office carpet and disappeared into a forward-leaning cup.

"Still got the touch," Mr Macintyre smiled, glancing at me.

I must confess that I was somewhat in awe of Mr Macintyre, maybe because he presented a confident air, or maybe because he was handsome. I noticed a photograph on his desk, which depicted

Mr Macintyre and his wife in wedding attire.

I was seventeen going on eighteen and starting to view the world, particularly men, in a different light. A crazy thought went through my mind. I'd only just met him, but I recognised that it would be so easy to fall in love with Mr Macintyre. Of course, he was old enough to be my father, and that thought poured a welcome shower of cold water on my foolish fantasy.

Setting the age difference aside, I asked myself an important question: would I accept a romantic dinner invitation from Mr Macintyre, should he make such a proposal? My answer was 'no'. And I offered myself a sound reason: Mr Macintyre was a married man, and I vowed that I would not become involved now, or at any point in the future, with a married man.

"This is a mere formality," Mr Macintyre said. "I've spoken with Mr Trimble in some detail; you've got the part. Of course, it's only a bit, but it's an important part in the context of the picture. I wanted to meet you, in person, to ensure that your stature was suitable." He paused and eyed me from head to toe. "And indeed it is; you are just the person I've been looking for."

"Thank you, Mr Macintyre," I said.

"While you're here," he said, swinging his golf club in playful fashion, "maybe you'd be kind enough to don that hat and shed some tears."

I stared at a Quaker's hat, which sat on Mr Macintyre's desk. I retrieved the hat and placed it on my head. Of course, I had no shortage of images or memories to call upon to produce my tears.

"Very good," Mr Macintyre said, "very impressive. Do you have an agent?"

"Er...ah...er...hum...no...not really," I said.

"Maybe you should consider finding yourself an agent," Mr Macintyre suggested. "You're talented, any fool can see that, but sometimes talent alone isn't enough to guarantee success."

"I will think about finding an agent," I said.

"Excellent," Mr Macintyre said. He retrieved his golf ball and lined up another putt. "I'll see you on the set, at Elmwood Studios, at the crack of dawn, a week from today."

"I'll be there," I said.

A Shock

Once again, I was faced with a dilemma: to honour my promise to Mr Macintyre or show up for work at Mr Penhaligon's herbal store?

As the main breadwinner for my father and myself, I couldn't afford to lose my job at the herbal store. Yet, I'd made a promise to Mr Macintyre. Added to that, my hunger for acting had returned – I really wanted this part.

In the event, matters unfolded in a most unfortunate manner.

Three days after my meeting with Mr Macintyre, I was serving a customer at Mr Penhaligon's herbal store when his telephone rang. Mr Penhaligon answered the telephone, scowled then offered me the receiver.

"Hi, Tula," Jackson Faron said.

"Hi," I said.

"Fancy going to the cinema on Saturday?"

"Sure," I said.

"And dancing after that?"

"Maybe," I said.

"Come on," he said, "you never go dancing with me."

"I'm busy," I said.

"You promised."

"I never. And I am busy." I glanced at Mr Penhaligon, who was glaring at me. This was the fifth time that Jackson Faron had phoned me at the herbal store in just over a week. "In fact," I said, "I'm very busy right now."

"Mary-Jane Sinclair reckons you're a dyke," Jackson Faron said.

"Mary-Jane Sinclair is wicked," I said.

"How many guys have you kissed?" Jackson Faron asked.

Once again, I glanced at Mr Penhaligon. Now, he was glaring at his pocket watch. My stomach churned. His angry expression conveyed a dreadful sense of foreboding.

"I must go," I said.

"If we go to the cinema on Saturday," Jackson Faron said, "will you kiss me?"

"I must go," I said. I broke the connection and handed the telephone to Mr Penhaligon.

"Thank you," Mr Penhaligon said. However, his irate tone did not convey any thanks. "You are an excellent worker, Miss Bowman. Nonetheless, I feel that your work is more suited to the telephone exchange than to this store. Kindly collect your coat and leave my employment."

Unemployed, I dare not break such bad news to my father. So, for the next three days, I pretended to travel to work; in reality, I spent my time in the local library. I read a number of books, including *A Christmas Carol* by Charles Dickens. I pictured Mr Penhaligon as Scrooge. At heart, he was a decent man, so to regard him as Scrooge was unkind of me.

The day arrived, my appointment with Mr Macintyre at Elmwood Studios. The studios resembled a workshop, rather than a glamorous film set. Carpenters and decorators, in particular, were very busy, constructing the scenery.

Mr Macintyre spotted me and acknowledged my presence with a wave of his golf club. He seemed to take his golf club everywhere. I wondered if he slept with it.

"There you are, Miss Bowman," Mr Macintyre said. "Ruthie will see to you; she'll arrange your costume and make-up."

Ruthie was a plump woman in her late thirties. She was matronly in appearance, and she made a great fuss of me. I found it very strange, for someone to make a fuss of me.

Ruthie dressed me as a Quaker's daughter. Then she escorted me on to the set. There, I met the director, Mr Paglino. He was plump, like Ruthie. He possessed dark, slicked-back hair and a crooked little finger. I noticed that he had a habit of using his crooked little finger to beckon people towards him. Now, he beckoned me.

"Miss Bowman," Mr Paglino said. "Your part is

straightforward. I want you to climb into that barrel. Your plan is to stowaway on that ship." He nodded towards the mock-up of a hull. "However, a crew member will discover you. Upon that discovery, you will climb out of that barrel and, crestfallen, cry."

"Why am I stowing away?" I asked.

"You want to become a whaler, like your father. He perished whilst whaling, and you want to honour his memory. However, the crew regard you as too young."

"Plus," I said, "I'm a woman."

"Yes," Mr Paglino said, "that is true too. Do you understand your part?"

"I understand it," I said.

I noticed that Mr Macintyre was looking on from the sidelines. This was my moment. I had to impress. I had to succeed. I had no job to return to. My only hope was that Mr Macintyre would offer me another bit part.

Mr Paglino discussed the scene with his cameraman, Archie Bleeker. Archie was a young, good-looking man with beautiful teeth and an easy smile. I'm not sure why I was drawn to his teeth. Maybe because they looked so fresh, so perfect.

Mr Paglino called the set to order. With his crooked finger, he indicated that I should climb into the barrel. This I did. Then one of the carpenters secured the lid.

I crouched in the darkness and waited for someone to open the lid. While I waited, I considered my character's motivation and emotional state. I didn't even know her name. Maybe the script referred to her as 'Stowaway', such was the lot of the actress who played bit parts.

A member of the ship's crew opened the barrel and stared at me in surprise. Upon my discovery, I was supposed to cry. However, I reasoned that my character would have more spunk than that. After all, she possessed the courage to stowaway on a whaling ship and the determination to become a whaler; therefore, I reckoned, she would put up a verbal fight.

I added flesh to my character. Instead of crying, I remonstrated with the sailor. I glared at him, waved my arms and clenched my fists. Having vented my spleen, I jumped out of the barrel, stormed off the ship, and ran along the dock.

I pictured an intertitle stating: *Looks like there's a storm brewing – Hurricane Henrietta!* I'd named my character Henrietta simply because of the alliteration.

Mr Paglino called 'cut' and I turned to Mr Macintyre to witness his reaction. He was swishing his golf club, whether in anger or approval, I could not tell.

Mr Macintyre waved his golf club and beckoned Mr Paglino towards him. The two men lowered their heads and engaged in an earnest conversation.

Looking on, I bit my lower lip. Maybe I'd overplayed my part. Maybe I'd added too much flesh to the bones. Maybe Mr Macintyre was furious with me.

Mr Macintyre said something to Mr Paglino and the director nodded. Then the handsome producer waved his golf club at me.

For a moment, I feared that Mr Macintyre would beat me with his golf club. Then, I reminded myself that he was a kind-natured man, not the sort to inflict violence on a female.

"Miss Bowman," Mr Macintyre said as I approached him and his swinging golf club, "I have a proposition for you: Mr Paglino will extend your part in this motion picture, possibly to five scenes. I feel that you're well suited to play bit parts in my future productions. Therefore, I'm willing to offer you a contract, $2,000 over six months."

"Two thousand dollars," I blurted, my eyes wide, my jaw dropping.

"Okay," Mr Macintyre said, misreading my reaction, "I'll up that to $2,500 over six months, but not a cent more."

"I'm so grateful, Mr Macintyre," I said. "I don't

know what to say."

Mr Macintyre smiled. He examined the grooves on the head of his golf club. Apparently satisfied with those grooves, and my performance, he offered his golf club a carefree swing.

"You will arrive on this set at dawn tomorrow," Mr Macintyre said. "Any questions?"

Words failed me. Mercifully, I was a 'silent' actress; therefore, I offered my thanks with a smile.

New Horizons

I arrived home to find my father sleeping in his armchair, a newspaper draped over his face. Upon hearing me, he snorted out of his sleep, pushed himself up and watched as the newspaper slid to the floor.

I retrieved the newspaper, folded it and placed it on a small table, positioned beside my father's armchair.

"Where have you been, Tula?" my father asked. He yawned and stretched his arms above his head. His shirt rode up, revealing the hairs around his bellybutton. For some reason, I felt compelled to turn away.

"Where have you been?" my father repeated.

"Elmwood Studios," I said. "I acted in a bit part. Mr Macintyre, the producer, liked my performance. He offered me a contract."

"How much?" my father frowned.

"Two thousand five hundred dollars over six months."

"Two thousand five hundred dollars!" My father's reaction mimicked my reaction, a mixture of surprise and delight. "This is wonderful news. We must celebrate."

My father reached for his whiskey bottle. From

the dresser, he removed two glasses and blew the dust off them. He poured four fingers of whiskey into each glass.

"Drink up, Tula," my father grinned, "let's celebrate."

I recalled the previous occasion when I drank whiskey, the night my mother died, and remembered how ill it made me feel, so I declined my father's offer.

"Not to worry," my father laughed, "I'll drink your share." He gulped down two fingers of whiskey and wiped the residue from his lips with the back of his hand. "Come on," he said, "tell me all about your acting and Mr Macintyre."

I sat beside the dining table, and while my father drank whiskey, I regaled him with my exploits at Elmwood Studios.

"That's wonderful," my father said. "With money like that rolling in, maybe we can find ourselves a better place to live, somewhere more suitable for a movie star."

"Mr Macintyre has only offered me bit parts," I said. "I'm not a movie star."

"All in good time," my father said, "all in good time." He topped up his whiskey glass and took a satisfying sip. "A movie star needs an agent," my father reasoned, "someone to manage her affairs."

"I've been thinking about that," I said.

"Think no longer," my father said. "I will be your agent. I will manage your affairs."

"But..."

Words escaped me. I didn't want to hurt my father's feelings. However, I realised that he was not qualified to handle my affairs. True, he could call upon years of wheeling and dealing on the streets, but those experiences did not qualify him to deal with complex legal contracts.

"I will look after you, Tula," my father said, "I always have and I always will."

My father's tone suggested that the matter was settled. So, I let it go, for now.

"You'll have to inform Mr Penhaligon," my father said. "He'll have to find a new assistant."

"Mr Penhaligon fired me," I said. "I've been going to the library, not his store, over the past three days."

"Why did he fire you?" my father frowned.

"Jackson Faron kept telephoning me at the store. I begged him not to, but he wouldn't listen."

"Jackson Faron is trouble," my father said. "All boys are trouble. You must keep away from them. Do you understand?"

I glanced down to our threadbare carpet and nodded.

"Good," my father said. "You have your career to think of. You're going to be a superstar, with your name in lights. You must focus all your thoughts, all your attention, all your energies on acting. You must not mix with the likes of Jackson Faron. Do you understand?"

I nodded. "I understand."

"We're going to have a wonderful time," my father said. He reclined in his armchair, balanced his whiskey glass on his stomach and sighed. "We're going to Hollywood. Maybe we'll move there and live there, full-time."

"I'm only a bit-part actress," I said, "on a six month contract. I'm not a member of the Hollywood elite."

"But you will be," my father insisted, "you will be." He straightened, gulped his whiskey and replenished his glass. "Maybe you should change your name; keep Bowman, but ditch Tula."

"My name is not important," I said. "As a bit-part player, I doubt that I'll receive a billing."

"Marie-Jean," my father said. "I wanted to call you Marie-Jean. I can picture it now, emblazoned across Hollywood in bright lights, 'Starring Marie-Jean Bowman'." My father turned to me and grinned. "What do you reckon, princess?"

"Who knows?" I shrugged. "I never thought I'd get this far. But, wherever this journey may take us, I want to be known as Tula. Tula is my identity. Tula is who I am. If I'm going to spend my days pretending to be other people, it's important that I retain a sense of the real me."

"Suit yourself," my father shrugged, "but I reckon you'd look good as Marie-Jean Bowman."

The excitement of the day had drained me, and I was ready for bed. However, before I retired, my father said, "As your agent, I reckon I should receive thirty-five percent of your wages, plus necessary expenses."

"Expenses?" I frowned.

"Yes," my father said. He offered a defensive shrug of his right shoulder. "I might have to travel on your behalf; I might have to head out of town."

"As my agent," I said, "I'll pay you twenty-percent, and no expenses. And that's the end of our discussion. I'm tired. I'm going to bed."

My father reached for his whiskey bottle. He glared at me. "You can be cruel, Tula Bowman. You can be a hard-hearted bitch, at times."

"A father shouldn't call his daughter a bitch," I said.

However, my father ignored me. He just sat there, drinking his whiskey.

Mr Macintyre kept me busy. My life became a whirl of activity. I played bit parts every day, sometimes for Mr Macintyre's production company, other times for other producers.

Mr Macintyre had a deal with the other producers – he'd loan me to them and they'd pay him a fee. I received my standard fee, regardless of the movie. I guess I should have asked for a percentage of the hiring fee but, in all honesty, I was just delighted to be involved in motion pictures.

During my six months as a bit player, I developed a reputation as a reliable actress. Producers were queuing up to enlist my services. Some days, I played in two movies – one in the morning, the other in the afternoon.

My parts were mundane, and not accredited, but I didn't mind. Often, I had to dance in the background, or walk past the main character and offer him a flirtatious look.

In the 'real world', I was approaching my eighteenth birthday and attracting many flirtatious looks. However, I kept my father's words in mind – I reserved my focus for my acting, and not for the men who were attracted to me.

My hair started to frizz. I think that was due to

the hair dye. I changed my hair colour every day. Sometimes, I changed my hair colour three times a day – my natural colour before I arrived on the set, dark brunette during morning filming, and platinum blonde for my afternoon role.

Six months went by in a flash. My contract was drawing to a close. Mr Macintyre had an option on my contract – he could renew it, if he so wished. However, before seeking to renew my contract, he wanted to see if I could perform in a major, credited roll.

Mr Macintyre arranged a screen test. Archie Bleeker would film that screen test. He was a jobbing cameraman and I'd bumped into him on a number of film sets. We knew each other well enough to smile and say "hello".

The night before my screen test, I sat on my bed and considered my situation – over recent months my father and I had moved from our slum to Bay Ridge, a decent, upwardly mobile district of Brooklyn. The rent was expensive and we could only remain in Bay Ridge if Mr Macintyre extended my contract.

I reasoned that Mr Macintyre was making good money on me, by hiring me out. Therefore, I considered that he would extend my contract, maybe for another six months. However, I wanted to become more than a bit-part player; I wanted to feature in major roles; I wanted a longer contract and a measure of security. To achieve my aims, I knew that I had to succeed in the screen test.

I arrived on the set. There, Archie Bleeker arranged the camera and the lighting. The set was a mock-up of a beach. I had to walk across the sand in a carefree manner, then gaze out to sea. After noticing a ship in distress, I had to convey that emotion, and call for help.

The scene was straightforward and I reckoned that I delivered a good performance. However, just before my final, pleading look, Archie's camera failed.

"Not to worry," Archie smiled. "It's always doing that. I know how to fix it."

While Archie repaired his camera, I sat in a deckchair and we chatted. In the main, we chatted about our backgrounds.

"Where are your folks from?" Archie asked.

"Brooklyn," I said.

"No," he grinned, "where are they from originally?"

"Britain," I said. "I'm not sure exactly where. Our family legend states that my mother was descended from kings and queens." I paused and offered Archie a sad look. "She's dead now."

"I'm sorry to hear that," Archie frowned.

"My mother reckoned that she was a princess.

At times, she acted like a princess."

"Was she an actress?" Archie asked.

"No," I said, "she just behaved in that sort of way."

I reflected on my comment. Maybe my mother had acted, to some extent. Maybe she'd shared my ambition to become an actress, then resented my aspiration when she realised that her dream had eluded her. Or maybe I was fantasising again. I knew that I had a vivid imagination; sometimes, I regarded that as a blessing, other times a curse.

"Where are your folks from?" I asked.

"The Netherlands," Archie said. "Our family legend states that our ancestors were among the first to settle in New York."

"It would have been New Amsterdam then," I said.

"Sure," Archie shrugged. "I'm aware of that."

"I'm not trying to belittle you," I said.

"I know that too," Archie said. "Everyone reckons that you're sweet, a real honey."

Was Archie offering me a compliment? I wasn't sure. Nevertheless, I smiled and accepted his words as praise.

Archie reshot the scene. My performance wasn't as good, second time around. That said, I reckoned that it was up to standard. However, Mr Macintyre would be the judge of that.

"I have other tasks to complete for Mr Macintyre," Archie said. "Come back tomorrow and we'll see what we've shot."

Already, in my brief career, I'd learned a valuable lesson from motion pictures – to succeed you required great patience.

The following day, I joined Archie and found him looking glum.

"The lighting was poor," Archie said. "Much of the time, your face was in shadow. That was my fault. I'd like to shoot the scene again, if you're up for it."

"Sure," I said. "I'll shoot the scene again."

I had no problem getting into character for any role I played. It came naturally to me. Of course, to date, I'd only played bit parts, and not characters that required a great deal of depth. Nevertheless, when a director called me on to the set, I could park my chewing gum and deliver a performance.

Archie reshot the scene one more time. I considered this performance to be the best of my three screen tests; the shadows in the second shoot had been a blessing in disguise.

I had to wait another day for Mr Macintyre to view my screen test. Now, my nerves were on edge. What would he make of my performance? Would he cancel my contract, or would he offer me a credited role in a motion picture?

I paced outside the screening room, my feet threatening to wear a groove in the carpet. I chewed on my lower lip. I bit my fingernails. I sipped water from the water dispenser then rushed to the restroom to relieve myself. When I returned, I found Mr Macintyre standing outside the screening room, chatting with Archie.

Offering an exuberant swish of his golf club, Mr Macintyre smiled at me and said, "Congratulations, Tula; you've got the part."

I stood there, my eyes wide open, my mouth agape. Meanwhile, Archie followed Mr Macintyre down the corridor. As they turned the corner, Archie glanced at me, grinned and winked.

Thanking Archie

I'd performed well in the screen test. However, it was thanks to Archie Bleeker and his skill as a lighting cameraman that I'd secured a credited role in a motion picture, and an extension to my contract. I had to find a way to thank Archie Bleeker.

I decided to buy Archie a small gift, a leather wallet. I'm not sure why I selected that gift. Maybe because I had money on my mind, thanks to my improved contract.

Now, I was earning more in a month than I'd earned in a year at the tin factory, or Mr Penhaligon's herbal store. I was rich. That said, I didn't consider that my riches stemmed from the money, they stemmed from the fact that I was blissfully happy, the happiest I'd been so far in my short life.

I found Archie repairing his camera. He wiped his hands on a rag, glanced at the grease, then stared at my gift.

"What's that for?" he asked.

"You went out of your way to ensure that the lighting was perfect. I wanted to thank you."

"Oh, shucks." Archie blushed; he actually blushed. I thought I was the only person in my family or social circle who blushed. "It's lovely," he said, "but I can't accept the gift."

"Why not?" I scowled.

"Because," Archie said. He paused and searched for an excuse. "Because...you shouldn't spend your money on me; I should spend my money on you."

"You're talking in riddles," I said, "I don't understand you."

"I'd like to invite you to dinner," Archie said. "And I'll pay for that dinner from this wallet. Those are my terms for accepting the wallet."

"You have a convoluted mind, Archie Bleeker, but I like your mind very much. I accept your dinner invitation. Where shall we dine? When shall we meet?"

"This evening," Archie said, "six o'clock. Meet me by Blackwell Brook, on Fairgrounds Road."

I nodded. "I'll be there."

I spent the afternoon preparing for my role as Daisy in *The Hedonists* by reading the script. At last, I was more than a bit player; I had an actual script. The script called for Daisy to spend a lot of time in the water. Thankfully, I could swim. We'd film on location, at Niagara Falls. I'd never been to Niagara Falls. At this point, I'd rarely ventured outside Brooklyn.

After reading the script, I rushed home to

prepare for my dinner date with Archie. I riffled through my wardrobe, searched for a suitable dress to wear. The early summer sun was warm, so I selected a light floral outfit. I held the dress against my petite frame and admired myself in my bedroom mirror. Without wishing to sound boastful, I reckoned that the dress made me look quite pretty.

"What are you doing?" my father asked.

I was so engrossed with my dress, and thoughts of my dinner date with Archie, that I didn't hear my father enter my bedroom. Indeed, I wasn't even aware that he was in the house.

"I'm dressing," I said, "for dinner; please leave the room."

"Dinner?" my father frowned, stepping further into my bedroom. "We're going out to dinner?"

"I'm dining with Archie Bleeker," I said. "He's a cameraman at Mr Macintyre's studios."

My father circled me. His frown developed into a scowl. He reached across and snatched my dress from my hands.

"Listen, Tula," he said, "we've had this conversation before. You're on the brink of something special. You're gonna become a major movie star. Boys can wait, especially boys like Archie Bleeker. When you date, it'll be with someone famous. When you marry, it'll be to a movie star. But that's for the future. First, you must perform in Mr Macintyre's movies. You must establish a solid reputation and earn your ticket to Hollywood."

"I understand all that," I said. "And I'd love to make motion pictures in Hollywood. But, in the meantime, I must thank Archie Bleeker because, if I do get to Hollywood, he's one of the reasons for my success."

My father continued to view me with deep suspicion. He clenched and unclenched his large hands, crumpling my dress. He was dirtying my dress; I'd have to select another.

"How do you intend to thank Archie?" my father asked.

"By dining with him," I said.

"Okay," my father said slowly. "But no kissing, and definitely nothing beyond that. Movie stars are not allowed to become pregnant. If they do become pregnant, they have abortions, and you don't want to have an abortion, do you, Tula."

"I have no intention of becoming pregnant through Archie Bleeker," I said. "Now, please leave my bedroom and allow me to dress."

My father had creased and dirtied my preferred dress, so I selected another, a peach-coloured dress with a high hemline. The dress was a little daring, but I was in the mood for daring – I wanted to show my father that I was my own person now, that I was a woman in my own right.

I met Archie beside Blackwell Brook, on Fairgrounds Road. He was dressed in his plaid three-piece suit, the suit he wore when filming for Mr Macintyre. Maybe he didn't see this as a special occasion. Maybe, most likely, he hadn't had time to return home and change.

"Where are we dining, exactly?" I asked.

"Over there," Archie said. He turned and pointed along Fairgrounds Road.

"But," I frowned, "but...that's a hot dog stand."

"Yeah," Archie grinned. "And after a coupla hot dogs we'll go on the rides." He took hold of my hand and led me down Fairgrounds Road. "You don't want to go on the big dipper on a full stomach, do you, Tula?"

I suppose Archie had a point. And I must confess, I did enjoy the hot dogs. And we had a great time on the rides. I screamed a lot, which seemed to please Archie. On the big dipper, he placed a protective arm around my shoulders and held me tight, which pleased me.

Archie bought me candyfloss, which was tricky to eat because the evening breeze threatened to blow it into my hair. At the end of the evening, he hailed a cab and paid the fare out of his new leather wallet. He joined me in the cab on the journey home. We sat close, holding hands.

On my doorstep, Archie said, "Can I see you again, Tula?"

"Sure," I said.

"When?" he asked, his voice troubled with nervous energy.

"On the set at Mr Macintyre's studio," I said, "tomorrow."

"What about away from the set?" Archie asked.

I smiled, swayed from side to side and withheld my answer. I was teasing him, and he knew it.

"Please," Archie begged, "I need an answer."

Eventually, I said, "Yes, Archie Bleeker, you may see me again."

"When," he asked, exhaling. For a good two minutes, it seemed, he'd been holding his breath.

"Saturday night," I said, "you can take me to the movies."

Archie grinned. He walked away from my house. At the street corner, he yelled with delight and threw his hat into the air.

Saturday night at the movies became a regular feature with Archie. While I watched the movies, he spent most of his time watching me. He sat with his arm around my shoulders and tried to kiss me on occasions. However, I laid down a firm rule: no kissing until we bid each other goodnight.

Archie wasn't thrilled about my kissing rule. However, he was always pleased to see me. My father was less enthusiastic. Whenever Saturday night rolled round, he gave me an angry look. Then he went to the local bars and got drunk.

With Mr Macintyre's production company, I spent a week at Niagara Falls, filming scenes for *The Hedonists*. The convoluted plot called for Daisy, my character, to fall into the water an awful lot. The hero would then chance by and rescue her.

Daisy was not the heroine in this movie. She was a protagonist whose main purpose was to annoy the heroine by flirting with the hero, and by falling into the water and being rescued by said hero.

Because Daisy was not the heroine, I would not receive top billing. However, my name would appear third on the titles and the movie posters. Stick that in your pipe, Mary-Jane Sinclair and smoke it.

Actually, the rumour was Mary-Jane Sinclair had been seen smoking a pipe. In all probability, it was only a rumour. Mixing with people in the movie business, I was fast learning that rumours of all sorts were commonplace, and far more plentiful than the rumours that circulated about Mary-Jane Sinclair on the street.

After each day's filming at Niagara Falls, I would dine with Archie. Rumours on the set circulated. Movie people gossiped. They suggested that we were lovers. Archie strutted around like the cock of the walk, giving the impression that we were lovers. I didn't like that. I preferred that we kept our feelings for each other, such as they were, to ourselves. However, Archie was high on emotion and determined to strut his stuff.

I was also concerned about my father, worried about his reaction should word of our 'affair' leak back to him. My father knew that Archie and I dated, but he didn't appreciate the depth of Archie's feelings for me.

I knew that matters would come to a head, and they did on the final day of location filming.

I was in my hotel room, packing, when Archie knocked on the door. I opened the door and glanced along the corridor. It was empty.

"May I come in?" Archie asked.

"No," I said.

"Why not?" he frowned.

"Because it would not be appropriate."

Archie sighed. "We're adults, Tula. You're eighteen now. What we're doing is not inappropriate."

Archie was right in that I was eighteen. In fact, I'd celebrated my birthday while we were filming at Niagara Falls. Mr Macintyre's production company had arranged a birthday party for me. I thought that was so sweet; I was deeply touched.

At my birthday party, the hero and heroine of *The Hedonists*, Alan and Julia, announced that they intended to marry in real life. I considered that so romantic, that people playing the roles of lovers could actually fall in love. I think that announcement stirred Archie too, and prompted his visit to my hotel room.

"We are adults," I conceded, "but it would not be appropriate for you to visit me in my hotel room. People will gossip. It could damage my reputation. I have my position as an actress to consider."

Archie laughed. "Listen to yourself, Tula Bowman. You're a young woman from the slums of Brooklyn talking as if she were born into the nobility."

"Maybe, one day," I said, "I will become a member of the acting nobility."

Archie laughed again. "Hark at you; it didn't take you long to put on airs and graces."

I frowned and reflected. Archie was right. My 'stardom', such as it was, had gone to my head. I was behaving in a haughty, inappropriate manner. I was not being true to myself. I vowed to correct my behaviour and remain on my guard. I should not forget my roots; at all times, I should remain true to myself.

"You cannot talk with me in my hotel room," I said, "but allow me to finish packing and I'll meet you outside the café."

The café overlooked Niagara Falls. It offered a stunning, spectacular view. I joined Archie and we strolled along the walkway, towards the falls.

As I stared at the cascading water, Archie blurted, "I love you."

I turned and stared at Archie. The setting was terribly romantic, so I could understand his words, and the timing of those words. I smiled at him, reached out, touched the back of his hand and said, "Thank you."

"Thank you?" Archie frowned. "You're a strange one, Tula Bowman; aren't you supposed to say 'I love you too'?"

Maybe I was supposed to say those words. However, the truth was I liked Archie, I didn't love him. I held on to the notion that love might develop, over time.

"Let's go back to your hotel room," Archie insisted. "Let me show you how much I love you."

"No," I frowned, "we cannot do that."

"Why not?" Archie scowled.

"Because I need to wait," I said. "Until I'm married. And I'm not getting married until I'm at least twenty-one."

"Twenty-one!" Archie blurted. "But that's three years! I can't wait that long."

"If you truly love me," I said, "you'll wait until I'm twenty-one."

Archie removed his flat cap. He crunched it between his fingers. He looked as though he wanted to throw his cap into the spray that rose from the waterfall.

"I love you," Archie said, "and you can't deny me the right to state my feelings. Equally, I can't wait three years."

"In that case," I said, turning my back on Archie Bleeker, "I think we should stop seeing each other."

"That's fine with me," Archie said. In a fit of pique, he did hurl his cap into the water. I watched as it tumbled through the spray and disappeared from view. "You know what people say about you, don't you, Tula Bowman, you know what the gossip is around the set."

"What is the gossip?" I asked.

"That you're a dyke. That you're only seeing me to cover for your lesbian lovers. They reckon that as soon as you reach Hollywood, you'll join the Sewing Circle."

"What's the Sewing Circle?" I frowned.

"You'll see," Archie said, "when you get there."

Before I could reply, and deny that I possessed any romantic feelings towards women, Archie stomped away. He disappeared through the mist that enveloped the walkway.

I wiped moisture from my face, spray from the waterfall. I felt bad about hurting Archie's feelings. I resolved to make it up to him, on my terms.

The Contract

Over the following six months, I continued to see Archie Bleeker, on and off. In the main, we met up on Saturday nights at the movies.

I heard a whisper that while Archie was seeing me, he was also seeing other women, but I didn't pry into that. I'd come to regard Archie as a friend, a movie buddy; he was welcome to date other women, if he so wished.

A week before Christmas, Mr Macintyre called me into his office. Whenever I received such a command, my heart sank; instinctively, I felt as though I'd done something wrong.

The Hedonists had been on general release for a month. It was fair to say that the reviews were mixed.

"Incomprehensible, convoluted, implausible," were some of the unkinder comments, while other reviewers stated that the movie was, *"capital entertainment, a fine romance, light-hearted escapist fun."*

In regard to the individual performances, I garnered the kindest reviews. *"Tula Bowman showed great promise in her first major role as Daisy." "Tulsa (sic) Bowman played the unsympathetic role of Daisy with immeasurable skill." "If Tula Bowman does not become a major movie star, I will eat my hat."*

Mr Macintyre had secured an advance distribution deal for *The Hedonists*. This meant that movie palaces throughout the country were obliged to screen the movie. Therefore, the negative reviews would offer little damage to the net income.

It was rare for motion pictures to enjoy a second tour of the movie palaces. Once screened, they were often disposed of, like used chewing gum.

Upon my return from Niagara Falls, Mr Macintyre farmed me out to other producers, and kept me busy with bit parts. I sensed that he was struggling to raise the necessary capital to shoot another major production, and fulfil his promise of offering me regular high-profile roles.

I entered Mr Macintyre's office with the dread that he was about to cancel my contract. However, I found him crouched over his putter, looking cheerful.

"Ha, Tula...one moment...let me just sink this putt...splendid...I still have the touch."

Mr Macintyre beckoned me towards his desk. I sat on a stout wooden chair, my hands resting in my lap. Mr Macintyre sat behind his desk in a luxurious leather chair. He swung that chair from side to side and studied a contract. Occasionally, he glanced in my direction and smiled.

"Tell me, Tula," Mr Macintyre said, "what do you make of acting in the movies?"

"I love it," I said. "I'm very grateful to you for offering me this opportunity."

"In terms of stardom and great riches," Mr Macintyre said, "Brooklyn is small potatoes; if you're looking to make it big in the movies, you need to act in Hollywood productions."

"I'm aware of that," I said.

Mr Macintyre smiled. He swayed from side to side and nodded. He studied the contract. "Would you like to work in Hollywood?" Mr Macintyre asked.

"I would love to," I said.

Mr Macintyre eased the contract across his desk. It skated over the highly polished surface and landed in my lap. I glanced at the contract. I noticed my name, printed in large capital letters.

"I've received an offer," Mr Macintyre said, "from a major production company in Hollywood, the Limelight Motion Picture Company. They were very impressed with your performance as Daisy in *The Hedonists*. They wish to acquire your contract."

Mr Macintyre paused, placed his elbows on his desk and leaned forward. "Do you understand what I'm saying?"

I glanced at Mr Macintyre, at the contract, frowned then nodded. "I think so," I said.

"Here's the deal," Mr Macintyre said. "The Limelight Motion Picture Company will acquire your contract, on improved terms – you will receive a twenty percent increase in your salary. You will work for the Limelight Motion Picture Company, in Hollywood, over a period of six months, in motion pictures that they deem suitable for your talents. Do you understand what I'm saying?"

I nodded. "I understand," I said.

"I will manage your affairs from this office. I will earn twenty percent of your earnings from this contract, and any subsequent contract that may stem from the original agreement; future contracts to be negotiated by all interested parties. Do you understand what I'm saying?"

I frowned then nodded. "I think so," I said.

"You may wish to consult with a lawyer," Mr Macintyre said. "Indeed, before you sign this contract, I insist that you do consult with a lawyer."

"I don't think that will be necessary," I said.

"I insist," Mr Macintyre said.

He offered me a very stern look; I'd never seen him look so serious.

"In that case," I said, "I will consult with a lawyer."

"Excellent," Mr Macintyre said. He leaned back in his chair and reached for a packet of Havana cigars. With his monogrammed lighter, he lit a cigar, sighed and blew a plume of smoke into the air.

While Mr Macintyre smoked his cigar, I tried to make sense of his offer. I'd receive a twenty percent pay rise, but that money would go to Mr Macintyre as commission; in effect, he would act as my agent.

I was still paying my father twenty percent, even though he wasn't managing my affairs. Maybe, financially, I could have secured a better deal but, at that moment, the thought of acquiring great riches didn't really occur to me. I was going to act in Hollywood; beyond that, I didn't have a care.

"Your first movie in Hollywood will be *The Ward*," Mr Macintyre said. "You will feature alongside Gregory Powell."

"Gregory Powell!" My jaw dropped. I had to steady myself to prevent myself from falling off the chair.

Gregory Powell was the biggest star in Hollywood. Furthermore, he was a fine actor, and had a reputation as a wonderful person. As a motion picture lover, he was my heartthrob.

"You'll play his ward, Clara," Mr Macintyre said, "a headstrong, rebellious tomboy. He'll fall in love with you, but he cannot marry you because the scandal of marrying his ward would ruin his political career. He sends you away, to Europe – these scenes will be filmed on a set in Hollywood.

However, when you return, he realises that he cannot resist you. For you, he sacrifices his political career. Do you think that you can manage that part, Tula?"

"Sure thing," I said.

Mr Macintyre and I chatted for another twenty minutes. He recommended a lawyer to read over my contract, and I promised that I'd make an appointment to see him.

I was still in a dream when I returned to the set to film a bit part. Archie was there, repairing his camera.

"I'm going to Hollywood," I said.

"Congratulations," Archie said. He didn't look up from his camera.

Archie sounded as if he didn't really care. He sounded as if I no longer meant anything to him. I realised that the rumours about him and other women were true and that he'd moved on and found someone else. I didn't blame him. Indeed, I wished him well.

"One thing, Tula," Archie said, struggling with his broken camera. "If someone in Hollywood needs a cameraman, mention my name."

"I'll do that," I said.

I was stuffing my belongings into a suitcase when my father entered my bedroom.

"So," he sighed, "you're leaving."

"I've received a generous offer from the Limelight Motion Picture Company – a six month contract and a leading role opposite Gregory Powell; I can't turn that down."

My father sat on my dressing table chair and stared at my reflection in the mirror. "I should go with you," he said.

"Your life is here," I said, "in Brooklyn, with your friends, singing in bars. You'd feel out of place in Hollywood."

"On the one hand," my father said, "you're right; I'm Brooklyn born and bred; this is my home. But, who's gonna look after you? Who's gonna look after your interests?"

"The Limelight Motion Picture Company has assigned me a chaperone," I said, "I'll meet her at the railway station this afternoon. As for my interests, Mr Macintyre will act as my agent."

My father glared into my dressing table mirror. He was decidedly unhappy. "What about our deal?" he asked. "What about my twenty percent?"

"I'll make arrangements," I said, sitting on my

suitcase in an effort to close it. "You'll still receive twenty percent of my earnings every month. That's more than enough to cover the rent on this place and your bar expenses."

I glanced at my father's reflection in the mirror. Running my words through my mind, I realised that they sounded harsh, cruel. However, my words represented the truth: my father needed money for the rent, a little food, and booze. Primarily, he needed money for booze.

My life was taking off, while my father's life was sliding into the gutter. Maybe he'd always lived in the gutter and now, now that my career was moving forward, I realised that a chasm was developing between us.

In retrospect, the cracks in our relationship had appeared the day my mother had died. I was leaving my father behind, physically and emotionally. And, although I felt excited about Hollywood and all it entailed, I felt sad about that.

"Things will work out," I said. "Once I'm settled in Hollywood, I'll call you and maybe we can arrange a visit."

My father picked up my hairbrush and toyed with stray strands of my hair. He teased the strands from the brush, kissed them and placed them in his jacket pocket. Then he turned and offered the brush to me.

"Go," my father said. "Enjoy yourself. Call me if you need me."

I placed my hairbrush in my suitcase and sat on the overstuffed valise again. Still, it wouldn't close properly. My father sat on my suitcase beside me and, at last, the locks met. We glanced at each other and laughed. My father kissed my forehead. I was on my way.

My father did not accompany me to the railway station. I think the idea of parting on the station platform, amongst hundreds of people, was too painful for him.

I threw three suitcases into a taxi and travelled to the railway station. There, amongst the commuters, I searched for my chaperone, Gloria Steenberg. Along with my finalised contract and a script for *The Ward*, the Limelight Motion Picture Company had sent me a picture of Miss Steenberg.

A short woman with wavy fair hair, Gloria Steenberg possessed hawk-like features – a hooked nose, close-set eyes and an intense stare. I wondered if we would get along. I placed Gloria's age in her mid-thirties. She was a 'Miss' and hadn't married. I wondered if she'd sacrificed love for her career.

In her photograph, Gloria's clothes – a skirt-suit, frilly blouse and cloche hat – balanced an old-fashioned look with the modern flapper look. She appeared smart, businesslike, but not overbearing. I was going to spend the next phase of my life with her, so I hoped that we would get along.

When I did catch sight of Gloria, I noticed that she was wearing clothes similar to the garments in her photograph. Maybe that was deliberate on her part. She smiled at me and we both waved.

Gloria walked towards me taking confident strides. Automatically, subconsciously, it seemed people moved out of her way.

From her walk alone, I sensed that Gloria knew where she was going in life and that she would not allow anyone to stand in her way. In the past, such a person would have intimidated me. However, thanks to my developing career and associated confidence, I felt that I could approach her as an equal.

"Hi," Gloria smiled. "I'm Gloria Steenberg. You must be Tula Bowman."

"That's right," I said.

Gloria nodded. "I recognised you from your movies."

Someone actually recognised me from my movies. I felt so excited; I felt fit to burst.

"I'll be your chaperone for the next six months," Gloria said. "I'll escort you on the train journey to Hollywood and help you to settle in. Do you have any questions?"

"When do we leave?" I asked.

Gloria checked her wristwatch. It was an elegant timepiece with a gold face and a thin leather strap. She glanced along the platform and the railway tracks. "The train is due in half an hour."

Our train arrived with a series of toots that sounded through a cloud of steam. Gloria helped me with my suitcases and we settled into our compartment. The Limelight Motion Picture Company had secured us a private sleeping compartment. I would travel in luxury.

Our journey across America took us seventy-two hours. We travelled through Philadelphia, Charlotte, Dallas, El Paso and Phoenix until we arrived at our destination, Hollywood.

During the daylight hours, I stared through the window, my eyes wide, my jaw slack, my senses utterly transfixed. During the night, I slept and, for a welcome change, I did not endure any nightmares. At various times, I also chatted with Gloria.

Through our conversations, I discovered that Gloria Steenberg hailed from New York. As a secretary, she'd worked for the Limelight Motion Picture Company in New York, and travelled with them when they'd relocated to Hollywood. I understood that Gloria had been living in Hollywood for five years.

Of course, as strangers getting to know each

other, we didn't discuss deeply personal matters. However, from our conversations, I gauged that Gloria was a 'modern woman' – to date, she'd not married and, currently, she was not stepping out with anyone.

Gloria and I laughed a lot during our journey and when we passed a significant landmark, she always offered me a snippet of information. For example, she informed me that the 'Five C's' – cattle, citrus, climate, copper and cotton anchored Phoenix's economy. I sensed that Gloria was an intelligent, highly educated person, and that I could learn a lot from her.

With the noonday sun kissing the tops of our heads, we disembarked from the train. I turned and stared into the mountains, at a large white building and, above it, a huge white sign. In capital letters the sign said, "HOLLYWOODLAND".

Gloria noted my bewildered expression. She smiled, guided me towards that sign and said, "Welcome to Hollywood."

A Party

From the first minute, my life in Hollywood was a whirl of activity. Initially, I needed somewhere to stay. Gloria solved that problem by offering me a room at her apartment in Glendale. Her apartment, large, spacious and adorned with fine art, overlooked a huge park, so naturally I was delighted to accept her offer.

I'd barely had time to unpack, or so it seemed, when I found myself at a party, a 'Baby Stars' party. The Limelight Motion Picture Company was hosting the party at a swish Hollywood hotel to introduce the 'Baby Stars' to members of the company, fellow actors and the media.

Chatting with the other 'Baby Stars', I gained an insight into Hollywood and how the system worked. Apparently, we'd been hired on six month contracts because we were talented actresses. That much, I could understand. What's more, we were 'cheap' – only one or two of us would go on to feature in more motion pictures. The rest of us would be discarded and replaced by the next wave of 'Baby Stars'.

Ten 'Baby Stars' attended the party. All of us had hopes, dreams and ambitions. Most likely, eight of us would leave Hollywood with exciting memories, and a sense of disappointment, a sense of what might have been.

At the party, I met the three men who would shape my immediate future in Hollywood and, potentially, my long-term career.

Mr Winter would direct me as Clara in *The Ward*. He was a small, jovial man with slicked-back hair, dark eyes that twinkled with amusement, and restless feet. Indeed, he had a habit of forever being on the move.

Mr Winter had arrived in Hollywood from Europe. He spoke excellent English, but with a pronounced accent. I couldn't place his accent – it appeared to be a blend of Polish, Austrian, Hungarian and German. Maybe Mr Winter's accent was an indication of his cosmopolitan lifestyle.

I was sitting on the floor, in the centre of the room, in awe of the motion picture stars as they swirled around me, when Mr Winter raised his champagne glass towards me and winked. We'd only met half an hour ago and briefly said, "Hello", and now he was greeting me as though I were a long lost friend.

Mr Vincetti was also a short man with slicked-back hair. His eyes were the palest of blues. They appeared cold, like chips of ice. Indeed, shivers ran up and down my spine whenever he glanced in my direction. He possessed small ears, a large nose and thick lips. I placed Mr Vincetti in his late thirties, while Mr Winter was a few years older.

Mr Vincetti also spoke, softly, with a mongrel, blended accent. He had yet to speak directly with me, but I'd overheard him talking with the other party guests.

Mr Vincetti did not sip any of the champagne, which was readily available to all the guests. Instead, he stood apart from the crowd, 'holding court'. Mr Vincetti was the head of the Limelight Motion Picture Company and, as such, the most important person at this party.

From my seated cross-legged position, I gazed at the motion picture stars as they swirled around me. Previously, I'd only seen these people on the silver screen, and now they were here for real, within touching distance, flesh and blood.

Of course, my gaze was drawn to Gregory Powell, the man I would act with in *The Ward*, the man I'd admired, from a distance.

Tall and lean with wavy dark hair, a pleasant smile and handsome features, Gregory Powell had risen to the top of the Hollywood tree. He could select the scripts that appealed to him, and demand a large salary. He could also choose the people he wished to work with. I wondered if he'd personally selected me.

As usual, Gregory's wife, Greta, stood at his

side. A fine actress in her younger days, she'd retired shortly after her wedding day. Like Gregory, Greta was in her early thirties. She possessed wavy, natural blonde hair, clear blue eyes and a flawless complexion. Indeed, her features appeared as fine and as delicate as porcelain.

I was staring at Greta, admiring her jewellery, noting how a few items – a gold necklace, a gold bracelet, plus a gold engagement and wedding ring – highlighted her class, when she glanced at me. She whispered a few words to Gregory then took a step in my direction.

"Oh, shit." I actually spoke the words aloud. I feared that my staring had caused offence and that Greta was going to admonish me. I scrambled to my feet and prepared to make a hasty retreat.

"Where are you going?" Greta asked.

"I...er...um...er...I...er," I said. "I was going to find something to drink."

"Drink this," Greta said, offering me a glass of champagne.

"Thank you," I said, accepting the glass, spilling champagne on to the parquet floor. The floor displayed a black and white zigzagged pattern. I imagined that the pattern would make your head spin after a few glasses of champagne. Of course, I was not of drinking age, but in Hollywood, normal rules did not seem to apply.

"Forgive me for saying this," Greta said, "but you appear nervous."

"I am nervous," I confessed. "I mean...all these people...all these stars, including your husband."

Greta smiled, then she laughed. "Let me tell you a secret," she said, "Gregory hates these parties. He's more nervous than you."

Greta turned towards Gregory, smiled and toasted her husband. He reciprocated and they both laughed. The love they shared was obvious. It was palpable. It was as though it contained a physical presence that travelled across the room.

"Soon," Greta said, "you will star alongside Gregory in *The Ward*."

"I know," I said. "I can't believe it. I can't believe that I've been offered such a lucky break."

"It has nothing to do with luck," Greta said, "it has everything to do with talent."

I frowned and eyed Greta over the rim of my champagne glass. She noted my frown and explained.

"I saw you in *The Hedonists* and recommended you to Gregory. I reckoned that you'd be ideal for the role of Clara and he agreed."

"So," I said, speaking slowly, trying to make sense of our conversation, "you secured this part, for me?"

"Yes," Greta smiled, "I guess I did."

Greta glanced towards Gregory, who'd attracted a throng of eager admirers. He looked anxious. Indeed, his eyes darted towards his wife, as though pleading for help.

"Oh dear," Greta laughed, "I'd better rescue my husband." She reached across and touched my arm in sisterly fashion. "Enjoy the party. I'm sure we'll meet again."

From the corner of my eye, I noticed that someone was filming the party. You're in Hollywood now, I reminded myself – cameras will be everywhere.

I was still adjusting to my surroundings when Gloria Steenberg approached me. She literally dazzled in her sequined outfit, which sparkled under the bright lights.

"What do you make of the party?" Gloria asked.

"It's...it's awesome," I said.

"It is swell, isn't it," Gloria said, glancing around the room. Her gaze returned and settled on me. Indeed, she offered me a glare. "Pity you look so dowdy, like Cinderella. Tomorrow, we're going shopping. Tomorrow, we're going to create a new image for you: Tula Bowman, movie star."

Placing My Bets

Ever since I set foot on the train in Brooklyn, I felt as though my life was hurtling at 100 mph. If anything, since my arrival in Hollywood, that pace had increased. It was exhilarating yet, at the back of my mind, I harboured the disturbing notion that, at some point, I would crash.

The morning after the 'Baby Stars' party, I went shopping with Gloria Steenberg. I say 'morning', but in reality it was noon before we explored the chicest stores in Hollywood.

Gloria insisted that I should adopt the latest flapper look, so I tried on a number of skirts and dresses that conformed to that fashion. The dresses were loose-fitting with drop waists and belts worn low on the hip. The length varied from the ankle up to the knee. However, none of the skirts or dresses were so daring as to sit above the knee.

In the main, the skirts were pleated with a hank hem. The dresses flattened my bust line. In the bust department, I needed all the help I could get, so I wasn't sure if this fashion really suited me.

I also tried on a number of cloche hats. I ended up buying a dozen. Gloria insisted that I should buy a velvet evening dress embellished with rhinestones, so we added that to our collection. At the checkout, the bill ran into hundreds of dollars.

"Who's going to pay for all this?" I frowned.

"You are," Gloria said.

"But..."

Gloria held up a hand to stop me. "No 'buts'," she said. "On your new contract, you can afford these items. Plus, you're going to become a big star, and a stepping stone on the path to stardom is to look like a big star."

Gloria paused. She placed her hands on my shoulders and looked me in the eyes. "I've been the chaperone to a number of 'Baby Stars' over the past four years, and all those 'Baby Stars' have gone on to secure long-term contracts. I will secure a long-term contract for you." Gloria squeezed my shoulders and smiled. "Trust me."

I decided to trust Gloria Steenberg. I paid the bill.

During the days, I spent my time rehearsing with Gregory Powell and our director, Mr Winter, plus other members of our cast and crew. Everyone was very professional and worked very hard. We worked long hours, from early in the morning until late in the evening. There was little time to socialise, or even indulge in any banter. By suppertime each day, I was ready for bed.

On the weekends, Gloria and I went to a movie palace to watch the latest release. In particular, I enjoyed Harold Lloyd in *Safety Last!* In some of the scenes, he had me on the edge of my seat, while in others I laughed aloud. The scene where he clutched the hands of a clock while dangling above moving traffic was incredible and had the audience gasping in amazement.

On my fifth Saturday in Hollywood, Gloria insisted that I should don my velvet dress. This I did. I admired myself in a mirror, fingered the rhinestones and said, "Where are we going?"

"To a casino."

"To watch?"

Gloria offered me a look that bordered on the pitiful. "No, silly; we're going to play."

I wondered about the wisdom of gambling in a casino, but held my tongue.

Gloria ordered a taxi and we travelled into a sleazy neighbourhood. The casino was garish, very loud and very bright. The clientele was smartly dressed, or at least they thought that they were smartly dressed. However, to my eye, the women wore too much make-up while the men looked like gangsters.

"I'm not sure about this," I said, hesitating in the foyer.

"Trust me," Gloria said. She took hold of my elbow and guided me towards a roulette table. As we walked towards the table, a photographer pounced. He took my photograph. The flash from his camera caught me by surprise and I blinked. The picture would not look flattering, but there was little I could do about it now.

Gloria acquired some chips and we sat at the roulette table. We watched people lose and curse, then joined the game.

"Follow my lead," Gloria said, "and you'll win."

Uncertain, and a little confused, I followed Gloria's lead. She placed a modest bet on twenty black, and won. We lost two spins in a row, then won on the next three spins. It was exciting. We bet our winnings on six black and won again. I couldn't help myself – I clapped and squealed with delight.

"You see," Gloria said, offering me a knowing look, "you're enjoying yourself."

To Gloria, I confessed that I was enjoying the thrill of placing my bets. However, I didn't like the look of the garishly made-up women, or the menacing-looking men.

I wondered how Gloria knew of this location. I wondered how she'd discovered it. I wondered about Gloria's background, and how she'd achieved her position in Hollywood.

The evening was drawing to a close and, between us, we'd won thousands of dollars, a small fortune. Other gamblers at our table had won too, but smaller amounts. However, the majority were disgruntled losers.

"One more bet," Gloria said, "seven red."

Gloria pushed her chips forward, but I hesitated.

"We could lose everything," I said.

"If we lose on this spin," Gloria said, "we'll still end the evening on evens; we're only gambling what we've already won."

Gloria had a point, I suppose, so I placed my chips alongside hers.

The roulette wheel spun. I held my breath as the little white ball bobbled, then I screamed with delight when it nestled alongside seven red. "We've won!" I said.

Gloria smiled. She nodded sagely, then collected our chips. The photographer swooped again and took my picture as I grinned at my chips. That picture would look good, if his newspaper or magazine decided to print it.

Gloria took our chips to a desk, presumably to cash them. Meanwhile, I hailed a taxi.

During our journey home, I turned to Gloria and said, "That was fun, but something, or rather someone, was missing."

"Who?" Gloria frowned.

"My father," I said. "I'd like him to join me in Hollywood."

"Not yet," Gloria said. "First, you must become a star. You must concentrate on becoming a star."

I wasn't sure about that. I wanted to act in motion pictures. I was desperate to act in motion pictures. However, I wasn't sure about stardom. I wasn't sure if I could cope with it.

At home, a thought struck me. I turned to Gloria and said, "Where's our winnings?"

"No winnings," Gloria said. "I handed in the chips, as arranged."

"As arranged?" I paused and tried to make sense of her words. "You mean, the whole thing was a set-up?"

"Of course," Gloria said. "The photographer captured a picture of you with your 'winnings'. That'll mean good publicity for you, and the casino. People in the motion picture business, and those who visit the movie palaces, will identify you as a winner. Project yourself as a winner, and you will be successful."

"But," I frowned, "but...that's deceitful."

"You're an actress," Gloria scowled. "Your job is to make the audience believe in you. You're building a career on wilful deceit."

The Kiss

I was nervous. We'd been filming *The Ward* for seventeen days and today was my big scene. Today, I would kiss Gregory Powell.

Of course, the kiss was 'only pretend' and with dozens of people hanging around the set, it would lack all sense of romance and passion. Nevertheless, our kiss had to look convincing. Also, during rehearsals I'd learned that Gregory was the ultimate professional. I didn't want to let him down. I didn't want to make a fool of myself.

I paced my dressing room in my long crepe dress and skilfully applied make-up. I reckoned that Mr Winter knew that I was nervous because he joined me for a pre-take chat, and he didn't normally do that.

"How's it going, Tula?"

Mr Winter parked himself on the edge of my dressing table and adjusted his porkpie hat. I'd discovered that during filming Mr Winter habitually wore a porkpie hat.

"Everything is going well," I said. "Thank you, Mr Winter."

"I noticed your picture the other day," Mr Winter said, "in *The Enquirer*. You were in a casino."

"That's right," I said. "Gloria Steenberg

escorted me there. We played roulette. It was fun."

"It's good to have fun," Mr Winter said. "You need to let your hair down. Most people think that making movies is a doddle, but it's loaded with stress. Right now, I'm waiting for my cameraman. He's late. Again."

Mr Winter removed his porkpie hat and fanned himself. He appeared harassed, frazzled, so I appreciated him taking the time and trouble to talk with me in this fatherly fashion. His talk made me think, yet again, that I should invite my father to join me in Hollywood.

"It's good to have fun," Mr Winter said. "Personally, I love swimming. However, my favourite bay sometimes attracts sharks. It's good to have fun, but at all times you must be aware of the sharks. Know what I'm saying?"

"I understand, Mr Winter," I said. "And I will remain wary of the sharks. I appreciate your concern."

"No problem," Mr Winter said. He plonked his hat on his head and tilted it at a rakish angle. He punched me playfully on the arm. "You're a smart kid; you'll go far."

Mr Winter eased himself off my dressing table. However, before he left my dressing room, I turned to him and said, "Regarding a cameraman, if you're looking for someone highly skilled and very reliable, I can recommend Archie Bleeker from Brooklyn."

"Archie Bleeker," Mr Winter said, caressing his jaw. "I'll keep him in mind."

Our cameraman arrived an hour late. From his hung-over state, it was clear that he'd been on a 'bender'. Mr Winter was furious. However, ever the professional, he kept his anger in check.

We filmed a scene, which required me to gather flowers in a meadow and look wistful. As I sniffed the flowers, I wondered about the people I'd left behind in Brooklyn. I wondered what they were doing. I wondered what they were thinking, in particular in relation to my movie career.

When I acted, I always called upon personal experience to generate the emotion. Then I channelled that emotion through my character. Sometimes, that emotion lingered with me after the scene. However, on most occasions, I could switch it off.

Gregory Powell arrived on the set. He greeted everyone personally and, in turn, each person greeted him. He was very popular on the set, and it was easy to understand why. Even though as the star Gregory carried every motion picture on his shoulders, even though he was the one under the greatest stress, he always found time for everyone. Nothing was too much trouble for him. He was an incredibly patient and considerate man.

Gregory looked handsome in his Regency robes. He looked every inch the Lord of the Manor, his role in *The Ward*. Briefly, we rehearsed the scene to make sure that Mr Winter, our lighting man and our hung-over cameraman were happy. Then we moved in for a take.

Gregory swept me into his arms, looked deeply into my eyes, uttered words of undying love – in the finished production, his words would appear as an intertitle – then kissed me on the lips.

I thought I would melt. I thought that Gregory would suck all the air from my body. I thought that my arms would lock around his powerful torso and that I'd never be able to let him go.

Gregory broke the kiss and gazed into my eyes, as required in the script. I was sorely tempted to ruin the scene so that he'd have to kiss me again. However, such behaviour would have been unprofessional.

As Gregory gazed into my eyes and offered more words of undying love, my heart responded. We were only acting, yet I could not deny my feelings, my emotions – I was in love.

Mr Winter called, "Cut!"

Gregory released me. He turned to the director and asked, "Was that okay for you?"

"Excellent," Mr Winter said. "*Wúnderbar.*"

"What about you, Tula?" Gregory asked.

"It was..." I struggled to find the right words. "Good," I said.

"Okay," Gregory said. "I'll change my costume and we can shoot the next scene."

Gregory walked off the set without glancing in my direction. For him, the kiss had been just another scene to shoot, another action for his character to perform. On a professional level, it meant a lot to him. Yet, on a personal level, clearly it meant nothing. And that, I reminded myself, is how it should be.

That evening, I found myself walking on the beach. I walked for miles, deep in thought. I was in love with Gregory Powell. I told myself that that was wrong – he was a happily married man. Furthermore, I genuinely liked his wife, Greta. She struck me as a warm, caring person.

I hated myself for loving Gregory. I considered jumping into the sea and sinking to the bottom of the ocean. But such an action would have caused my father deep distress.

I tried to convince myself that my infatuation with Gregory was just that, an infatuation. Many people were besotted with motion picture stars, even though they'd never meet them, even though they'd never truly get to know them. Being besotted with your favourite star was all part of the appeal.

I tried to convince myself that I was infatuated with Gregory, but I knew that that wasn't true. It was more than infatuation; it was love. This was the real thing.

I considered screaming at the ocean in an effort to release my frustration. Then I caught sight of a pebble. The waves had fashioned the pebble into a perfect shape, a heart. I picked up the pebble and caressed it, ran my fingers over its smooth contours. I kissed it. I hugged it to my breast.

Then an idea possessed me. I knelt on the sand and, in front of a rocky outcrop, dug a deep hole. I placed my pebble in that deep hole. It was a symbolic act. I was burying my love for Gregory, a love that could never be.

I smoothed the sand, straightened and dusted myself down. My love for Gregory was dead and I would mourn its loss. To compensate, I would throw myself into my work and become a great actress.

Negotiations

I kept my promise – I dismissed all romantic thoughts of Gregory Powell and threw myself into my work.

Six months went by in a flash. Mr Vincetti supplied me with a series of supporting roles. I worked every day, sometimes on weekends.

The Ward was touring the movie palaces and receiving great reviews. Most of the praise was, deservedly, reserved for Gregory. However, I did garner my fair share of praise. *"From 'Baby Star' to Mega Star, for Tula Bowman that can only be a matter of time."*

"In 'The Ward', Tula Bowman displayed a range of emotions we have not witnessed since Sarah Bernhardt graced the silver screen."

I also received some insults. *"Audiences are tiring of over-emotional waifs as portrayed by Miss Tula Bowman. What the modern movie-goer is looking for is a young woman with spunk. It's time that these ingénues and the actresses who portray them are consigned to the dustbin of motion picture history."*

On balance, eighty percent of my reviews were good; ten percent were indifferent while the other ten percent castigated my performance. It's funny how words of criticism tend to linger in the memory, far longer than words of praise.

Aside from the critics, I sensed that Mr Vincetti didn't really rate me, hence his decision to offer me supporting roles, and not headline parts. By this stage, I was convinced that I only secured the role of Clara in *The Ward* thanks to Greta Powell and her influence on her husband. I could not have Gregory as a lover, I knew that, so I consoled myself with the thought that at least he was with a wonderful woman, a woman who truly deserved his love and affection.

When not filming, I spent time with Gloria Steenberg at home, in restaurants, at parties, at the stores and at movie palaces. Gloria was also keen to visit the casinos. However, heeding Mr Winter's warning about 'sharks', I refused.

Four months after the completion of *The Ward*, I heard that Archie Bleeker was in town and working with Mr Winter. The director had acted upon my recommendation, and I was pleased about that. I was keen to work with Mr Winter again, if the opportunity should arise, and catch up with Archie, if time allowed. But first, before any other consideration, I had to secure a new contract.

On a dark stormy day, I met Mr Vincetti in his fifth floor office, an office that overlooked the ocean. The waves were wild, tossing the ships without mercy. I thanked my lucky stars that I harboured no ambitions to become a sailor.

Gloria Steenberg accompanied me to the meeting. I'm not sure why. I think she wanted to offer moral support. Also, at the close of my 'Baby Star' contract, her contract as my chaperone would expire.

"Please be seated," Mr Vincetti said. He sat on a high-backed leather chair, behind his enormous desk, while Gloria and I sat on modest wooden chairs, in front of the mahogany desk. Mr Vincetti was the boss and, through chairs alone, he displayed that fact.

Mr Vincetti adjusted his shirt cuffs, eased them down from under the sleeves of his jacket. He wore gold cufflinks adorned with large diamonds.

As usual, Mr Vincetti spoke slowly and quietly, his voice barely rising above a whisper. He also stared at me through cold, ice-blue eyes. Whenever he stared at me, I shivered. It was an involuntary gesture on my part.

"Your contract is up," Mr Vincetti said.

"Yes," I said, "it expires at the end of the month."

In his leather chair, Mr Vincetti swayed gently from side to side. He steepled his fingers, placed them against his chin and stared at me. He pursed his thick lips. He licked his lips. His actions reminded me of a reptile.

"I have a mind not to renew your contract," Mr Vincetti said.

"But Tula deserves a new contract," Gloria said. "She's worked hard over the past six months. She's received praise from the critics and her directors for all her roles. And she's received fan mail," Gloria added, producing a large bag stuffed with letters. "Motion picture fans love her. She's developing a devoted following."

Mr Vincetti ignored Gloria. He stared at me. "The success of *The Ward* was down to Gregory Powell," Mr Vincetti said. "When Powell plays in a movie, I can place any skirt opposite him. As long as she's good looking and can display emotion, the picture will be a success."

"Tula is more than 'a piece of skirt'," Gloria said. "She's a very talented actress. The fan magazines are queuing up to interview her. If you do not offer her another contract, I know of at least two production companies who will."

"Who?" Mr Vincetti frowned. "Name those companies."

"I cannot," Gloria said. She matched Mr Vincetti, glare for glare. "Those offers are privileged information."

"I see," Mr Vincetti said, eyeing Gloria through narrow eyes, leaning back in his chair.

Mr Vincetti picked up a fountain pen and

unscrewed its top. Ink dripped on to a blotter. He looked at the ink with a certain distain. I sensed that Mr Vincetti was a perfectionist, and maybe that was my problem – in my performances to date, I had not achieved perfection.

"I don't believe in ceding any ground to a rival," Mr Vincetti said. "Therefore, on this occasion, I will consider extending Miss Bowman's contract, on the same terms as previously."

"On improved terms," Gloria said. "Tula is through with bit parts and support roles; to progress, she needs leading roles. And she needs to work with Gregory Powell and Uwe Winter again; they bring out the best in her, encourage her finest performances."

"You drive a hard bargain, Miss Steenberg." Mr Vincetti threatened to smile. However, he did not allow himself that luxury.

"We want a two-year contract," Gloria said, "plus the guarantee that Tula will work with Gregory Powell and Uwe Winter on at least four more movies."

"Maybe Gregory Powell and Uwe Winter are not keen to work with Tula again," Mr Vincetti said.

"I have spoken with them," Gloria said. "They are very keen."

Mr Vincetti covered the ink stains with blotting paper. He watched as the blotting paper absorbed the ink, as the stains formed new patterns.

Of course, everyone in Hollywood was there to make money, especially the executives. However, some people were there for the love of their art. I figured Mr Vincetti for a hard-headed businessman. Yet, as he watched the ink patterns form, I reasoned that maybe he also had the ability to appreciate art.

"Very well," Mr Vincetti sighed. "I will inform our people to draw up a new contract. Miss Bowman's wages will remain the same. The contract will run for twelve months. It will guarantee at least two motion pictures with Gregory Powell and Uwe Winter."

"We accept," Gloria said.

I was aware that these negotiations were going over my head, passing me by, and that I had no say in my future. In addition, while I appreciated Gloria's support, I did feel uneasy about her regarding me as a commodity.

Gloria and I walked out of Mr Vincetti's office into the storm. Shielding behind an umbrella, I turned to her and asked, "Which production companies made the additional offers?"

"No one made an additional offer," Gloria said. She took hold of my arm and flashed me a broad, cheeky grin. "To win big, sometimes you have to bluff."

I was absorbing Gloria's words when, to my

surprise, she kissed me.

"Come on," Gloria said, dragging me by the elbow, "let's celebrate."

Another Kiss

Mr Vincetti was determined that I should earn my wages. He found regular work for me, mostly in supporting roles. Also, during lulls, he hired me out to other producers.

As per the terms of my contract, Mr Vincetti scheduled two motion pictures in which I would take the female lead opposite Gregory Powell. Mr Winter would direct those pictures. Furthermore, I'd learned that Archie Bleeker had become Mr Winter's ace cameraman, so the making of those pictures would become a reunion, of sorts.

After three months of nonstop work, I succumbed to an illness, a bad dose of the flu. I lay in bed for a week, barely able to move. During that time, Gloria tended to me. She became the brick, the foundation I could rely upon.

During my recuperation, I lost wages, as per the terms of my contract. That was annoying. But, more disturbing was the subtle change in Gloria's behaviour. She'd always been controlling. Indeed, at times I sensed that she manipulated me as one might manipulate a mannequin.

Gloria had always been tactile in that she would touch me whenever a situation presented itself. Her touches were never inappropriate. They were merely displays of emotion, of excitement, or offers to assist me with awkward buttons on a favourite dress.

However, now Gloria started to hit on me, in the same way that men hit on me at the parties we attended. Everything came to a head on a particular Saturday night, after our weekly trip to a movie palace.

I was in my bedroom, preparing for bed, when Gloria entered. She'd been drinking whiskey, and I could smell it on her breath. She'd taken to smoking cigarettes in long cigarette holders. She reckoned that smoking cigarettes in such a manner made a woman look elegant, nonchalant.

Gloria insisted that I should smoke cigarettes through a long cigarette holder. I tried it for a week then abandoned the practice because cigarettes made me cough.

Gloria was smoking a cigarette on that particular Saturday night. She was blowing smoke rings into the air and viewing me through heavily lidded eyes.

With an extravagant gesture, Gloria sat on the edge of my bed and raised a leg. The long split in her skirt revealed her thigh.

"You look beautiful," Gloria said, as I reached for the buttons on my dress.

I undid a button then hesitated. "This is not

appropriate," I said. "I should undress alone."

"Continue," Gloria insisted. She placed her cigarette holder across an ashtray and offered me a sensual smile. "Or maybe you'd like me to help you."

Before I could reply, I found Gloria on top of me. She pushed me on to the bed and kissed me with great passion. In her eagerness to undress me, she tore my dress.

I fought the urge to panic. I tried to push Gloria away from me, but she was too strong, and too determined. I pummelled my fists against her back, but that only seemed to spur her on. I glanced to my right and noticed the ashtray. I reached for the ashtray and positioned it above Gloria's head.

I struck Gloria with the ashtray. With a grunt, she rolled off me and fell on to the floor. My initial reaction was, I'd killed her. However, to my great relief, I noticed that she was breathing. Then, to my horror, I noticed that her cigarette had rolled from the ashtray and set the lace curtain alight.

I rushed from the bedroom to gather glasses of water. I threw the water over the curtain and Gloria. After several glasses of thrown water, the fire faded and Gloria revived.

"What happened?" Gloria asked, grimacing, caressing the back of her head, glancing at the smouldering curtain.

"You dropped your cigarette," I said.

The troubled look on Gloria's face told me that recent events were now revealing themselves to her in all their brutal clarity.

"I'm sorry," Gloria said. "I thought you wanted me to kiss you."

"Whatever gave you that idea?" I scowled.

"You never protested before," Gloria said, "when I touched you. And when we attend parties, you're always cold towards the men. You always reject men, at every party. I got the idea that you don't like them."

"I like men," I said, "but I'm particular in my tastes. Besides, I'm here to concentrate on my career. Like I said to a gentleman the other week at a buffet: 'I'm looking for a piece of cheese, not a husband.'"

Despite herself, Gloria laughed. Despite myself, and the situation, I laughed. Then, we both became serious.

"Please forgive me," Gloria said.

"I forgive you," I said, "but we must adjust our relationship. I don't know what your official position is with me right now; I don't know if you are still my chaperone. If you are, that can continue. However, I need my own place to live; I need to move out."

Gloria struggled to her feet. I helped her. She

fell over the heel of her shoe and twisted her ankle. Literally, Gloria was aching from head to foot. She hobbled towards my bedroom door. There, she paused and turned to stare at me.

"I misread you," Gloria said, holding the back of her neck – with the ashtray, I'd really thumped her hard. "And for that, I apologise. However, you were violent in your reaction. Tell me," she frowned, "has someone hit on you like that before?"

"My mother used to attack me," I said. "What you did sparked a flashback. Maybe I shouldn't have hit you that hard but, in that moment, I became possessed."

Gloria's actions provoked negative thoughts of my mother. The singed curtain and its pungent smell brought to mind the fire that had claimed Finn's life. It was all too much. I began to cry.

Gloria took a step towards me, to comfort me. However, she sensed that I would not appreciate her gesture. So, she left my bedroom and closed the door, offering a soft, "Goodnight."

Eventually, my tears subsided and I reflected. We were ruled by passions – passions for our art, entertainment, and love. We were ruled by our passions and, if not careful, they could destroy us. Gloria's passion had ruined our relationship. I feared that my passion for acting would ruin me.

I would move out of Gloria's apartment and

find a place of my own. However, the thought of living alone in a metropolis like Hollywood did not appeal to me. I would find a place of my own and invite my father to live with me.

Over the next month, Gloria and I became more distant. After the incident in her apartment, I suppose that was inevitable.

From Mr Vincetti, I discovered that, officially, I was no longer a 'Baby Star'. Therefore, I did not require a chaperone. Gloria would move on and chaperone one of this year's 'Baby Stars'.

I wondered if the pattern of slow seduction, over many months, would repeat itself. I wondered if such a pattern had become engrained in Gloria's lifestyle. I wondered if I should inform Mr Vincetti.

Sometimes, I found it difficult to take vital decisions on my own. This was a vital decision that would affect Gloria's career, her lifestyle. Rightly, or wrongly, I decided not to inform Mr Vincetti.

It was a struggle to find somewhere suitable to live, at an affordable price, but I managed to rent an apartment in Pasadena, near the library and art museum. On quiet days, I enjoyed looking around the library and art museum. I promised myself that if I truly established myself as an actress in Hollywood I would acquire a home near the coast. However, for now, Pasadena would do.

With my home established, I sent for my father. I'd spoken to him on the telephone, but hadn't seen him for about a year.

I waited on the railway platform in a state of nervous anticipation. I was about to welcome my father, yet so much had happened to me recently, it felt as though I were about to greet a distant relative.

Physically, and emotionally, I'd moved away from my father. Maybe spending time together would help us to bridge that gap.

Through a cloud of white smoke, my father's train arrived. He stumbled on to the platform carrying a battered brown suitcase. He looked around, his features displaying confusion. Then, he caught sight of me and smiled.

My father ambled towards me, carrying his suitcase. He walked like a drunken sailor, favouring his back. In all probability, my father was drunk. Maybe over the coming months I could help him to become sober. He was drinking his life away, and it was my duty as his daughter to put a stop to that.

My father placed his suitcase on the railway platform and opened his arms to greet me. However, I walked up to him and shook his hand. My father stared at our handshake, his aged features revealing his confusion.

"Is that the way daughters greet fathers in Hollywood?" he asked.

I didn't reply. I couldn't say why, but I felt that

that was the way I should greet him.

"Let me help you with your suitcase," I said.

I carried my father's suitcase to the taxi rank and we hailed a taxi. In the near future, I would learn to drive; I wanted that sense of independence.

During our journey to Pasadena, I asked, "How are you keeping?"

"I'm okay," my father shrugged. "My back hurts now and again but, apart from that, I'm fine."

"You've had no problems cashing my cheques?"

"Your cheques arrive the first of the month," my father said. "I cash them, no problem. I want you to know, I'm grateful for the money. And now that I'm in Hollywood, I intend to take my managerial duties seriously."

I allowed my father's comment to slide. Since signing my new contract, I'd cut my ties with Mr Macintyre in Brooklyn. Basically, I was managing my own affairs. That was a challenge, and a great strain. I needed someone to assist me with my affairs, but I recognised that that someone could not be my father. Even though his heart was in the right place, he did not have the business acumen to swim with the sharks that circled the murky waters around Hollywood.

Changing the subject, I asked, "How are the folks in Brooklyn?"

"Aunt Tula is well," my father said, "though as miserly as ever. Gadsden has retired. His store now belongs to one of the major chains. Mary-Jane Sinclair was arrested for soliciting, but the charges were dropped. Submarine Lil is still doing a roaring trade."

"That's a shame about Mary-Jane Sinclair," I said.

My father shrugged. "For some women, it's inevitable; they're born to go on the game."

We arrived at my apartment, a modest bungalow, and my father admired the front lawn. "That grass will need cutting," he said. "I'll do that for you. And I'll paint the picket fence."

My father would not complete either task. We both knew that. However, I offered no comment; I merely smiled.

My father turned and grinned at me. "My little girl has got her own apartment in Hollywood, complete with a white picket fence." His grin grew broader. "I'm so proud of you; I want you to know that."

"Thank you," I said.

I led my father into his room and placed his suitcase on the bed. He took a quick look around the room then asked, "Where do you keep the booze in this house?"

"No booze," I said. "I drink alcohol at parties,

268

but I don't drink at home."

Of course, technically, the authorities had banned the sale of alcohol, although resistance was strong in our city, in New York. Hollywood too was awash with booze. As they say, where there's a will, there's a way.

"Not even wine?" my father frowned. "Surely, you drink the odd glass."

"I guess we can share a bottle of wine," I said, "on special occasions. But I want you to get sober while you're in Hollywood. We can't pretend anymore; we must acknowledge the fact that you are an alcoholic."

"I can hold my drink," my father said, his tone indignant.

"Let's not argue on our first day," I said. "Take a shower, relax, and we'll dine out this evening."

My father removed his tie and jacket. He tilted back his hat. He offered me a long look, loaded with appraisal. "You've grown up," he said, "in appearance and attitude."

"I've learned a lot in recent months," I said, "about life and acting."

My father wrapped his tie around his fingers, akin to a boxer wrapping bandages around his fist. "Do you have a boyfriend?" he asked.

"No boyfriend," I said.

"But you must have received offers."

"I've received many offers," I said, "and turned them all down."

"That's wise," my father said. "You need to wait, until you're the Queen of Hollywood, then you can choose anyone to be your King."

"I have no ambitions to become the Queen of Hollywood," I said. "I want to act in motion pictures. I want to make movies that people will love. So many people lead hard lives. Saturday night at the movies is the highlight of their week. I want to give these people something they can look forward to, something that will tide them over their next difficult week."

"And what about a husband?" my father asked.

"When I marry," I said, "it'll be for love."

My father laughed. "That's my Tula, forever the romantic." He placed his fist, wrapped in his tie, to my chin and gave it a light, playful tap. "Hold on to your ideals," my father said, "marriage can wait. For now, you have me to look after you."

The Fundraising Ball

Greta Powell arranged a fundraising ball at the Excelsior Hotel. My father and I were invited. The funds raised from the ball would assist ex-soldiers wounded in the Great War. It was a noble cause, and, in my own modest way, I was delighted to offer my support.

I noticed a number of familiar faces at the ball, including Gregory Powell, of course, Greta, Mr Winter, Mr Vincetti, Gloria, and Archie Bleeker.

Archie glanced in my direction. He offered me a lopsided grin then, with long loping strides, he wandered over and stood at my side.

"Care to dance?" he asked.

"Sure," I said.

Archie danced with 'two left feet'. On a number of occasions, he trod on my toes.

"Ouch!" I said.

"Sorry," he frowned.

During the slow numbers, Archie held me tight and we smooched across the dance floor. We attracted a number of stares, not because we were great dancers, but because we looked incongruous, Archie being so tall, me being so short. Also, it must be said, Archie danced like a klutz.

"I want to thank you," Archie said, "for

recommending my services to Mr Winter."

"My pleasure," I said. "But if you tread on my toes one more time, I'm going to kick you in the shins."

"Sorry," Archie said. "Maybe we should sit the next one out."

Archie and I retired to the fringes and admired the other dancers. Gregory danced with Greta and they looked glorious together. Indeed, their graceful movements and sense of harmony elicited spontaneous applause.

I also noticed that Gloria was dancing with Mr Vincetti. Furthermore, she was raking her long fingernails across the back of his neck in the most suggestive fashion. I formed the impression that Gloria was seeking to seduce Mr Vincetti, and become his mistress.

During my time in Hollywood, I'd overheard a number of rumours and lots of gossip. Many people in the community expressed a preference for men and women. I reasoned that, maybe, Gloria was one of them.

I'd also heard that people married in an attempt to hide their true sexuality. Known as 'Lavender Marriages,' these unions were a sham, their main purpose being to allow the 'husband' and 'wife' to indulge in clandestine, same-sex affairs.

I considered it a shame that people could not be

open about their sexuality, due to the mores of society, and that they had to indulge in such charades as 'Lavender Marriages'.

Gloria took hold of Mr Vincetti's hand and led him towards the exit. The implication was obvious. Greta noticed, but everyone else was too wrapped up in the merrymaking to care.

Greta glanced at me and arched an eyebrow. I shrugged. Gloria and Mr Vincetti were adults, and if they wished to conduct an affair that was none of our business.

Greta's raised eyebrow and my shrug highlighted our curiosity. However, we were similar in temperament in that we were private people. We would not gossip. We would leave that to the people in Hollywood who made a living from rumours and innuendos.

Breaking my reverie, Archie said, "Thanks for the dance, Tula. Maybe we can link up again, go to a movie."

"Maybe," I said.

For some reason, Archie appeared juvenile to me now, probably because I'd grown up over the past year. Also, I reckoned that it would not be wise to rekindle our previous relationship. I looked forward to working with Archie again, but in terms of romantic relationships, we both needed to move on.

Mr Winter performed a magic trick, which attracted a large audience and plenty of laughter. He produced a rabbit from his hat. How on earth did he manage that?

I was trying to figure out the secret to Mr Winter's magic trick when Greta wandered over to me. Dressed in a long gown decorated with pearls, she looked very glamorous.

"Are you okay?" Greta smiled.

"I'm fine," I said. "I was just trying to work out how Mr Winter produced that rabbit, and where it's gone now."

Greta laughed. "Uwe is full of tricks. I gave up trying to understand his magic a long time ago. Now, I just sit back and admire his skill."

Mr Vincetti reappeared, along with Gloria. They separated, then offered each other secret smiles.

"I noticed that you were pensive earlier," Greta said, frowning at me. "Do you have anything else on your mind?"

"I was just thinking about my affairs," I said.

"Your business affairs?"

"Yes," I said. The complex nature of my legal contracts was playing on my mind.

"Do you have an agent?" Greta asked.

"No," I said.

"I could manage your affairs," Greta suggested.

"After all, I manage Gregory's affairs."

Greta's generous offer made me gasp. "I couldn't impose on you."

"It would not be an imposition," she smiled.

"If you're sure," I said.

Greta reached out and placed a reassuring hand on my arm. "I'm certain."

Assistance with my legal affairs and contracts would ease my burden. It would free-up my mind for acting. Furthermore, I trusted Greta, a statement I could not make about everyone in Hollywood. I'd liked Greta from our first meeting. Now, I found myself warming to her even more.

My father wandered across the dance floor, a glass of champagne in his hand. I must confess that he looked out of place, in his shabby suit. He needed a new suit. At the first opportunity, we'd visit the department stores.

Greta recaptured my attention with a curt comment. "May I be blunt with you?" she asked.

"Sure," I said.

"All of Gregory's leading ladies fall in love with him at some point. At first, that upset me. However, now I accept it because when I raised the subject with Gregory, he made it plain that we share a special bond. I know that you have feelings for Gregory, and I know that he likes you. Equally, I know that Gregory is a man of honour and that he'll respect me and his marriage vows. Do you understand what I'm saying?"

Greta's comment took me aback, not because of her tone, or that I disagreed with her words, but because I felt as though she'd peered into my mind.

"I think so," I said.

"Good," Greta smiled. "In that case, we can be friends, and business partners?"

"I'd like that," I said.

Greta trusted her husband and he respected her. To me, that sounded like the basis for a stable relationship.

An outcry attracted our attention. We turned to witness my father and Mr Vincetti standing toe-to-toe. They were arguing and pushing each other.

"I think your father is going to punch Mr Vincetti," Greta said.

"Father!" I ran across the dance floor and dragged my father away from Mr Vincetti. "I'm sorry, Mr Vincetti," I called out over my shoulder, "I'm truly sorry." To my father, I said, "You can't do that."

Mr Vincetti offered my father an ice-cold glare. He straightened the lapels on his jacket and reached for a glass of champagne. Gloria appeared at his side. She glared at my father too. I made my excuses to Greta and dragged my father out of the hotel, into the cool night air.

"I wanted a drink," my father explained, "and that monkey man pushed me."

"This is not a backstreet bar in Brooklyn," I said. "This is the Excelsior Hotel in Hollywood. And that 'monkey man' is Mr Vincetti, one of the most important people in Hollywood."

"I wanted a drink," my father said.

"You're drunk," I said.

"I only wanted a drink," my father said.

"Drink that," I said. Annoyed with my father, I pushed him into a fountain.

"I'm drowning! I'm drowning!" My father yelled, flapping his arms, kicking his legs.

"No, you're not," I said, dragging him from the fountain.

My father stood in the moonlight, looking dumbfounded, staring at his wet clothes, which dripped on to the concourse and formed a puddle.

"There's a club in Hollywood," I said, "for people who can't control their drink." I grabbed my father's arm and dragged him towards a taxi. "First thing tomorrow, you're gonna join that club."

Greta renegotiated my contract with Mr Vincetti. She secured a two-year extension to my original deal, with increased wages and the right to work with the leading actor and director of my choice on at least six movies a year.

For his part, Mr Vincetti had the right to hire me out, and allocate parts that he considered worthy of my talent. As a result, I made sixteen movies in eighteen months, eight of them with Gregory, Mr Winter and Archie Bleeker.

Greta and I became good friends. My father attended the group for alcoholics each week. And I secured the lease on an apartment adjacent to Venice Beach, an apartment complete with a modest-sized swimming pool.

I was twenty, going on twenty-one. I was exhausted from all the work, but blissfully happy.

On a warm June day, I reclined on my sunlounger and allowed my fingers to ripple the cool clear water of my swimming pool. Dressed in a bathing costume, I would swim after lunch. However, for now, I would enjoy a story written by F. Scott Fitzgerald.

Mr Winter had suggested that I should become acquainted with F. Scott Fitzgerald's work because he had plans to adapt his stories into movies.

At some point, I must have dozed because I awoke to find a shadow falling over me. I lowered my sunglasses and gazed at the man who'd cast that shadow. Tall and broad-shouldered, I placed him in his early twenties, not much older than me. He had freckles on his face, primarily across his cheeks and the bridge of his nose, and a large gap between his two front teeth.

Startled, I reached for a towel and covered myself. "Who are you?" I frowned.

"Terry," he smiled, his smile emphasising the large gap between his two front teeth.

"How did you get in?"

"The gate was open," he said.

My father must have left the gate open. Despite my warnings, he was forever doing that.

"What do you want?" I asked.

"Your autograph," Terry said.

Terry sat on a deckchair beside me. From his jacket pocket, he produced an autograph book and thrust it into my hands.

"I bought this book in the drugstore this morning," Terry said. "Yours will be the first name in it. Yours will be the only name in it. Please, sign it for me."

Terry offered me a pen and I signed his autograph book.

During my time in Hollywood, I'd appeared in a number of successful movies and featured in the movie magazines. However, I had yet to appear on the cover of a movie magazine. According to Greta, that honour would present itself in the near future.

I received fan mail, virtually every day. I tried to reply to my fans in person, but even writing short notes was exhausting. When I mentioned this to Mr Vincetti, he offered a solution – a standard letter signed by me, along with a picture. This wasn't ideal, but at least it acknowledged the kindness displayed by my fans.

I had fans, but they were largely anonymous. This was the first time I'd met a fan on a one-to-one basis, in person, and it made me feel uneasy.

"Are you making a movie at the moment?" Terry asked.

"Currently," I said, "I'm resting. We begin shooting again next week."

"Oh," Terry said. "What's the movie called? What's it about?"

"I'm not allowed to say," I said. "Some things must remain secret, until it's time for the movie to be released."

"I loved you in *Dancing Daughters*," Terry said. "I've seen that movie five times."

Dancing Daughters was a movie I'd made for one of Mr Vincetti's associates. Neither Gregory nor

Mr Winter were involved. In *Dancing Daughters*, I played a rebellious flapper. In the majority of my recent movies, I played a flapper, mainly because flappers were all the rage.

I liked the outlook associated with flappers – the rebellious attitude, the fashion, the fact that women were standing up for themselves. However, I also enjoyed playing the sensitive heroine, roles I usually fulfilled alongside Gregory.

"In *Dancing Daughters*," Terry said, "you did a lot of dancing."

"Yeah," I sighed.

Obviously, when you play the lead in a motion picture entitled *Dancing Daughters*, it does rather telegraph the part. *Dancing Daughters* was a fun movie to make, but hard on my legs.

"You showed a lot of your legs in that movie," Terry said. He leaned forward and peered at my thighs. Feeling disconcerted, I covered my thighs with a towel.

The regulators had not been happy with some of my scenes in *Dancing Daughters* because I'd revealed too much of my legs. Consequently, we had to reshoot some of the scenes, while I was filming another movie. That meant working into the evenings and on weekends.

"You danced beside a swimming pool in *Dancing Daughters*," Terry said, "would you like to dance for me?"

"No," I said, "and I think you should leave."

"Oh," Terry sighed, "can't I stay for five minutes longer?"

"Okay," I said, "but no dancing today; my doctor advised me to rest."

I'd visited the doctor because after *Dancing Daughters* I developed a pain in my right hip. For some reason, he prescribed sleeping tablets. I took the tablets for a week, but they left me feeling grotty, so I discarded them. My hip healed over time. I was wary of medications. I knew of some people in Hollywood – producers, directors and actors – who could only function by popping pills.

"I think you're beautiful," Terry said.

"Thank you," I said.

"Can I call on you again?"

"It's not really allowed," I said. "The studio doesn't like its stars getting too close to the fans."

"Oh," Terry sighed. He lapsed into silence and pondered that point. Gathering his pen and autograph book, he stood and said, "In that case, I'd better leave."

Terry departed. The whole episode struck me as strange, and disconcerting. In all probability, Terry meant no harm, but I resented the intrusion.

Later, while swimming in my pool, I tried to rationalise my thoughts. I valued my privacy, yet I was becoming public property. I wanted to forge a successful career as an actress, yet I craved anonymity. I'd placed myself in a dilemma, and I feared that it would not be possible to square the circle.

I celebrated my twenty-first birthday with a modest party. I invited my father, of course, Gregory, Greta, Archie, Mr Winter, Gloria and Mr Vincetti. Everyone arrived, except Gloria and Mr Vincetti. Their affair was ongoing, and I guessed that they had no wish to be seen together in public.

Gregory and I made another motion picture, *The Grass is Always Greener*. The movie was a Western, about the Gold Rush. The two main characters, played by Gregory and me, didn't find gold. However, they did find something more precious – a love for each other.

The movie magazines ran features describing Gregory and me as 'Hollywood's Favourite Movie Couple'. This was hyperbole, of course, concocted by Mr Vincetti to promote *The Grass is Always Greener*. Mr Vincetti's tactic worked – the movie was a box-office success.

One night, I arrived home after a local screening of *The Grass is Always Greener* to find the lights on in my house. This puzzled me because my father was out, attending his weekly meeting for alcoholics.

Displaying great caution, I opened the front door and tiptoed into my house. I made my way up the stairs, careful to avoid the seventh stair, which always creaked, and walked towards the light.

Someone was in my bathroom. I was pondering what to do, considering whether I should barge into the bathroom and confront my intruder, or call for help, when the door opened and a young woman, around my age, stood before me. Mexican in appearance, she clutched a towel to her naked breasts and screamed. She was still screaming when my father appeared beside me.

"It's okay, Margarita," my father said, "it's okay. This is Tula, the movie star. Tula," he explained to Margarita, "the star of the silver screen."

"Tula," Margarita said. "*Si, Si*...Tula...Tula..." She smiled, bowed, then curtsied before me. "Tula...Tula...*Estrella de cine...estrella de cine*..."

The whole situation was bizarre, and embarrassing. I was tired after another long day, which also included photo-shoots and costume fittings. I had no mind to cope with this.

"Tell Margarita to get dressed," I said to my father. "Then, we must talk."

While Margarita dressed, my father and I talked in our living room. I could smell whiskey on his breath. He hadn't been to the meeting for alcoholics, he'd been to a speakeasy. He'd let me down. He'd let himself down. I felt so disappointed.

However, before we could address that problem, we had to address our Mexican issue, namely Margarita.

"Who is she?" I asked.

"My girlfriend," my father said.

"Your girlfriend?" I stared at my father, aghast. "She's no older than me. She speaks very little English. She's probably here illegally. What are you playing at?"

"I'm going to marry her," my father said.

I sighed. "I need a drink."

As I said those words, I looked at my father and realised that alcohol was not the solution. Indeed, alcohol had probably gotten us into this mess in the first place.

"Where's Margarita from?" I asked.

My father shrugged. "Hollywood, I guess."

"Originally," I said. "Where was she born?"

"I don't know," my father said.

"Mexico," I said. "She probably sneaked over the border when no one was looking."

"You shouldn't decry all Mexicans," my father said, "they're lovely people."

"I'm not decrying them," I said. "I know they're lovely people. I've worked with them, men and women. Mexicans are warm and generous people; I love them. But here we are addressing a specific problem – Margarita. I have a 'no scandal' clause in my contract. I can't do anything that would invite scandal. If my name appears in the newspapers for the wrong reasons, Mr Vincetti could tear up my contract."

I paused for breath, then continued, "Besides, everything about your relationship with Margarita is wrong. If you want companionship, you should seek it with someone closer to your own age."

Margarita appeared in the doorway, fully clothed. She smiled and bowed at me. She stared at me through doe-eyes. This was embarrassing and wounding. I felt as though I were being cruel and heartless. Like me, Margarita had arrived in Hollywood looking for a break. Did I have the right to deny her, to reject her?

"Maybe we could employ Margarita as a maid," my father suggested. "If we do that, it might satisfy the authorities."

"Very well," I said. "You can look into it. But, right now, Margarita must leave our house. I'm tired. I need my bed."

While my father explored legal ways for Margarita to remain in the country, I wrestled with the idea that he wanted her as his girlfriend, and the fact that he'd fallen off the wagon. He was drinking himself to death. Maybe I could concoct a deal – allow Margarita to stay, as long as my father quit the booze.

I was sitting beside my swimming pool, mulling over my problems, when Terry reappeared. Along with his autograph book, he also carried a camera. He smiled at me and pretended to take a photograph.

"Look what I found," Terry said, holding up his camera, "in the drugstore."

"It's very nice," I said.

"I'd like to take your photograph," Terry said.

"That's not allowed," I said. "Mr Vincetti controls the rights to my image; I can't allow anyone to take my photograph."

Strictly speaking, that was not true. However, Terry was starting to annoy me; I was beginning to feel increasingly uncomfortable about his intrusions.

"Oh," Terry said. "Maybe I can take just the one picture of you, in your swimming costume?"

"I think you should leave," I said. "I have a lot on my mind. I need time to sit and think. I need time alone."

"I thought you loved me," Terry pouted.

"Whatever gave you that idea?" I frowned.

"I love you," Terry said. "I thought you loved me."

I picked up a rake, the one I used for removing leaves from my pool. I held it in a defensive position. I felt in need of protection.

"Please leave," I said. "I appreciate your love of my movies, but I do not love you. You should abandon that thought. You should not walk around with that idea."

"If you won't marry me," Terry said, "I'll kill myself."

"Go," I said, shaking the rake at Terry. "Go now, before I call the police."

Terry departed, looking morose. I ran into my house and opened my medicine cabinet. I stared at the sleeping pills and wondered if I should take one, in the hope that it would calm my nerves. I was shaking like a leaf. I feared that everything was getting to me. I succumbed and popped a pill.

I made another motion picture with Gregory, Mr Winter and Archie – *The Lighthouse Keeper*. Gregory played the title character while I played the only survivor of a shipwreck. In the midst of a storm, Gregory rescued me and, over the course of my recovery, our characters fell in love.

To complicate the plot, my character held strong Quaker beliefs, while Gregory's character was an atheist. In the end, we married against convention. I realised that that was becoming a theme of my motion pictures – quite often, my characters were rebellious and went against convention.

During the making of *The Lighthouse Keeper*, Terry attempted suicide. Thankfully, he did not succeed. From newspaper reports, I gathered that Terry's action was not a serious attempt to claim his life; it was a cry for help. Hopefully, now he would receive that help and find peace.

The episode regarding Terry upset and unnerved me. I found myself relying on sleeping tablets to sleep at night. The tablets left me feeling lethargic and my acting suffered accordingly. My performances dipped below my usual professional standard. Mr Vincetti, quite rightly, was not pleased. Nevertheless, he insisted that I should meet members of the media to promote *The Lighthouse Keeper*.

I sat beside Gregory and Mr Vincetti on the set of *The Lighthouse Keeper*. Mr Winter's team had constructed a lighthouse, and the interiors. We'd filmed the sea scenes in a large water tank. I'd picked up a chill from spending many hours in the cold water. I was drifting into poor physical and mental health.

Members of the press sat on rows of chairs, their notepads and cameras at the ready. They would ask us questions and we would respond with witty answers; at least, that was the plan.

"Charlie Saddler, *The Enquirer*," the first reporter said, raising an arm. "I have a question for Miss Bowman."

"Go ahead," Mr Vincetti said. He was acting as 'master of ceremonies' and, if necessary, would field any awkward questions. "What would you like to ask Miss Bowman?"

"How do you feel about Terry Rogers and his attempted suicide?" Charlie Saddler asked.

"Miss Bowman feels very sad about the events surrounding Mr Rogers," Mr Vincetti said, interjecting before I could answer. "However, as I understand it, Mr Rogers was in poor mental health before this incident occurred and, therefore, Miss

Bowman should not feel any guilt or shoulder any blame. The matter should now rest with Mr Rogers and his doctors. Furthermore, I would request that members of the press grant Mr Rogers some privacy so that his mind can heal."

"James Falk, *Screen and Stage*. What is Mr Powell's opinion of Miss Bowman as an actress?"

Gregory turned to me, smiled and said, "Miss Bowman is a very gifted, natural actress. She is a pleasure to work with and I hope we will appear in many more productions together."

"Miss Bowman is becoming a star in her own right," James Falk said. "It's the convention that motion pictures should contain one star and a cast of supporting players. My question is this: for Miss Bowman to achieve stardom, does she need to move out of your shadow and claim top billing in her own right?"

"I...er...," Gregory hesitated.

"Allow me to answer that question," Mr Vincetti said. "As you are aware, the Limelight Motion Picture Company is at the forefront of innovation. And one of our innovations is the concept of the multi-star motion picture. In future, our movies will feature not one, but two or more stars, therefore offering the public even greater value for their nickel."

"What about talkies?" James Falk asked. "Do

you have any plans to introduce sound to your movies?"

"We are exploring that possibility," Mr Vincetti said. He smiled at the press corps. "As the saying goes, 'watch this space'."

"Dorothy Cooper, *The Hollywood Reporter*. I understand that Miss Bowman has recently come of age. I'm sure her fans would love to know, does she have any plans to marry?"

"I have no plans to marry at the moment," I said. "I have my career to think of."

"But you must have received many proposals," Dorothy Cooper persisted.

"I've received proposals from admirers," I said, "and I'm grateful for them. But at this time, I'm not in love."

"When you look at Mr Powell on the silver screen," Dorothy Cooper said, "when you embrace him, when you kiss him, it would appear that you are in love."

"That's called acting," I said. "I am an actress. It's true that I'm very fond of Mr Powell. Equally, I'm very fond of his wife, Greta. I'm proud to regard them as my friends."

"What about your cameraman, Archie Bleeker?" Dorothy Cooper asked. "I understand that in Brooklyn the two of you were good friends."

"We were just that," I said, "we were good

friends."

"So," Dorothy Cooper said, her pen poised above her notepad, "you have no plans to marry at the moment."

I sensed that Dorothy Cooper dipped her quill in acid, rather than ink. However, for now, I allowed that thought to pass.

"I expect that I will marry," I said, "when I find the right man, when I receive a proposal that my heart can accept."

"Will you marry me?" A member of the press corps called out.

We all turned to stare at Earl MacInnes, a middle-aged portly man with a bushy moustache and a balding head. Spontaneously, members of the press corps laughed. Even Earl laughed.

I giggled then said, "I'm sure that you have the qualities of a wonderful husband, as your wife will attest."

Everyone laughed again. Even Mr Vincetti seemed pleased with my performance. As I relaxed into my role, I realised that it was a performance. And I felt comfortable with that. More and more, I felt comfortable playing a part than being myself.

"Maybe members of the press would like to ask Mr Powell and Miss Bowman about their latest motion picture," Mr Vincetti prompted, making sure that *The Lighthouse Keeper* featured in the press reports.

"Some of the scenes in *The Lighthouse Keeper* looked dangerous," Charlie Saddler said, "especially the scenes where Miss Bowman was swept off a ship in a storm. Would you kindly inform our readers – do you perform your own stunts?"

"I don't regard them as stunts," I said. "I regard them as actions performed by my character. As for the danger, I used to spend my evenings in the dark alleys of Brooklyn. I ask you, gentlemen, which would you prefer – immersion in cold water or running with the rats from a mob?"

As intended, everyone found that amusing, everyone except Dorothy Cooper, who continued to exude an air of malevolence.

"One more question," Charlie Saddler said, "for Mr Powell. I understand that your wife, Greta, was confined in hospital recently due to a miscarriage."

"That is a private matter," Gregory said. "I will not go into the details."

And on that note, Mr Vincetti called an end to the press conference.

A Dinner Invitation

Gregory and Greta invited me to dinner. Greta picked me up in her silver Oldsmobile Deluxe and drove me along the coast road to her house in Rustic Canyon. I was learning how to drive and, in the near future, intended to acquire a car.

I was aware of Greta's miscarriage, but made no mention of it to anyone. As Gregory rightly said at the press conference, it was a private matter. Indeed, I did not discuss it with Gregory, or Greta.

Outwardly, Greta displayed no physical or emotional scars. She appeared to be in good health. However, I knew that, inside, she was hurting.

We dined on roast chicken and salad, standard fare. Despite their exalted status, Gregory and Greta did not exude any airs or graces. Indeed, they were a regular couple, down to earth in many respects.

After dinner, we retired to the drawing room. I wondered about the true purpose of this invitation, and was eager to find out. However, all in good time. I urged myself to remain patient and reminded myself that I was a guest.

"Have you heard the latest?" Greta asked as we sipped our gin rickeys, "Vincetti and Gloria intend to marry."

"I thought he was already married," I said.

"He is," Gregory said. "Obviously, he intends to obtain a divorce."

"Far be it for me to gossip," Greta said, "but I reckon that Gloria is a social climber."

"I reckon you're right," I said. "She's using him to advance her career."

"Maybe you should reserve such chatter for when you ladies are together," Gregory said. "Whenever talk moves on to relationships and affairs, I always feel out of my depth."

"Nonsense, darling," Greta laughed. "You enjoy a good gossip as much as anyone."

Gregory offered his wife a sheepish look. He shrugged a shoulder then sipped his gin rickey.

I stared into my drink and wondered if people gossiped about me. I wondered what they said about me, and my father.

As though reading my thoughts, Greta said, "I understand that your father has settled into the community."

"He has," I said.

"I understand," Greta said, "that he intends to marry."

"I don't think that will happen," I said. "He's taken up with our maid, Margarita, but she's in the country illegally. I believe the authorities will deport her."

"If Margarita marries your father," Gregory

said, "maybe she'll have the right to stay."

"I feel as though my father has placed me on a Ferris wheel," I said, "one that keeps spinning, one that will not allow me to get off."

"Is that why you're taking the pills?" Gregory asked.

"Pills?" I frowned. At first, I considered offering a denial. Then I realised that to Gregory and Greta, I could not lie. "I'm taking sleeping pills," I said. "From childhood, I've suffered from insomnia."

"Many people in Hollywood take pills," Greta said, "uppers and downers."

"Vincetti takes uppers," Gregory said. "That's the only way he can work eighteen hours a day."

"It makes you wonder how he finds any time for Gloria," Greta said. "And," she added pointedly, "his wife."

"What about Mr Winter?" I asked. "Does he take any pills?"

"Not that I'm aware of," Gregory said. "Uwe and I are from the 'Old School' – we don't believe in artificial stimulation."

I nodded, stared into my gin rickey and said, "Maybe I should abandon my sleeping tablets."

"That's between you and your doctor," Gregory said. "All I'll say is, you were a better actress when you were not taking the tablets."

"In that case," I said, "I will abandon them. I'm here to make motion pictures, and take pride in my work. If my acting is suffering because of the sleeping tablets, I will discard them."

I considered that that was the true purpose of this dinner invitation – to discuss my dependence on sleeping tablets and the way they were affecting my performances in Gregory's pictures. However, having cleared the air of such talk, Gregory surprised me.

"You've heard the rumours," Gregory said. "Everyone's talking about them, on the sets and in the studios."

"The community is always abuzz with rumours," I said, "which ones are you referring to?"

"The talkies," Gregory said. "Vincetti mentioned them at the press conference. He said that the Limelight Motion Picture Company intends to invest in, and produce, talkies in the future. Also, some companies are already offering screenings in New York, of pictures enhanced with sound."

"Don't you think that's exciting," I said, "adding our voices to our gestures and expressions? We'll be able to convey more feeling, more emotion, and make better motion pictures as a result."

"You'll have no problem adapting to the talkies," Gregory said. "You're a natural. However, I'm a bit long in the tooth for that game. I'm set in my ways. I'm not sure that I'll be able to adapt."

Sensing her husband's distress, Greta offered him a hug. I wanted to reassure Gregory too, so I thought and sought the right words.

"You've acted on the stage," I said. "Indeed, you were invited to Hollywood because of your outstanding stage performances. You are familiar with acting and the spoken word. You have a beautiful speaking voice. You have a photographic memory, and therefore no trouble in remembering a script. The talkies were made for you. I'm certain that you will adapt."

"Tula's right," Greta said. "The talkies will be the making of you. They'll cement your reputation as a great actor. You need to take your time, find the right script, and work with people you trust."

"Tula," Gregory said, "Uwe Winter and Archie Bleeker; if I'm to make talkies, I want to work with them."

"If Mr Vincetti is agreeable," I said, "I'd be delighted to work with you."

Greta nodded. "I agree. I think that's the best way forward."

Gregory studied his gin rickey. He pulled a disgruntled face. He wasn't sure. The only way to convince him would be on the set.

"In all likelihood," I said, "Mr Vincetti will arrange screen tests for the talkies. Let's wait and see how we get on with them."

"Very well," Gregory said. "But if I flop in the screen tests, I'm quitting the movies. I have business interests away from motion pictures; I will pursue them."

The thought of never working with Gregory again distressed me. I vowed that I would help him through the screen tests.

Gregory needed my help. I needed to be at my sharpest. Therefore, I resolved to dispense with my sleeping tablets.

Without the pills, I suffered from shivers, aches and chronic insomnia. However, all these symptoms eased over the course of a month.

Gloria and Mr Vincetti married. It was a marriage I did not understand. Gloria was a social climber, yet her sexual preference was for women. Mr Vincetti spent all his waking hours at the studio – he was married to his job. Maybe I was missing something obvious. Maybe I was being naive.

Then I overheard a casual remark made by one of the prop men – Mr Vincetti enjoyed the company of men. His marriage to Gloria was a front. Maybe they were deceiving themselves. Maybe they were deceiving each other. In Hollywood, we created worlds of pretence, yet the greatest pretence took place before our eyes, in our real lives.

The authorities deported Margarita before my father could arrange a marriage. Practical considerations and organisation were not his strong suits, so I was not surprised when his marriage plans fell through.

On the one hand, I felt sorry for Margarita. She

was seeking to better her life, and there was nothing wrong with that. On the other hand, I had to concede that she could do better than my father – no woman should tie her future to an alcoholic.

Depressed at Margarita's deportation, my father turned to his primary source of comfort – booze. With my allowance to bankroll him, his drinking became excessive. Success was troubling me and destroying my father. Our lives were not the stuff of dreams; we were not creating the images I'd conjured up in my teenage fantasies.

As anticipated, Mr Vincetti arranged a screen test so that we could experiment with his new sound system. Along with the regulars, a new member joined our crew – Alistair Renwick. Originally from Scotland, on day one Alistair arrived on the set wearing a kilt, which broke the ice and raised a laugh from the crew.

Mr Winter would direct, Archie Bleeker would shoot the scene and Jack Dresden would oversee the lighting. Jack was a very good lighting technician – he knew how to illuminate my face so that I always looked my best on the silver screen.

The slightest blemish is highlighted a thousand times on the silver screen, so a lighting technician who is sympathetic to an actress' appearance is worth his weight in gold.

We worked with the script for *The Lighthouse*

Keeper because the set was still standing and because we were familiar with that motion picture. A scenario writer had added dialogue, replacing the intertitles, plus some of our expressions and gestures, with words.

Gregory and I took our cue from Mr Winter and Archie's camera began to roll.

"You know that I am grateful to you," I said in character, "you know that I love you, and want to marry you, but I cannot do that if you do not share my beliefs."

"I am not a Quaker," Gregory said in character, "I can never become a Quaker, therefore it is best that you should go."

"Cut!" Mr Winter yelled.

The director walked over to Gregory and whispered into his ear. "Let the words do the talking. Fewer gestures, fewer physical movements; cut down on the pacing – the sound engineer can't keep track of you. And lose the dramatic sweeps of your hand."

Gregory nodded and we reshot the scene. However, he repeated the errors of the first take. He was so used to a certain style of acting, it was so ingrained in his being, that he found it difficult to adapt.

After the third take, which was also a failure, Gregory stormed off the set. This was most unlike him; cool and composed, on previous shoots he'd always remained calm.

I glanced at Mr Winter and he nodded. Gathering up my skirts, I ran after Gregory.

I found Gregory standing beside a tailor's dummy, looking morose.

"I can't do it," he said. "You'd be better off shooting the scene with this dummy."

"You can do it," I said, "and you will. "

Gregory turned and offered me a wan smile. "I'm grateful for your support, Tula; you've always been a sympathetic actress; you've always given me a chance to shine. When you act, you always think of the other players. Not many actresses are like that. In fact, few are. Few have the ability to act like that. But talking pictures are not for the likes of me; they are for the likes of you, actors and actresses who are relatively new to motion pictures, artists who are making their name."

I sighed, took a deep breath and wondered what to say. I realised that it was now or never. I realised that it was time to offer a confession.

"I love you," I said. "I accept that you love Greta and that you will always be together. I've reconciled myself to that notion and learned how to accept it. The only way I can live with my feelings is to express them when we act together. If you walk away from acting and deny me that outlet, I will become distressed; I will go insane. I do not wish to sound melodramatic, but I think that I will lose my mind."

Gregory paused. He offered me a long, deep stare. "I see," he said. "I sensed that you had feelings for me, but I never imagined that they ran that deep."

"You and Greta are beautiful together and I want you to remain together, but please do not deny me my world of fantasy, the world I enter when I act with you."

"Maybe you need a fiancé," Gregory said. "Maybe you need to move into the real world."

"You are probably right," I said. "But at this stage of my life, I cannot do that." I sighed and offered Gregory an imploring look. "I guess I am frightened of the real world."

Gregory nodded. He caressed my cheek. I caressed his hand and kissed his fingers. We were not acting now. This was for real and, even though I realised that this was as intimate as we would ever get, I had to admit that it felt good.

"I will never leave Greta," Gregory said.

"I know," I said.

"I love her," he said.

"I know," I said. "You were made for each other. I have learned to accept that. But, please, for the sake of my sanity and career, allow me to act with you."

Gregory took hold of my hand. We returned to the set. Mr Winter gave Gregory a moment, allowed him to compose himself, then we went for another take.

At the end of the take, Mr Winter placed his thumb and forefinger together and formed the letter O. "Perfect," he said. "*Perfekt*. Thank you, lady and gentlemen; that's a wrap!"

My driving lessons were going well and I was nearly ready to purchase a car. I had enough money to purchase a luxury item such as a car. Sometimes, I had to pinch myself to confirm that this was real. Sometimes, I could not believe my good fortune.

My confession to Gregory did not affect our working relationship, or our personal relationship, for that matter. He remained committed to Greta, deeply committed. Indeed, whenever he had the opportunity he displayed his affection for her, through flowers, gifts and, more importantly, through the time he devoted to his wife.

I did not feel any jealousy. Maybe I should have felt that emotion but, in all truth, I was content with my lot. I pondered why that should be and concluded that I was frightened of forming a deep, intimate relationship. I knew that to be true, but I did not understand where that truth stemmed from.

We slipped into the habit of Greta picking Gregory and me up from the studio each day and driving us home in her Oldsmobile Deluxe. Sometimes, she offered Archie Bleeker a lift too.

During breaks between takes, Gregory tried to get Archie and me together, but that ship had sailed. To his credit, Archie was fully aware of that fact and sought nothing more than friendship.

We were driving through Beverly Hills when snow drifted on to the windscreen. Snow in Hollywood was usually very light and melted away in seconds but, for five minutes, the snow fell.

Greta leaned forward and peered through the windscreen while Gregory sat on the passenger seat and I reclined in the back. I was very tired after a long day's filming; with the car rocking me to sleep, I dozed.

I awoke to find that we were approaching Rustic Canyon. The snow had stopped. Gregory and Greta were in heated conversation, talking about Christmas.

"What about you, Tula?" Greta asked. "What are your plans?"

I rubbed the sleep from my eyes and frowned. "For Christmas?"

"Yes," Greta said, "do you intend to go anywhere or stay with anyone?"

"Not really," I sighed. "I guess it'll be me and my father again."

"Would you like to spend Christmas Day with us?" Greta asked. She smiled into her driver's mirror and winked. "You could help me with the dinner."

"I'd love to," I said. "But what about my father?"

"Bring him along too," Greta said. "Christmas is about family and being together. Your father would be most welcome."

Greta knew my feelings for Gregory, yet she went out of her way to make me feel welcome in her home. In my suspicious moments, I wondered if she had an ulterior motive. However, I soon realised that the explanation was more prosaic – Greta trusted her husband; she realised that they shared an unbreakable bond.

Hollywood and its acting community was littered with casual relationships, with people using each other, so to discover such a bond was close to unique. If I ever found the courage to launch into an intimate relationship, I wanted it to mirror the connection shared by Greta and Gregory.

"I'd love to spend Christmas Day with you," I said. "Thank you for the invitation."

"My pleasure," Greta said. She smiled at me through her driver's mirror. "That's settled then."

Even though the snowfall had been light, the road was icy in places, and Greta's Oldsmobile slithered as we rounded the bends. She was a good driver though, very steady, very patient, so I felt relaxed on the back seat, so relaxed in fact that once again, I dozed.

I awoke from a nightmare. In my nightmare, Gregory yelled, "Look out!" as a child ran into the road. The child was chasing a hoop that was rolling along the icy street.

Greta hit the brake and swerved to avoid the child. Thankfully, her Oldsmobile did not harm him. However, the car did slide off the road and connect with a tree.

I was sitting in the middle of the road – somehow, the impact had thrown me from the car. Gregory was sitting beside the tree. His right leg presented itself at an unnatural angle – clearly, because of the accident, his leg was broken.

Gregory was holding Greta in his arms. He was kissing her and urging her to move. "Wake up," he said. "Wake up. Please, wake up."

At that moment, I blinked, and realised that I was fully awake. I also realised that this was no nightmare – it was all too real.

I scrambled to my feet, slipped, and ran over to Greta and Gregory. I squatted beside them and became vaguely aware of a crowd as people rushed to the scene.

I stared at Greta. She was dead. I'd seen dead bodies in Brooklyn – I knew what death looked like. She was dead. Greta Powell was dead.

I couldn't believe it. She'd been alive only seconds ago, without a care in the world, discussing plans for Christmas. She'd been alive, but now she was dead.

I could understand how a life could fade, over time, and appreciate that that was natural. But, how could a healthy, vibrant person leave this life in the blink of an eye. It did not make any sense to me. I struggled with the concept. I stared at Greta. I began to cry.

A man pushed past us. "I'm a doctor," he said. "Let me see if I can help."

The doctor examined Greta. However, he was no miracle worker – he could not bring her back to life.

I wondered about the role of God in all this. On the screen, I'd played a number of characters who'd held strong religious beliefs. They were challenging roles to play because I found it difficult to identify with them.

Where was God in all this? How could he allow such a thing to happen? I stared at the grey sky and yelled, "I hate you, God!"

Everyone stared at me as though I'd lost my mind.

At that point, I did hate God. At that moment, I broke all my ties with religion.

"That leg is broken," the doctor said to Gregory. "Remain still. We'll get you fixed up in no time."

I wished that we could turn back time. I wished that we'd never embarked upon this journey.

Gregory ignored the doctor. He held Greta in his arms, rocked her and cried. I dropped to my knees to comfort him. Gravel dug into my skin, but I didn't care. The level of discomfort, minor in the great scheme of things, told me that I was alive.

Greta was dead; I could do nothing about that. And Gregory was dead inside. I'm not sure when I hit upon this notion, maybe later that night, maybe the following day, but I vowed to make it my life's mission to bring Gregory back to life.

A Bitter Farewell

Everyone in the Hollywood community attended Greta Powell's funeral, and by that, I mean literally everyone. She'd been so well liked, universally loved.

Of course, Greta's funeral stirred dark memories of my mother, and the depressing thought that my father would leave me, sooner rather than later. His alcoholism was now rampant – no one could drink to that excess and survive.

I'd be alone in Hollywood, albeit surrounded by casual friends and acquaintances, so I'd be luckier than some. Nevertheless, I would be alone. I would have to summon up all my determination to survive. Indeed, I would summon up that determination because, deep down, I was a fighter.

Gregory attended the funeral service on crutches. His sister, Eva, attended too, and she offered physical and emotional support.

At the end of the service, Gregory limped over to me. The wind caught his black tie, and he straightened it. He bowed towards me and wiped the tears from his eyes.

"Thank you," Gregory said. "Thank you for being a tower of strength."

"Anytime," I said. "Anytime you need me, call

me, I'll be there."

Gregory nodded. With Eva's support, he limped away.

The following day, Mr Vincetti called me to his office. He was in a sombre mood. Revealing his frame of mind, he closed the blinds.

"Please," Mr Vincetti said, "be seated."

I sat in front of Mr Vincetti's desk while he sat on his leather chair. We sat in silence for a good two minutes.

After that period of reflection, Mr Vincetti looked at me and said, "We're all in a state of shock, we're all overcome with great sadness, with grief, but even at a time like this, we must turn our minds to practical considerations."

"I understand," I said.

"Physically, Gregory will not be able to act for three months. Mentally, I suspect that it will take him much longer than that. We cannot remain idle for months on end; we must continue to make motion pictures."

Mr Vincetti paused and assessed my reaction. He gathered from my intense stare that he had my full attention.

"The Limelight Motion Picture Company is solvent, but we are moving into uncertain territory. In the coming year, talking pictures will become all the rage. We must move with this trend and produce talking pictures."

"Our books suggest that you are the best equipped actress to move with this trend. Therefore, I intend to make you our lead actress. I will remunerate you, and adjust your contract, accordingly. I intend to place the Limelight Motion Picture Company on your creative shoulders. The future of our company will depend on you and your creative talents." Mr Vincetti paused and stared deep into my eyes. "Do you think that you are ready to accept that challenge?"

"I will do my very best," I said. "I will not let anyone down."

"I know that to be true," Mr Vincetti said. "That is why we are holding this conversation." He adjusted the signet ring on his right hand, slid it up and down his little finger. He secured the ring then asked, "Is there anything you'd like to add? Are there any demands you'd like to make of me?"

"I would like to work with Mr Winter and his crew," I said, "as often as possible. And I feel we should recruit new scenario writers – an actress is only as good as her script."

"Do you have anyone in mind?" Mr Vincetti asked.

"F. Scott Fitzgerald," I said, "I feel that we should secure the rights to some of his work. And Thornton Lovell – he produces interesting stories,

stories that are sympathetic to actresses, stories that engage with the audience."

"I will look into it," Mr Vincetti said.

We stood and Mr Vincetti adjusted the blinds, allowed a little light to shine into his office.

On the set, I met Mr Winter. He was studying a script, placing ticks and crosses beside the various scenes.

"We'll need to reshoot some of the scenes for *The Bostonian*," Mr Winter said, "to cover for Gregory's absence. It'll mean long hours, and shooting on the weekends."

"That's not a problem," I said. "I'll make myself available."

Mr Winter nodded. He pushed back his hat and fanned himself with the script. "I can't believe it," he said. "I can't believe that Greta is no longer with us. I can't believe that she's gone."

"I can't believe it either," I said. "I'm just grateful that Eva is staying with Gregory and that he's not alone in that big house."

"Greta was so kind and generous," Mr Winter said. "She didn't have a malicious thought for anyone, or a wicked bone in her body. When I arrived in Hollywood from Europe, she took me in, showed me around, made me feel welcome. She opened doors for me, introduced me to the movers and shakers. She got me started on my Hollywood career."

"I've cried a lot since she died," I said. "I expect you have cried too."

"You'd better believe it," Mr Winter said.

We sat in silence. Archie Bleeker joined us. He sat in silence too.

Eventually, I said, "We need to do something to raise Gregory's spirits. We need to make a movie that will lift his heart."

"Any ideas?" Archie asked.

Mr Winter removed his hat and scratched his head. He thought for a minute, then said, "I have a script in my office, written by Greta. It needs some work, but maybe we could adapt it and make it into a movie."

"Great idea," Archie said. "The movie would serve as a lasting tribute to Greta."

"Mr Vincetti would have to approve the script," Mr Winter said.

"Leave it with me," I said. "I'll make sure that Mr Winter will approve the script. And," I added, "I want to star in this picture. I don't care if it adds to our workload, I'll toil all day and night, if necessary, but we must make this movie."

Mr Winter nodded. "We will," he said.

In the parking lot, Mr Winter placed his hands on my shoulders. "You are taking a lot on to these shoulders," he said. "You may look frail, but I know that deep down inside, you are strong."

"I am strong," I said.

"Nevertheless," Mr Winter said, "promise me that after we've navigated through this crisis, you will rest."

"I will rest," I said.

In retrospect, I should have kept that promise.

The Engagement

We reshot the scenes for *The Bostonian*, to cover for Gregory's absence. We also filmed *Roses*, Greta's script about a young woman and her friendship with a woman in her nineties. The woman in her nineties was a keen gardener who cultivated roses. After her passing, the young woman, my character, kept her garden in bloom.

We worked long hours, all of us. Some of the crew popped pills, but I got by on adrenaline, and a determination to honour Greta's memory, and help Gregory. In the midst of all this, Mr Vincetti presented me with another project, *The Engagement*.

The Engagement was a light comedy. I was in no mood for humour, so I required all my skills as an actress to convincingly convey the part.

Mr Vincetti also presented me with a stiff challenge – he insisted that I should announce my engagement to Grant Arliss, my leading man in *The Engagement*. Mr Vincetti ensured me that our engagement would only be for publicity purposes – when our promotional tour was complete, we could break it off.

Grant Arliss was twenty years older than me, but that sort of thing rarely mattered in the movies. He was suave and debonair, with immaculately groomed hair and a pencil-thin moustache. He was also four times married, and four times divorced.

We announced our engagement to the press, posed for photographs, and made sure that we were seen together at all the right parties and social gatherings.

At the end of our promotional tour, Mr Vincetti said that I could call off the engagement and cease seeing Grant Arliss during my personal time. However, I didn't call off the engagement. I don't know why. Maybe I was so drained, so exhausted, I didn't have the emotional energy to go through the trauma.

I sensed that there would be trauma because Grant had warmed to his role and made it plain that he was very fond of me. Maybe I didn't have the energy to call off the engagement because I was lonely and Grant had cast a spell on me.

Whatever the truth of the matter, I found myself sailing on Grant's yacht during my leisure hours, those precious hours when I took a break from the studio.

Time had moved on, I was twenty-two approaching my twenty-third birthday. It had been eighteen months since the accident. Physically, Gregory had healed and resumed his acting career. However, these days our paths rarely crossed – our schedules conspired to keep us apart.

I was sunning myself on Grant's yacht, sipping a gin rickey, dreaming of I don't know what – due to my exhaustion, my head was often fuzzy these days. In the distance, Catalina Island offered the perfect backdrop. The water was blue and clear. Dolphins appeared, toyed with us, then swam away.

Sucking on his pipe, his nautical cap positioned at a suitably rakish angle, Grant navigated his yacht along the Californian coast. He was master of his vessel. I sensed that he thought that he was my master too.

"It's a beautiful day," Grant said.

"Indeed, it is," I smiled.

"It's a beautiful day for romance," Grant said.

I turned and glanced up at a seagull. I admired the way the bird spread its wings, how it floated on the air, how it appeared to be free.

"I've been thinking," Grant said.

"What about?" I frowned.

"Us," Grant said. "Our engagement. I feel it's time that we set a firm date for our marriage."

"Are you sure about that?" I asked. "Do you really want to marry me?"

"Most assuredly," Grant grinned. "Most assuredly."

Grant made a slight adjustment to the wheel so that his yacht sailed past an outcrop of jagged rocks.

He was an expert sailor. Indeed, he'd spent some time in the navy before embarking on his acting career.

"What do you say, Tula?" Grant asked. "December 26th. Let's name that as our wedding day."

I shrugged. "Okay."

What was I doing? What was I agreeing to? I was looking to placate Grant. I was looking to buy time. Right now, I didn't want to fight. I didn't have the energy for such battles.

"Splendid," Grant said.

Grant beckoned me towards him so that he could offer me a kiss. His kiss lingered. I feared that we might crash into the rocks, so I pulled away.

Another yacht sailed past us. Grant waved to the skipper and called out. There was a great camaraderie amongst the sailing community, I noted, akin to the camaraderie shared by the acting community. I suppose that was natural, when people shared a common cause.

Grant eyed me as I adjusted my bathing costume, as I straightened the strap on my bathing bra.

"That's a very fetching costume," Grant said.

"Really?" I frowned. "It's not too revealing?"

"It's perfect," Grant said. "Why don't we drop anchor, and make it official."

"Make what official?" Through my mind fog, I continued to frown.

"Our forthcoming nuptials," Grant said. "Why don't we go below deck?"

In an instant, my mind fog cleared and Grant's meaning became all too obvious. I fought the urge to panic. I searched my mind for a solution that would not cause offence.

Jumping up, I dived into the water. "First," I laughed, "you must catch me."

Make a game of it, I thought. Tease Grant. Suggest to him that I regarded his proposal as a bit of fun. For his part, Grant laughed too. Of course, he would not abandon his yacht and swim after me, so I knew that I was safe.

I was safe in the water, swimming with the dolphins. But, for a moment on the yacht, I'd been genuinely frightened, frightened at the thought of intimacy. I had no idea where that fear stemmed from. And, in all truth, I was too scared to search my mind, too scared to look.

Since moving to the coast, I swam whenever I had the opportunity. I'd become a strong swimmer, so I knew that I could make it safely back to the shore.

On the shore, Grant secured his yacht. Then he joined me. "That was naughty," he said. "And naughty girls deserve a punishment. Do that when we're married," he grinned, "and you can anticipate a severe punishment."

I offered Grant a sweet smile, a saccharine smile, a false smile. I didn't like this man. I didn't want to spend any more time with him. Yet, we planned to marry in December.

I was making a huge mistake, but the emotions of the past two years and non-stop acting had drained all my mental energy. I couldn't help myself. Despite myself, I was going to become the fifth Mrs Arliss.

The Interview

Thankfully, my acting schedule kept me away from Grant Arliss. I spent the autumn months on location in Texas, filming *Aces*, a picture about pilots and their exploits during the Great War. This was a 'man's picture', a 'buddy picture'; I was in the cast to provide some romantic interest and add a little froth.

We stayed in the Saint Anthony Hotel in San Antonio, which was quite luxurious. I must say, the cast misbehaved. We were there for three months, so no one could have expected saintly behaviour. By the time we left, most of the elevator operators, young impressionable women, were pregnant. Back in Hollywood, I heard that the hotel's management planned to replace the young women with elderly men.

In early December, Mr Vincetti arranged an interview with Dorothy Cooper. The idea of the interview was to promote our new movie, *Aces*, and feature me as the Limelight Motion Picture Company's lead actress. I didn't care for Dorothy Cooper – her articles were often bitchy. Nevertheless, to please Mr Vincetti, I agreed to the interview.

I met Dorothy Cooper in a French restaurant on

Marina Del Rey. It was a stormy day. Rain lashed the windows while the small boats bobbed on the water. The storm clouds and accompanying mist reduced visibility to a matter of yards. We were cocooned in the restaurant, hunched over our coffees and croissants.

In her early forties and dressed in the latest slim-line fashions, Dorothy Cooper looked like a motion picture star. Indeed, she looked far more of a star than I did. Her clothes were black, which matched her pageboy-styled hair and her patent leather accessories. Although only a small woman, Dorothy Cooper exuded a huge sense of power. She knew that the ink that flowed from her pen could make or break an actor's career.

Dorothy Cooper smoked a cigarette placed in a long, elegant cigarette holder. She flicked ash into an ashtray then tapped her notebook with a pen.

"Tell me about your upbringing," Dorothy Cooper said. "I understand that it was difficult."

"It was difficult, at times," I said, "but no more so than the lives experienced by many of our young people."

"Nevertheless," Dorothy said, "you must notice a huge contrast between your life now and your life then."

"There are contrasts," I said, "and similarities."

"Please elaborate," Dorothy said.

"Well," I said, "in regard to the contrasts, I no longer have to worry about every cent, every nickel. Thanks to my contract with the Limelight Motion Picture Company, I can live comfortably. As for the similarities, I worked hard in Brooklyn and I work hard here."

"Tell me about your latest picture," Dorothy said.

"It's an amazing movie," I said, "full of daredevil stunts. I can promise you, some of the flying will leave you perched on the edge of your seat."

"Did you do any of the flying?" Dorothy asked.

"No," I said, "I remained grounded."

"Only the men went up in the aeroplanes?"

"That's right," I said. "In the Great War, the pilots were men."

"Didn't you ask one of the pilots to take you up for a joy ride?"

"We didn't have time for that," I said. "We were shooting to a tight schedule."

Dorothy took a drag on her cigarette. She blew a plume of smoke, which curled into the air. I coughed and brushed the smoke away from my face.

"I understand," Dorothy said, "that your location hotel was bedevilled with scandals."

"I wouldn't know about that," I lied. "I didn't

see anything untoward."

Dorothy offered me a knowing smile. She took another drag on her cigarette. "What goes on in Texas, stays in Texas; don't worry, honey," she said, "I know the score."

Dorothy made a note in her notebook. I tried to read her notes, but they were illegible; she wrote in a thin, spidery scrawl.

"In your recent motion pictures," Dorothy said, "your performances have been variable. Do you accept that as fair comment?"

"I always offer my best," I said. "Sometimes, I don't meet the movie industry's exalted standards."

"Do you regard the movies as an industry?" Dorothy asked.

"I suspect that most of the players regard motion pictures as an art; without wishing to sound pretentious, we see ourselves as artists. However, motion pictures are expensive to produce, so there is an industrial aspect to them as well."

"What are your views on the talkies?" Dorothy asked. "A number of talking pictures are currently taking the country by storm."

"I think talking pictures are an exciting development," I said. "I'm delighted that the Limelight Motion Picture Company is at the forefront of this new venture."

"Nice plug," Dorothy said, taking another drag

on her cigarette. "Don't worry, honey, I'll make sure that I insert your studio's name in my final copy."

"We're approaching the anniversary of the accident that claimed Greta Powell's life," Dorothy said. "Would you care to talk about that accident?"

"No," I said. "Out of respect for Gregory Powell, I would prefer if we did not mention the anniversary."

"Fair enough," Dorothy shrugged. She reached for her coffee and took a sip. Her lipstick left a big red kiss on her coffee cup.

"Tell me about your upcoming marriage to Grant Arliss," Dorothy said. "When did you fall in love?"

"We fell in love during the making of *The Engagement*," I said. "It was such a romantic movie; I guess the atmosphere was right."

I was acting now; I was not being Tula Bowman. I was lying to Dorothy Cooper. I didn't like myself. I wanted this interview to end.

"Grant Arliss has a reputation as a ladies' man," Dorothy said. "How will you tame him?"

"Love will tame him," I said. "I'm a great believer in love."

Dorothy lit another cigarette. She was a chain smoker; despite her elegant looks, her chain smoking was evident from the stench that wafted from her clothes.

Leaning back in her chair, Dorothy said, "Allow me to be candid with you. The interview is over; you can speak freely now. Grant Arliss is seeing at least three other women, to my knowledge; do you really wish to marry someone like that?"

"Your information does not surprise me," I said.

"But you intend to go through with the wedding?" Dorothy scowled. She looked genuinely angry. To my surprise, she looked upset. "Don't actresses have any self-respect?"

"I respect my profession," I said, "the projects I work on, and my audience. I make many sacrifices to offer that respect."

"Do you intend to continue acting after your wedding?" Dorothy asked.

"That is my intention," I nodded, "yes."

"How does Grant Arliss feel about that?"

I shrugged. "We haven't discussed it, yet."

"Honey," Dorothy Cooper sighed, "I want you to know that I'm on your side."

"If you say so," I said.

"I am," Dorothy said. "Really, I am. And I reckon that you're being a bloody idiot. Allow me to make the speech I make to all young actresses. Few of them listen, but I reckon that you have the intelligence to take my words on board."

"I'm on the side of women. The trouble is, I've

seen so many young actresses enter the Hollywood machine only to get chewed up and spat out on the other side. Looking at you, right now, I reckon that you're on that conveyer belt. I hope you'll find the strength, the courage, the intelligence to jump off and save your sanity."

"If I jump off," I said, "that'll mean the end of my career."

"Maybe," Dorothy conceded. "But not if you take control. As I see it, you can blaze like a comet and be gone within a year. Or you can shine like a diamond, like a distant star, and enjoy that star's longevity. The choice rests with you."

The Big Decision

In December, to mark the anniversary of Greta's passing, I made my way to the graveyard, carrying a bunch of flowers, carnations, her favourite.

I found Gregory in the graveyard, paying his respects. I stood back and allowed him a moment with Greta. Then he reciprocated and allowed me to place the flowers. In silence, we walked out of the graveyard.

We walked through a park. Laurel trees lined our path. The sky was grey, a mass of clouds laden with rain. Raindrops fell. Gregory produced an umbrella and we sheltered together.

"I understand that congratulations are in order," Gregory said.

"Congratulations?" I frowned.

"Your upcoming marriage to Grant Arliss."

"Oh," I said, "yes, it's only a matter of weeks until our wedding day."

"I don't wish to interfere," Gregory said, "but you know who Grant Arliss is, you know what he is?"

"I'm fully aware of Grant's reputation," I said.

"And it doesn't bother you?" Gregory frowned.

"Why should it bother me?" I asked.

"If you need to ask that question," Gregory

said, "then I suggest that we should curtail this conversation."

I looked up into Gregory's sad eyes and frowned. "Are we arguing?" I asked.

Gregory smiled. His smile touched his eyes and I felt so grateful. I felt grateful because, in that moment, the sadness dropped away from his eyes and revealed the Gregory Powell of my youth.

"I don't think we're arguing," Gregory said. "I think we're enjoying a frank exchange of views."

"That is a relief," I said, "because I have no wish to argue with you."

We walked on, under the laurel trees. Raindrops fell from the laurel trees and pitter-pattered on Gregory's umbrella.

"Do you love Grant?" Gregory asked.

"I promised myself that I'd only marry for love," I said, evading the question.

"Why are you marrying him?" Gregory asked.

That was a very good question, and I felt that Gregory deserved an honest answer. "Maybe I'm lonely," I said. "Maybe I feel that it's time I settled down, time I accepted a man into my life."

Gregory nodded. We walked on, towards a lake. Raindrops splashed in the lake. I marvelled at the concentric circles formed by the splashes. I marvelled at the wonder of nature.

"How's your father?" Gregory asked.

"He's holding on," I said. "His drinking has become acute. I've tried to control him, but failed. I've bullied him and encouraged him. I've tried everything I can think of." I sighed. "I don't know what more I can do."

Gregory twirled his umbrella. A raindrop splashed on to my face, under my right eye. He leaned forward and brushed the raindrop away. We stood in silence and held each other's gaze.

"I'm going away soon," Gregory said.

"Where?" I frowned.

"To Utah, on location. I'll be gone six months."

"What's the movie?" I asked.

"*The Fields of France*," Gregory said. "It's a Great War movie about fighter pilots."

I nodded. Talkies, musicals and movies about the Great War were all the rage. Somewhat cynically, I thought, if someone could set a musical during the Great War, they'd have a box office hit.

"I'll miss you," I said.

"I'll miss you too," Gregory said. "But I need this movie; I need to get away; I need to find myself again, and I don't think that I can do that here. Plus," he added, offering a wan smile, "the part calls for me to fly an aeroplane, so I'll be taking flying lessons."

"You are not doing any stunts." That was an order on my part, not a question. "I've acted in a stunt movie, *Aces*; I know how dangerous the stunts can be."

"I won't participate in any stunts," Gregory assured me. "I'll leave all the dangerous stuff to the experts."

I breathed a huge sigh of relief. Six months without Gregory would be painful to endure, but at least I'd know that he'd be safe.

What was I thinking? Gregory's career and absence should be irrelevant to me. After all, while he was away I'd be making a new home as Mrs Arliss.

"I'd like to phone you," Gregory said, "while I'm away. May I?"

"You may," I said.

"Grant will not object?"

"You are my friend," I said, "a very good friend; Grant will not pick and choose my friends."

Once again, we paused and gazed into each other's eyes. I sensed that we were 'talking in tongues' – we were communicating, but neither of us had the courage to say what we were really thinking.

"May I drive you home?" Gregory asked.

I nodded. "You may."

At home, I paced the floorboards. My father was in his room, in a drunken stupor. I checked on him from time to time, to ensure that he was still alive. It was so wearing on my nerves, to check on him and anticipate that, one day, I'd find him dead.

I paced the floorboards and stared at my telephone. I had a decision to make. I was drifting; I was drifting like a great ship towards an iceberg. A collision was imminent; I had to change course.

I sat in my armchair and picked up my telephone. I dialled Grant's number. No answer. I replaced the receiver, then tried again.

Grant picked up his telephone on the fifth ring. He mumbled something to someone in the background, and I heard female laughter. Then he spoke into the telephone.

"Hello."

"It's Tula."

"Hi, sugar, how are you?"

"I'm fine," I said.

"Are you on for Saturday night?"

"No," I said.

"Why?" Grant asked. I could sense his frown.

"I don't wish to see you again," I said. "Our relationship is over."

"You're pulling the plug on our marriage?"

"Yes," I said. "It's off."

"I see," Grant said.

Once again, I heard female laughter in the background.

"I've been anticipating your call," Grant said.

"In fact, I've been wondering why it's taken you so long."

"I've been thinking," I said, "thinking deeply about my life."

"That's your problem," Grant said. "You think too much. You should go out and enjoy life."

"I intend to do just that," I said.

Grant laughed. Then, he erupted with anger. "There's a word for women like you, Tula, and it's not a very pleasant word."

Before I could reply, Grant slammed his telephone down.

I stared at my receiver, pictured a future without Grant Arliss, and breathed a huge sigh of relief.

Another Big Decision

While Gregory was away, he phoned me every day. We spent so much time on the telephone, he'd have to make another movie just to earn the money to cover the cost of his telephone calls.

Gregory's telephone calls soon became the highlight of my day. I was busy in the studio, making movies for Mr Vincetti. I was making movies at such a pace, they were becoming a blur to me.

I'd always been very good at leaving my characters behind in the studio. But now, I was taking them home with me, I was thinking about them constantly, I was dreaming about them, I was losing my sense of self.

Mr Vincetti was 'cracking the whip' and placing me in as many motion pictures as possible because he had a distribution agreement with the movie theatres. Basically, to screen a Tula Bowman movie the theatres had to screen other movies produced by Mr Vincetti.

Mr Vincetti placed me in his marquee movies. His other movies were cheaper productions. He made good money on my movies. He also earned a small fortune on his low-budget movies, simply because of the distribution agreement tied to my films.

If I'd been more savvy, I would have asked for more money. However, I was exhausted from the endless round of rehearsals, costume fittings, shootings, and interviews. Also, I had my father to tend. Talking with Gregory at the end of the day was a blessed relief.

During the filming of *The Flirtatious Flapper*, I passed out. The part called for my character to flirt shamelessly with all the male members of the cast. She was doing this to make her true love, the manager of a department store, jealous. He was ignoring my character, so she wanted to capture his attention.

The part also called for me to dance in a number of scenes. Dancing was not my strong point, and the energy expended soon wore me out.

With the aid of smelling salts, I recovered from my faint and we continued shooting. However, I believe that Mr Winter, who was directing me, had a word with Mr Vincetti and recommended that on the completion of filming, I should be allowed a long break.

I was approaching my twenty-fourth birthday when Gregory returned from shooting *The Fields of France*. Tanned from all his outdoor activities, he looked in good health. In fact, he looked in terrific shape.

The sun was shining, the seagulls were squawking, the yachts were bobbing on the water, their masts in full sail, when Gregory invited me to walk along the beach. Naturally, this was an invitation I was only too glad to accept.

"*The Fields of France* was an interesting movie to film," Gregory said.

"Oh," I frowned. "How so?"

"Filming the movie offered me a great insight into the bravery displayed by the pilots and soldiers during the Great War."

"I hope you never have to fight in such a war," I said.

Gregory nodded. "I hope humanity is not stupid enough to engage in a war of that scale again."

We walked along the beach, following the curve on the sand created by the incoming tide. Children played on the beach. I smiled as they built sandcastles.

I wondered if, some day in the not too distant future, I'd give birth and raise a family of my own. I wondered if I'd be able to sustain a career and raise a family. Many actresses retired from motion pictures upon marriage. Indeed, many engaged in motion pictures with the sole intention of netting a suitable husband.

Whatever the future might hold, I considered

that I would not retire. Movies were deeply ingrained in me. They were a part of my soul, my very being. I could not imagine a life without movies.

Some of the critics had made mention of the fact that I did not appear in stage plays, and therefore I was not 'a proper actress'. They reckoned that talkies would be my downfall. I vowed to make a success of my talkies and make the critics eat their words.

"While I was away," Gregory said, "I thought about Greta, a lot."

"I can understand that," I said.

"I thought about myself and the direction my life is taking."

I nodded and held my tongue.

"I thought about us, a lot."

"What about us?" I asked. My voice sounded strange to me; my words appeared as a strangled whisper.

"We are very good friends," Gregory said.

"We are," I agreed.

"You are my favourite actress to work with."

"The feeling is mutual," I said.

"I would like to share my life with you on a more permanent basis," Gregory said.

I frowned. "Gregory Powell, what are you saying?"

Gregory placed one knee on the sand, took hold of my hand, and proposed to me. "I would like you to be my wife."

I gasped. At night, after talking with Gregory on the telephone, I'd dreamed of this moment. And now he was making the moment all too real.

"But," I blurted, "but...I'm not like Greta."

"No one is like Greta," Gregory said. "I'm not looking for anyone to replace Greta. I'm looking for someone to love, someone to share the rest of my life with. And I want that someone to be you."

"I see," I said.

Although I'd been dreaming of this moment, I stood there, my feet sinking into the wet sand, stunned.

"What do you say?" Gregory asked. "Will you marry me?"

"Yes," I said.

Before I could add any further words, Gregory swept me into his arms and offered me a passionate kiss.

I was getting my breath back when my eyes wandered over to a rock. "I wonder," I said.

"You wonder?" Gregory frowned.

"Bear with me," I said.

I took hold of Gregory's hand and dragged him towards the rock. There, I knelt on the sand and started to dig. After all this time, would it still be there, or would the sea have washed it away?

The waves had created more erosion, and with that erosion, more sand, so I had to dig deeper than initially anticipated. However, eventually, I found it, my heart-shaped rock.

I stood and presented the rock to Gregory. "A symbol of my love for you," I said.

Gregory accepted the rock with a smile. "I shall treasure it," he said, "as I shall treasure you."

We walked along the beach, hand in hand. As we walked, I considered how and when I should share my happy news with my father.

Back to Brooklyn

Mr Vincetti paired Gregory and me together in a motion picture, *The Bridge*. We would spend two months filming the movie, in Brooklyn,

Summer was drawing to a close and I'd yet to tell my father of my impending marriage to Gregory. I sensed that my father would not be pleased. I based my feeling on my father's desire to control me, and his need to regard me as his financial and emotional provider. Nevertheless, I vowed that as soon as we established ourselves in our hotel in Brooklyn, I would tell my father about my love for Gregory.

My father was still drinking heavily. However, in Brooklyn he made an effort to look more presentable. He dressed in a smart suit and clean shirt. He polished his shoes and straightened his tie. He even combed his hair.

I sensed that my father wanted to show off to anyone who might know him, to display to them what a success he'd made of his life. I had no problem with that, even though my father's success was no more than reflected glory, no more than shadows cast from my limelight. I was just pleased that he was looking after himself and taking pride in his appearance.

My father and I entered the dining room at the Regency Hotel and the waitresses fussed over us. Nothing was too much trouble for them. They would do anything to accommodate a movie star.

I found the notion of people regarding me as a movie star faintly ridiculous. I was just like them, a gal from Brooklyn, a gal doing a job. The only difference – my job description was 'actress'. But I was just like the waitresses. Remembering that fact kept me sane, stopped my mind from floating away on the clouds.

Gregory would join us tomorrow, so now was the moment to inform my father of our impending nuptials. I could delay no longer. I had to reveal our secret to him.

I waited until my father had consumed three glasses of wine, then I informed him of my decision. "I'm going to marry," I said. "Soon."

"Oh?" My father paused then poured himself another glass of wine – the waitresses had left two bottles so that he could serve himself at his leisure. "Who's the lucky man?"

"Gregory Powell," I said. "We'll make firm marriage plans the moment we return to California."

My father frowned. He loosened his tie. "Are you sure about this?" he asked. "Are you certain?"

"I'm sure," I said, "I'm certain. Gregory is the

man I love. He's the man I wish to marry."

"But," my father frowned, "he's a widower; he should continue to mourn his wife."

"Gregory will mourn Greta for the rest of his life," I said. "But through his sadness he must also find special moments and take pleasure from them."

My father sat back. He reached for a napkin and spilled wine over the dining table. A waitress rushed forward and cleaned up the mess. I made a note to offer the waitress a generous tip.

"I think you should wait," my father said, "until you find a man more suitable."

"No one could be more suitable than Gregory Powell," I said. "I have very strong feelings for him; he's the man I love."

"But what about us?" my father asked. "We are good together. I've guided your career; I've made you a star."

If my father wished to hold on to the fantasy that he was my Svengali, then so be it. In reality, he'd contributed little to my career. In Hollywood, he boasted to anyone who'd care to listen that he was my manager, and I allowed him to broadcast that boast. Since Greta's death, Gregory and I had made contact with a leading agent in Hollywood, Mr Bertram, and he was managing our business affairs.

"If you marry Gregory Powell," my father said, "where will I live?"

"You can live in my house," I said. "I'll move in with Gregory."

"And what'll I do for money?" my father scowled.

"I'll continue to offer you an allowance," I said. "You'll want for nothing. You can continue to live the life you've grown accustomed to."

My father gulped his wine. He spilled some over his shirt and tie. The idea of making himself look more presentable now forgotten, he ignored the stains, reached for a bottle and poured himself another glass of wine.

"When I wanted to marry," my father said, "you prevented me."

"The authorities deported Margarita," I said. "And anyway, she was not right for you."

"Gregory Powell is not right for you," my father said. "There are things you should know about him."

"What 'things'?" I frowned.

"Things," my father said. He stared at his wine glass, his bloodshot eyes, his morose features offering a weary countenance.

"There are no 'things' to know about Gregory," I said. "The Hollywood community is a hive of gossip-making and scandal-spreading, and during my time there, I've not heard one bad word spoken about Gregory."

"He's too good to be true," my father said. "Believe me, I know his type – when he gets you behind closed doors, he'll beat you."

"The wine is talking," I said, "and your words are upsetting me. I think you should quit drinking and we should quit talking. Whatever you say, I intend to marry Gregory; my mind is made up."

"If you marry Gregory Powell," my father said, "he'll expect you to be a wife in every room of the house."

"I'm a passable cook," I said. "I can cook for him."

My father laughed. Then, he became more serious. "In every room of the house, Tula. Every room."

My father stared deep into my eyes. He held my gaze. Goosebumps appeared on my skin. I felt hot, then cold. Perspiration poured from my skin. I felt faint. A waitress rushed to my aid and prevented me from collapsing on to the dining room carpet.

"My daughter is tired," my father explained to the waitress. "It's not easy being an actress. They work long hours and are in the spotlight all the time. Help me to help her to her room; she needs to lie down."

My father and the waitress helped me to my room where I reclined on my bed. My father fanned me with a newspaper and, in time, the episode faded.

"Just like your mother," my father said, "you're just like your mother; you can't handle undue stress. Being a dutiful wife is very stressful, Tula. I don't think you're ready for that commitment, yet. You need to complete this movie, then you need a long period of rest."

"Yes," I said, "I need to rest."

These fainting episodes were becoming more acute and more frequent. I needed to banish them from my life. I needed to rest. I would inform Gregory of my decision. I would place our marriage on hold. I felt sure that he would understand.

On the Ledge

Mr Winter was directing *The Bridge*, with Archie Bleeker serving as his chief cameraman. I was grateful for that; I was grateful to be surrounded by familiar, friendly faces, by people I could trust.

The fainting episode in the hotel dining room had unnerved me. I felt vulnerable. I wanted to go home, yet I had no firm idea of my home. I felt lost.

The moment Gregory arrived in Brooklyn, he noticed the change in my behaviour. He sat beside me in my hotel room and took hold of my hands. "What's the matter?" he asked.

"I'm just tired," I said. "I'll feel fine after a couple of days' rest."

"We're shooting tomorrow," Gregory said. "On Brooklyn Bridge." He caressed my cheek and gazed into my eyes. "You're pale and clammy. You're not well. Maybe you've picked up a bug. Sometimes, a change of environment can make a person feel unwell. Sometimes, a sensitive person needs time to adjust."

"I can't marry you," I said.

I was hoping to prepare my words and utter them softly, say them in a manner that reduced any distress. However, in my agitated state, my words came tumbling out.

"Why not?" Gregory frowned. "Why can't you marry me?"

"I'm not in the right frame of mind," I said. "I need to get well before I can commit to you."

"What's happened?" Gregory asked. "Is it something to do with you being back in Brooklyn?"

"It's nothing to do with Brooklyn," I said. Even as I said the words, I began to cry.

"It's everything to do with Brooklyn," Gregory said. He held my hands tight and urged, "Tell me, what's the problem? Tell me, what's wrong."

"Nothing's wrong," I said. Even to my ears, my words sounded pathetic, false; it was clear that something was seriously wrong.

"I'll call Uwe Winter," Gregory said, "we'll postpone the filming."

"We can't do that," I said. "Location filming is expensive. The cast and crew are all set. We can't let them down."

"Very well," Gregory said. "But I want to know what's troubling you; I want to know what's on your mind."

I sighed. "There's nothing on my mind."

"You're lying, Tula." Gregory sounded angry. I'd never seen him or heard him display such anger before. "I want the truth," he insisted. "I will not tolerate lies."

I continued to cry.

"What's the matter?" Gregory asked. He took me in his arms and rocked me, like a baby. "Tell me, what's wrong."

"It is Brooklyn," I said. "It's the bad memories."

"What bad memories?" Gregory asked.

"My mother," I said. "Several times, she attacked me with a knife."

"No one will attack you now," Gregory said, "you're safe with me."

"I feel safe with you," I said.

Gregory kissed my forehead. He hugged me tight. "I'm pleased to hear that." He kissed me again and smiled. "So, no more stupid talk about postponing our wedding."

"Do you really want to marry me?" I asked.

"Yes," Gregory said. "I want to be with you for the rest of my life."

I dried my eyes and frowned. "Even though I have problems with my mind?"

"A problem is an item in need of a solution," Gregory said. "We'll find that solution, together."

I sighed and relaxed in Gregory's arms. I felt safe with him, calm. I just needed to rest, I told myself, I needed to rest in Gregory's arms.

"I was thinking of Paris," Gregory said.

"Paris?" I frowned.

"For our honeymoon."

I leapt up and ran to the window. I stepped on

to the ledge and looked down. It seemed such a long way down. The people looked like ants, scurrying around. If I jumped, it would put an end to this misery, yet my death would cause Gregory so much pain. And he'd already endured so much pain.

My mind was skittish, not my own. I had no idea what I was doing. I'd lost control. I felt frightened. I felt scared. I felt like a puppet at the mercy of a puppeteer as he pulled my strings.

"What are you doing, Tula?" Gregory asked, standing beside me. "Your behaviour is irrational. You need to step inside. You need to calm down."

"Don't touch me!" I yelled. "Don't touch me! If you touch me, I'll jump!"

"I'm not going to touch you," Gregory said, "I'm not going to hurt you. Come on...step inside. Sit on this chair."

I glanced over my shoulder to a richly upholstered Regency armchair; I stared down to the ground. A crowd had gathered. They were staring up at me. I wondered if they recognised me. I wondered about the publicity. I wondered if this was the end of my career.

The situation was totally crazy. I was inches away from ending my life, yet my main thought was centred on my career. Maybe all actors and actresses were egotists, at heart. After all, we were presenting ourselves to the public and saying 'look at me'.

Yet, I didn't want people to look at me, I wanted them to look at my character. I wanted to express myself, artistically. Painters painted, writers wrote. I wanted to act, then preserve the privacy of a painter or a writer.

I wondered how people would remember me. I wondered if they'd appreciate my films. The style of movie acting was already changing, thanks to the talkies. I wondered if future generations would regard my performances as over-dramatic or camp. I wondered if they'd dismiss me as a poor actress.

That thought upset me. My foot wandered off the window ledge. I pictured myself spiralling to the ground. I fell into a faint. And woke up on my bed.

Gregory must have caught me. He'd saved my life. He was pacing the room, looking anxious, when I turned to face him. Aware that I was awake, he rushed to my side.

"How are you?" he asked.

"I'm fine," I said, offering a tentative smile.

"Your behaviour is irrational, Tula," Gregory said, caressing my brow. "You're hot one minute, cold the next. Your skin is clammy. I will send for a doctor. You need some medication."

"No," I said, grabbing Gregory's arm, pulling

him towards me. "No doctor. I'm fine now. I thought I was losing my mind. I was frightened. But I'm calm now."

"Are you sure?" Gregory frowned.

"I'm sure," I said. "Don't worry about me. I won't do anything to hurt you. Let's complete the shooting of *The Bridge* here in Brooklyn. We'll discuss marriage and our plans for the future when we return to California. Okay?"

"Very well," Gregory said. "But if anything like this should happen again, I will call a doctor."

"I'm fine now," I said. "Nothing like this will ever happen again."

The Telegram

We filmed several scenes on Brooklyn Bridge, which attracted a lot of attention. I had to sign numerous autographs, to placate the crowd. Throughout, Gregory kept a close eye on me.

Naturally, I appreciated Gregory's concern, but my crisis had passed; I was feeling well again. I was into my character, a woman fighting for her family and the building of the bridge. I was into my acting stride. I was offering quality performances. From instinct, from experience, I knew that my performances were good.

I also knew that I was acting well from Mr Winter's kind words. He was delighted with my performances. He felt sure that I would win an award.

On rainy days, Mr Winter planned to film the interiors. He'd hired a converted ballroom for the purpose. The ballroom measured fifty feet by thirty-five feet with rolls of canvas, paint and wooden joists placed out of camera range, on either side.

Archie had positioned his camera on a five-foot square platform. The platform moved on rollers, for the tracking shots.

Two dozen arc lights hung from pulleys. The arc lights were very hot. Sometimes, acting under the arc lights made me feel faint, so I drank lots of water before each take.

The set contained a dozen Cooper-Hewitt mercury-vapour lamps that, on occasion, also made me feel faint. These lamps were mounted on ceiling banks and floor rollers.

The Cooper-Hewitt lamps were strange. When in use, they clicked like castanets. Most of the actors liked that beat because it offered a sense of rhythm. The sound recordists hated the beats because they were difficult to filter out.

We were still adjusting to the talkies, still coming to terms with them, still developing best practices and new techniques.

Our dressing rooms, wardrobe and prop rooms were located in the cellar. The whole building was a hive of activity as Mr Winter prepared to shoot a dramatic scene, a scene in which my character would confront the local councillors, opponents of her plans, and give them a piece of her mind. I was in a feisty mood. I was up for this scene.

Our other main opponents were the ferry owners, who feared a loss of trade. We would shoot a scene with them, on the river, later in the week.

Gregory would participate in the councillor scene, after I'd delivered my big speech. He would walk up to my side and offer me moral support. Of course, during our shared ambition to build a bridge over the East River, our characters would fall in love.

Kissing in motion pictures was the most unromantic, most unerotic thing imaginable. With dozens of people looking on, it was difficult to conjure up a sense of romance. Without doubt, I found the kissing scenes in motion pictures the most challenging, the most difficult to deliver, especially when my lead man was not Gregory Powell.

Regulators were not happy with some of the scenes that were currently appearing in motion pictures. They thought that passionate scenes on the silver screen would inflame the audience. They also complained about the portrayal of single mothers, divorced women, and women of 'easy virtue'. As an actress, I resented the regulators' interference; I felt that they were poisoning our art.

That said, the directors were very inventive and often created scenes, with the casual use of a cigarette lighter, for instance, that were far more suggestive than a simple kiss. To me, that proved that the regulators had no idea what they were doing. They were bigoted men, often men with double standards, men who insisted upon imposing their will on everyone else.

Tom Boyd played my opponent, the leader of the town council. Portly, with a bald pate and large side-whiskers, Tom was a great character actor.

However, he did have a way of making me laugh during the serious scenes. This was very naughty of him, of course. To counter Tom's tomfoolery, I'd developed a technique that called for maximum concentration. Invariably, this meant that I delivered some of my best scenes when acting with Tom.

"Okay," Mr Winter said, "everyone ready? Great. Action!"

"You are stuck in the past," I said, in character, "your minds are in the eighteenth century. It's time that you moved into the nineteenth century. It's time that we built the bridge."

The Bridge was a period movie, which meant that I was clothed in a heavy crinoline dress and a tight corset. I could barely breathe in the corset. I had no idea how Victorian women coped, day in, day out.

"I will raise a petition in favour of the bridge," I said. "I will get everyone in Brooklyn to sign it. What is more, I will campaign against you at the forthcoming elections and ensure that you lose your council seat."

"Cut!" Mr Winter yelled. He tilted his hat back, smiled and said, "That was excellent. Tula, you're on fire today."

I was on fire, in an acting sense and physically. The heat from the lamps and my clothing had me perspiring by the bucket load, which necessitated a reapplication of my make-up.

While Lillian reapplied my make-up, Archie approached and offered me the thumbs up. Archie was dating Lillian, and I'd heard a whisper that they would wed.

"That was excellent, Tula," Archie said. "I reckon you're a better sound actress than silent actress. I reckon the talkies will make you a superstar."

"Thanks, Archie," I said. Then I vacated the make-up chair so that he could spend a moment with Lillian.

Back on the set, I prepared for my next scene. I looked around for Gregory, because he would join me in this scene. I found him standing beside Mr Winter. Both men looked troubled.

"A telegram," Gregory said, as I approached, "addressed to you. I took the trouble of reading it."

"I don't mind," I said. "I have no secrets to hide from you."

"It's your father," Gregory said.

Suddenly, I knew why Gregory and Mr Winter looked so troubled. Suddenly, I knew why Gregory had decided to read my telegram.

"He's dead," Gregory said.

I swooned and fainted. I believe Mr Winter caught me. I believe I heard the assembled cast and crew mutter, "She's not well; she needs medical help."

My Journal

I felt cold, sitting alone in my room, in the asylum. I stared at my journal, which sat on my lap. Dr Brooks had read my journal and, soon, he would talk with me. He would help me to understand why I'd suffered a mental collapse.

Of course, I knew why I was feeling mentally and physically unwell – my father's death. I found that keeping a journal calmed me. It helped me to unburden my thoughts at the end of the day. Therefore, even though Dr Brooks had said that I no longer needed to write out my experiences for him, I decided to keep this journal for myself.

I reflected on my journal. Had I told Dr Brooks the truth? To the best of my memory and ability, I reckoned that I had. What he'd make of my truth was a matter of his opinion as a skilled physician. Whatever he said, I wanted to go home. I wanted to leave this depressing place.

Of course, I lost my part in *The Bridge*. My performances, possibly my best performances to date, were consigned to the cutting room floor. Thankfully, we were not too deeply into the filming when my emotional collapse occurred, so Mr Winter was able to hire another actress and reshoot my scenes. The other actress, Jennie de Haven, took my part in the motion picture, and my status as the Limelight Motion Picture Company's lead actress.

My career had suffered a major setback, but I was a Bowman, I was a fighter, I would claw my way back to the top.

Throughout, Gregory stood by me. I could not have complained if he'd walked away. A lesser man would have abandoned me. Gregory's loyalty proved to me that he was indeed a wonderful man.

The door opened and Dr Brooks stepped into my room. He smiled at me and asked, "May I sit with you?"

"Of course you may," I said.

Dr Brooks sat opposite me, about four feet away. He adjusted the seams on his trousers and accepted my journal as I leaned across and handed it to him. Even though Dr Brooks had read my journal, I felt that it should be in his possession as we talked.

"Thank you for your journal," Dr Brooks said. "I believe that it will greatly assist us as we ease you towards recovery."

"I collapsed because my father died," I said.

"Indeed," Dr Brooks said. He offered me a reassuring smile while steepling his fingers against his chin. "I wish to discuss your journal; are you happy with that?"

"Perfectly happy," I said.

"Very well," Dr Brooks said. "Let us begin."

I knew that we had to discuss my journal; I knew that the discussion was an essential part of my therapy. I'd told Dr Brooks that I felt happy to discuss my journal. However, the truth of the matter was, I felt extremely nervous.

"Let us start with your mother," Dr Brooks said. "Your relationship with her was..." He paused and searched for the right word. "Unconventional?"

"I loved my mother," I said, "and I believe that she loved me."

"Your mother attacked you," Dr Brooks said, "on numerous occasions. She threatened to kill you."

"She did," I conceded. "However, I do not believe that she would have perpetrated an attack to the point where it would have claimed my life."

"Your mother found it very difficult to offer love," Dr Brooks said, "to you, and your father."

"She was often cold towards him," I conceded. "I cannot deny that."

"And what of your father?" Dr Brooks asked. "Was he cold or affectionate?"

"My father was drunk most of the time," I said, "so his behaviour resembled that of a drunk."

"When inebriated," Dr Brooks said, "a man's behaviour can vary; some men become friendly and docile, while others become angry and aggressive.

In regard to your father, what was his prevalent mood, when drunk?"

"His mood varied," I said. "Usually, he was docile."

"You lacked for love in your family home," Dr Brooks said. "Would you regard that as a fair assessment?"

"At times," I said, "I felt lonely; I cannot deny that."

"Your need for love," Dr Brooks said, "is a very human need; did you seek to make a career in motion pictures to compensate for that lack of family love?"

"I entered motion pictures because I loved the magic of the silver screen. However," I confessed, "now I can understand what you're saying; I can appreciate that I was also looking for affection from the audience, that I wanted someone to love me."

"Gregory Powell loves you," Dr Brooks said.

I smiled and nodded. "I believe he does."

"Do you love him?"

This time, I nodded with more vigour. "Indeed, I do."

"And yet," Dr Brooks said, "you are reluctant to marry him." He paused and studied my features closely. "Why might that be?"

"I'm scared," I said.

"Scared?" Dr Brooks frowned. "Scared of what,

exactly?"

"Scared," I said, "of the intimacy."

"But," Dr Brooks said, "intimacy is an act of love. Why would you be frightened of such love?"

"I don't know," I said. "Maybe it has something to do with what my mother said when I was younger."

"And what did your mother say?" Dr Brooks asked.

"She said that if I was intimate with a man, I could turn into a whore."

"And do you really believe that?" Dr Brooks asked. "Do you really believe that if you were intimate with Gregory Powell, as husband and wife, you would turn into a whore?"

"I do not believe that I would become a whore," I said. "I believe that I would remain true to my husband."

"So," Dr Brooks frowned, "why the fear? Why do you collapse at the thought of intimacy?"

"I do not collapse at such a thought," I said. "I collapse when, physically, I feel uncomfortable."

"I'm talking about mental collapse," Dr Brooks said. "Your mind falls into fragments when you consider intimacy. Tell me, Miss Bowman, why should that be?"

"I don't know," I said. "This conversation is making me feel very uncomfortable. I would like to stop now."

"We will stop," Dr Brooks said. "It is not my wish or intention to make you feel uncomfortable. However, as your physician, I must say this: I believe that you do know why you fear intimacy. I believe that the reason is buried deep in your subconscious. I believe that you placed it there, in a chest, if you will. You securely locked that chest, locked away the thought that disturbs you and, metaphorically, threw away the key. It is my task to find that key, to unlock that chest, to allow that disturbing thought to enter your conscious mind so that you can confront it, so that you can dismiss that demon, so that you can return to full physical and mental health."

"Tell me, Miss Bowman," Dr Brooks said, "will you help me to find that key?"

"If it will make me well again," I said, "I will."

"Good," Dr Brooks said. He stood and placed my journal in my hands. "Mr Powell wishes to see you. Do you wish to see him?"

"Yes," I said, "I would love to see Gregory."

"In that case," Dr Brooks said, "I will allow you to talk with Mr Powell. Then, we will go in search of that key."

Gossip

Gregory entered my dank room. He smiled at me then occupied the seat recently vacated by Dr Brooks.

"How are you feeling?" Gregory asked.

"Much better," I said. "I think I'm ready to go home."

"Dr Brooks will sanction your request," Gregory said. "But, before he does that he feels it's important that we fully understand your problem, to prevent the prospect of a relapse."

"I understand that," I said. "And I feel that we do fully understand my problem – I collapsed due to the stress of my father's death. It's as simple as that."

"Dr Brooks thinks that other factors are at play," Gregory said.

"Dr Brooks is a kind man," I said. "But he is wont to chase after shadows that don't exist." I straightened my posture and offered Gregory a winning smile. "I understand myself better than anybody understands me. Sometimes the solution is simple, but we look for complications. I believe that the solution is simple in my case."

Gregory paused. His facial features tightened. His expression told me that he was not convinced.

I felt that I'd talked enough about my problems for one day, so I sought to change the subject. "Have you completed the filming of *The Bridge*?"

"Yes," Gregory said, "that's all wrapped up. Vincetti and Uwe Winter are very pleased with the movie. They reckon it will be a big hit."

"Did you enjoy acting with Jennie de Haven?" I asked.

"At times," Gregory said, "she was temperamental and very demanding, but we completed the picture without too many flare-ups."

"And what about your next project?" I asked.

"I've put everything on hold," Gregory said, "until you're well again."

"I am well," I said. "I'm ready to leave now."

"You are better," Gregory said, reaching across to touch me, "but not completely well. We still need to understand what triggered your collapse."

Even though I loved Gregory, I shied away from his compassionate touch. My action suggested that, maybe, I was not completely well.

"I've received an offer," Gregory said, "to make a light-hearted mystery movie. It's possible that the movie could develop into a series. Certainly, the material is there. The central characters are a husband and wife team. I would like to embark on this project, but I feel that it will only be a success if I embark on it with you. You are perfect for the role of my wife. You have the looks, natural wit and intelligence. I feel that the chemistry between us is perfect for this series. That chemistry would carry the stories regardless of the plots which, incidentally, are very good."

"That sounds ideal," I said. "We'd be able to spend more time together."

"Yes," Gregory said. "I want to be with you. I want to act with you. But before we make any firm commitments we must ensure that you are well."

"What else is happening at the studio?" I asked.

"Archie is to wed Lillian."

"I'm pleased for him," I said.

Gregory nodded. "I'm pleased for him too. Also, Vincetti and Gloria are to divorce."

"That was inevitable," I said.

"I'm not happy with Vincetti," Gregory said. "He should have stood by you. He should have offered you more support."

"Mr Vincetti is a businessman," I said. "He's not an artist. He doesn't have an artist's sensibilities. I can understand his position. His focus is always on the accounts ledger. He's in movies to make money. While I'm in here, in this asylum, I can't make any money for the Limelight Motion Picture Company. I don't resent his attitude towards me, or feel any animosity towards Jennie. I feel that Archie is right – I'm a better talkie actress than silent actress. Once I'm fully well, I feel certain that I can reclaim my place in the industry and produce my best performances."

Gregory nodded. "I agree. I must confess, with the talkies, when we act together, you carry me."

"You're being too modest," I said. "You're still top of all the fan and distributor charts. The public and the businessmen love you. Gregory Powell is still a colossus in the movie industry."

Gregory sat back and laughed. He had a way of keeping everything in proportion. Despite his great success, he never allowed the adulation to go to his head. He remained grounded; a humble man who'd got lucky in that someone had recognised and nurtured his talent. The bright lights were just for show, and he knew that. He knew that true success stemmed from being true to yourself.

"There's also talk of producing movies in colour," Gregory said. "The technology is advancing by the day. They have cameras now that can film using a three-colour technique. I'm not familiar with the science, but I've seen the end product, and it's impressive."

"It will probably mean more time in the make-up room," I said, "if they intend to film us in colour."

"I'm sure that the audience will love colour movies," Gregory said, "but I wonder if we'll lose something; for instance, the use of shadows."

"You are very good with the technical aspects of movie making," I said. "Maybe you should become a director."

"Maybe," Gregory mused. He paused then smiled. "There's one thing I forgot to tell you about Jennie."

"Oh," I frowned, "what's that?"

"She insisted on only being filmed from one side, her left-hand side. She has a slight imperfection on her right cheek and is paranoid about it appearing on the big screen."

"I guess all actors are paranoid," I said, "about something."

"You don't have to be mad to work in this industry," Gregory said.

I smiled and finished his sentence for him. "But it helps."

Gregory smiled too. Then his features became serious. "The authorities plan to demolish your old home in Brooklyn," he said. "Dr Brooks would like you to visit the building, before they turn it into rubble. Will you visit your old home?"

I paused and thought deeply about that question. It would mean revisiting my old haunts, becoming reacquainted with memories from my troubled past, with old demons and ghosts. I shivered at the prospect, but understood the reasoning behind Dr Brooks' request.

"Will you accompany me?" I asked.

"If Dr Brooks is willing," Gregory said, "of course I will."

"In that case," I said, "I will revisit my old home."

My Old Home

We arrived in a limousine, which, on reflection, wasn't the greatest idea because the car attracted a crowd. Word got around that movie stars were in the neighbourhood and soon the streets were full of excited people.

The locals knew me from my youth. They knew that I was plain, ordinary Tula Bowman. As my mother used to say, "Ya jest a woikin goil from Brooklyn. Don't put on no airs or graces; you ain't nothing special."

However, Gregory Powell was a superstar with a superstar's mystique. The crowds flocked into the streets in the hope of catching a glimpse of him.

To his credit, Gregory took time to greet the people and sign autographs. From the shadows, Dr Brooks looked on, quietly observing, always assessing, forever wrapped up in his role of psychiatrist.

From the sidewalk, I stared up at our old brownstone. It looked dangerous, in a state of ruin, on the brink of collapse. I wondered about the wisdom of visiting my old home, I wondered about meeting the ghosts from my past; I wondered if it was a good idea.

I was lost in that thought when Gregory took

hold of my elbow and guided me into the building. Before I knew it, and with Dr Brooks following in our footsteps, we were climbing the stairs.

Outside, the crowd cheered, and Gregory waved from a window. Inside, I stared at the water stains and mould that patterned the kitchen walls.

I recollected: my mother used to cook at that stove; I used to cook at that stove; we used to eat our dinners at that table; as a youngster, I used to play on that floor; during his scallywag days, my father used to hide items in that hole in the wall.

I wandered over to the wall and examined the hole. What did my father used to hide in there? Probably booze. With the passing of time, I'd come to realise that in my youth my father was a bootlegger.

I peered into the hole in the wall. There was no booze in there now. The homemade gin had long gone. Probably, I reflected with sadness, my father had consumed it all.

Our living room offered a jumble of memories, mainly of my mother sitting in her chair, staring into the middle-distance, entranced, locked in one of her episodes.

My poor mother, a victim of a broken mind. I paused and reflected. Was my mind broken? No, it was damaged, and a damaged mind offered the hope of a healthy repair.

I pictured myself in a cot. I had no idea that I possessed such an early memory. I pictured my mother welcoming a man into our home and drawing a curtain across my cot, so that I couldn't see him. I recalled the sounds that the man – that the men – and my mother made, sounds of pleasure mingled with agony.

The memories disturbed me. I looked around in a state of fright. Perspiration poured from my body. My skin became clammy. I felt faint. Gregory hurried to my side. He placed an arm around my shoulders and I felt calm again.

I remembered the occasions when my mother had attacked me with a knife. Those memories disturbed me too, but not to the same extent as the memories of my mother entertaining her male guests.

I glanced at Dr Brooks. He was observing me, gauging my every reaction. He offered me a reassuring smile and I wandered into my old bedroom.

"How do you feel, Miss Bowman?" Dr Brooks asked.

"I'm okay," I said.

Dr Brooks nodded. He brushed away an imaginary speck from his trousers. He was in the habit of brushing away imaginary specks from his clothing. Maybe it was a nervous habit. Maybe psychiatrists had hang-ups too.

"Do you have any special memories of this room?" Dr Brooks asked.

I glanced around my old bedroom and reflected. "I used to read my movie magazines, in secret. I used to read about you." I turned to Gregory and smiled. "I used to dream of meeting you."

"And you made that dream real," Dr Brooks said.

I circled the bed and looked at a lopsided picture on the wall. The picture featured a religious image. I had no memory of that picture. I concluded that a recent tenant must have placed it there.

"Do you have any other special memories?" Dr Brooks asked.

"I used to gather dye from the walls," I said, "and use it as make-up."

"Did you used to entertain boyfriends in this room?" Dr Brooks asked.

"Of course not," I said. "My mother and father would not allow it."

"Did you used to sit in this room while your mother entertained her male guests?"

"I know what you're saying," I said, "and I don't like the implication." For the first time, I became angry with Dr Brooks. "My mother was not a whore."

"What was she?" Dr Brooks asked, his voice gentle, his look sympathetic.

I bit my lower lip and stared at the threadbare carpet. I could not find an appropriate answer to his question.

"I've read your mother's case notes," Dr Brooks said. "Various factors contributed to your mother's illness. One of those factors was related to diseases transmitted by her male clients. Some of those diseases can have an adverse effect on the mind."

"I don't like what you're saying," I said, "and I want you to stop now. I will not allow anyone to bad-mouth my mother."

"Yes," Gregory said, supporting me. "Steady on. We're here to uncover the root of Tula's problem, and not denigrate her mother's memory."

"It is not my intention to denigrate anyone's memory," Dr Brooks said, "but for Miss Bowman to fully understand the source of her problem, she must have a firm knowledge of her past. She must recognise and acknowledge who her parents were, the type of people they were."

"I know who my mother was," I said, "and I know what she was. Now, can we please move on?"

"Very well," Dr Brooks said. "Did your father enter this room?"

"Of course," I said. "We all wandered into every room in the house."

"Did you welcome your father's visits?"

"Of course," I said. "He was my father."

"When your mother died," Dr Brooks said, "during that period of mourning, did your father visit you in this room?"

I began to perspire. My skin became clammy. My stomach did summersaults. I found it difficult to breathe. An image appeared in my mind, an ugly, disturbing, upsetting image, an image of my father and me in this room. My eyes widened as I pictured the image. My mouth opened and I released a silent scream.

I'd suppressed that image for so long, buried it deep in my subconscious. However, now it was staring at me, glaring at me. I couldn't face it. I fell into a faint.

Why?

Gregory caught me. He carried me into the kitchen and placed me on a chair. The chair was none too steady. I was none too steady. I leaned on the table and Gregory for support.

Dr Brooks applied smelling salts and offered me a bottle of water – he'd come prepared. Vaguely, I remained aware of the crowd waiting outside the brownstone, eager to catch another glimpse of Gregory.

"Are you all right, Miss Bowman?" Dr Brooks asked.

I sipped some water and nodded.

"Good," Dr Brooks said. "Take your time. There is no rush."

I took my time. I sipped the water and stared into the middle distance. The image appeared again. The image frightened me. Dr Brooks sensed that I was reliving that disturbing moment from my past. He sought to reassure me.

"Don't fear the memory," Dr Brooks said. "Allow it to surface. Allow it to wander around this room. Allow it to take its place within this house. And remember this: when the demolition men destroy this building, they will destroy the hurt within that memory. You will not banish the memory – that is not possible or desirable – but, over time, the hurt will fade. You are strong, Tula; you have the courage to face up to that painful memory, and allow it to fade."

I stared at Dr Brooks. I realised that that was the first time he'd called me by my given name.

"You can do this, Tula," Dr Brooks said. "You've displayed great courage and determination to make a success of your career. You will find the courage and determination to face up to, and release, this painful memory."

"Why?" I asked. That question gnawed away at my mind. "Why did he do it?"

Dr Brooks glanced at Gregory then at me. He offered a shrug of his lean shoulders and sighed. "Only your father could offer the truthful answer. I can only offer an educated guess."

"Offer your guess," Gregory said. "Tula needs to know. She deserves an answer."

"Very well," Dr Brooks said. "After your mother died, your father was emotionally upset. That upset might have disturbed the fragile balance of his mind. He was angry with you for jumping into your mother's grave. Drunk most of the time, it is my guess that he was also sexually frustrated. Any one of those things, or a combination of those things, could have led to the incident."

"Call it what it was," I said. "Put a name to that

incident."

"Very well," Dr Brooks said. "It's good that you are willing to face up to the full truth of that incident. It is my professional opinion that any one of the factors I previously mentioned could have led to the rape."

"My father raped me," I said.

"Yes," Dr Brooks said.

"And I buried the memory."

"You buried the memory deep in your subconscious," Dr Brooks said, "but you could not expunge it from your mind."

"And that memory resurfaced when my father died."

"It was looking for a release," Dr Brooks said, "a way to emerge. Now that that memory is out in the open, to make a life for yourself, to become Mrs Gregory Powell, you need to confront that memory. You need to acknowledge the truth and allow the pain to fade, over time."

"Will the pain ever fade?" I asked.

"It will," Dr Brooks said, "over time."

I clenched my fists. My face became angry, ugly. "I hate my father," I said.

"That's understandable," Dr Brooks said.

"I hate my mother," I said.

"Your mother is the source of many issues," Dr Brooks said.

"Why?" I repeated. "Why?"

"To answer that question," Dr Brooks said, "you must also consider that your father's feelings towards you were always misplaced."

There was so much to take on board, so much to comprehend. I felt overwhelmed. I wanted to run from this building, run all the way to Hollywood. However, a thought made me stay: maybe I'd been running all my life. Maybe my father's inappropriate feelings towards me had been the main reason why I'd felt the need to run away.

"We've uncovered the source of Tula's distress," Gregory said. "What happens now?"

"I recommend a return to the asylum," Dr Brooks said, "for a period of rest, a course of hydrotherapy and, if necessary, medication."

"No," I said. "No asylum, no hydrotherapy, no medication. I want to go home, with Gregory."

Gregory took hold of my hand and caressed my fingers. I eased my fingers into his hand and tightened my grip.

"May I suggest a compromise," Dr Brooks said. "I would like to observe you, at close quarters, for at least a week. If I consider that you are well enough after that week, I will allow you to return to Hollywood, with Gregory. However, for the long-term good of your health, I would recommend regular contact, weekly telephone calls. Are you willing to accept that compromise?"

"No drugs," I said, "and no hydrotherapy. And after a week, I will leave the asylum."

"I will look after Tula," Gregory said. "I will ensure that she rests, totally. I will keep the media and Hollywood jackals away from her. I will guide her towards her recovery."

"I'm sure you will," Dr Brooks said. "And it's because of your support that I'm willing to compromise and grant Tula's request."

I took another sip of water and gathered my thoughts. I had so many questions. Maybe I could share them with Gregory. My main question was, did my father feel sorry about the rape, did he feel any remorse?

I wished that I could talk with him now, and hear his answer. I wished that I could slap him across his face.

I wondered if my father had buried the memory of what happened between us. It was the only time that it happened; certainly, he did not approach me in that manner ever again.

Before the rape, I worshiped my father. After the rape, I sensed that there was always an emotional distance between us. Now, I could understand that emotional distance, from my point of view. I wondered why my father maintained that emotional distance. Did he fear that he would force himself upon me again?

Gregory stood and walked over to the window. He waved to the crowd and they offered a big cheer.

The fans formed images of their favourite motion picture stars and, doubtless, pictured them in paradise. They had no idea that we suffered. They had no idea that we went through the same emotional turmoil that they went through.

We offered the fans a release from their turmoil, a break from their grinding reality; we offered their minds stories and scenarios that transported them away from their problems – that was our main job.

I'd been in the fans' shoes. I'd looked up to stars like Gregory to transport me away from my reality. I understood the vital role that motion pictures stars played in the lives of many people.

"I'll meet the people outside," Gregory said, "talk with them and distract them. Dr Brooks, you travel with Tula back to the asylum. I'll catch up with you later."

Gregory smiled at me and took hold of my hands. "Rest now. Follow Dr Brooks' advice. In a week, we'll return to our home in Hollywood. In a week, we'll embark upon a new phase in our lives; we'll make ourselves whole again."

Recuperation

My week in the asylum passed peacefully. I displayed no unseemly behaviour. I did not suffer from an adverse reaction to my revelation. I spent many hours in meditation. I spent many hours writing in my journal. Over the course of a day, I wrote a letter to my father.

Dear Father,

I know that you will not read these words, but Dr Brooks suggested that it would be a good idea for me to put pen to paper. He suggested that writing to you would offer me a form of therapy, an emotional release.

Father, I hate you. I hate what you did to me. I also pity you, for allowing yourself to commit such an act, for allowing yourself to become the man you ultimately became.

Why did you do it? Why? I need an answer to that question before I can move on.

Was it lust? Was it as simple as that? I don't believe that your act was driven by lust alone. I know now that you used to visit Submarine Lil and her friends frequently. They satisfied your lust, at the basest level.

Were you so overcome with grief at my mother's passing that you succumbed to such barbarity? I know that you truly loved her, and that she did not love you.

I do not believe that my mother hated you. I believe that, because of her illness, she was incapable of displaying love.

I wake up at nights in cold sweats, truly frightened. I'm frightened that I will become my mother and not display any love towards Gregory. That thought deeply upsets me. I've discussed that thought with Dr Brooks and he's reassured me that I will not develop into my mother. He feels certain that I can enjoy a happy life with Gregory.

Father, did the drink drive you to rape me? Lost in an alcoholic haze, were you fully aware of the barbaric nature of your act? Is that why you appeared embarrassed for many months after the incident?

Did you get me drunk on purpose? Did you plan the rape, or did it 'just happen?' I think the latter. I was very drunk. I felt nothing at the time, but in the morning, I felt very unwell. My memories of the rape are a jumble, akin to a muddled nightmare. I'm aware, now, that something did happen but, for years, I could not put the pieces together; maybe my lack of clarity was due to deliberate suppression on my part, a deliberate attempt to smother the emotional pain.

Father, you cannot supply me with answers but, maybe, with Gregory and Dr Brooks' help, I will come to learn the truth. I am aware that there are no instant answers or solutions, and that recovery will take time. I am fortunate in that I have Gregory to support me. With him in my life, I feel truly blessed.

I have much more to say, but right now, I'm too tired to say it, so I will close this letter.

Yours truly,

Tula

I reread my letter several times. I wrote more letters, similar in nature. After reading them and thinking about them, I ripped them all to shreds and placed them in the wastepaper basket. I found the act of writing the letters and ripping them up cathartic. Bit by bit, word by word, I released the demon from my mind.

After the week in the asylum, Dr Brooks allowed me to return to Hollywood with Gregory. We decamped to his bolthole in Topanga, to a beautiful home that nestled in the hillside. There I rested. I wanted for nothing. Indeed, Gregory treated me like a princess.

Two weeks after my return to California, Mr Vincetti made a request to visit me. After much discussion with Gregory, I persuaded him that we should allow Mr Vincetti to visit.

We sat on the patio in the sunshine. The scene was very civilised. Indeed, Mr Vincetti looked the epitome of civility in his pink shirt, straw hat and fashionable sunglasses.

"How are you feeling?" Mr Vincetti asked.

"Good," I said. "I'm feeling good. I'm feeling much better."

"That's splendid," Mr Vincetti said. He lowered his sunglasses, slid them down the bridge of his nose, as though to get a better look at me. "Do you feel well enough to return to the studio?"

Before I could reply, Gregory said, "Tula needs another three months of rest, at least."

"I see," Mr Vincetti said. "I was afraid you would say that." He leaned back in his chair and placed his hands together, as though in prayer. "I'm sure you're aware of the clause in your contract."

"Which clause?" I asked.

"The absence clause," Mr Vincetti said. "If you are away from the studio for a period of three months or longer, and the studio is not responsible for causing that absence, we have the right to cancel your contract."

"That would be madness," Gregory said. "Tula

is your best asset. She's a natural for the talkies. In the future, she'll clean up at the awards. You're making a bad short-term decision; you're not looking at the future."

Mr Vincetti smiled and shrugged. "All I will say to you is, Jennie de Haven; Jennie is now our leading actress."

"Jennie's beautiful," Gregory said, "and a very talented actress, but her voice is as squeaky as a mouse."

Mr Vincetti continued to smile and shrug. "The fans love Jennie, they love everything about her. Besides, we need to balance the books. Developments in talking pictures and colour movies are very expensive. We need to release one of our stars."

"I understand," I said. "Will I receive a severance payment?"

"That can be arranged," Mr Vincetti said. "I will make the payment as generous as possible."

Mr Vincetti returned to his office. For a good ten minutes, Gregory was furious. He marched across the patio with his hands in his pockets, kicking at the weeds that poked through the crazy paving.

"Please sit down," I said. "You're giving me a headache."

"I will not sit down," Gregory said. "And you

will not boss me."

"Gregory Powell," I said, "if I'm to spend my life with you I will do so as your equal. I will speak up for myself and challenge you, if need be."

Gregory paused. He stared at me, his mouth agape. Then he burst out laughing and hugged me. "You're getting better," he said. "Your spirit is returning."

I laughed too. "It is," I agreed.

In the sunshine, on the patio, Gregory and I talked for an hour. It was an earnest conversation. At its conclusion, I summarised our thoughts.

"The severance payment will mean that I can rest, for another three months at least. When your contract is up next year, you can leave the studio. We can make the light-hearted mystery series as independents. I've read the scripts. They're very witty. The series is sure to be a hit."

Gregory nodded. He turned and glanced across the bay, to the horizon. "The sun is setting," he said.

"It is," I said. "But it's rising for us."

The media received word that Gregory and I were living together. Such was their wont, the reporters decided to camp outside Gregory's house every morning. They were looking for answers, a smidgen of scandal, a morsel of gossip.

"Maybe I should unfurl the hosepipe," Gregory said, "and give them all a good soaking."

"Don't do that," I smiled. "After all, when we return to the set, we'll want them to write nice words about us."

"Very well," Gregory shrugged. "But they are disturbing you. I'll have a word with them."

"Later," I said. "Talk with me first."

"Okay," Gregory said. "What shall we talk about?"

"Baseball, the stock market, the latest movies...I'm up for anything. I just like to hear the sound of your voice."

Gregory sat beside me on the chaise lounge. This had become our regular seating arrangement. It was intimate, and I felt comfortable with it.

"Let's talk about you," Gregory said. "You're continuing to make progress."

"I feel much better," I said. "I feel stronger, mentally. I get moments when I feel tearful, but those moments are now few and far between."

I took hold of Gregory's hands, looked him in the eyes and said, "You've been wonderful to me. I don't know how I can thank you."

"You could marry me," Gregory said.

"I could," I said, lowering my eyes, "but I still need to think about that."

"I understand," Gregory said.

The reporters outside were more vociferous than usual and, even though our neighbours were distant, I feared that we'd be getting a bad name in the neighbourhood.

"I'd better have a word with them," Gregory said, sensing my discomfort.

"Okay," I said, "but make sure it's a friendly word."

Gregory set his jaw and offered a look of determination. "Don't worry," he said. "I will."

Although annoyed that the media were disturbing me, when Gregory ventured outside, he was all sweetness and light.

I sat on the window seat and listened as Gregory fielded questions from the reporters. I recognised several familiar voices, including Charlie Saddler, James Falk, Earl MacInnes and Dorothy Cooper.

First, the reporters greeted Gregory with a round of applause. Then Charlie Saddler said, "We understand that Miss Tula Bowman is staying with you. How is she?"

"Tula is fine," Gregory said. "She's well."

"The rumour is she suffered a nervous breakdown," James Falk said. "Is that true?"

"Tula collapsed on the set," Gregory said. "A combination of over-work, extreme tiredness and her father's death was responsible. Whether or not that constitutes a nervous breakdown, I don't know. The medical aspects and details are in the hands of her physician."

"When will we see Miss Bowman on the screen again?" Earl MacInnes asked.

"You can see Tula on the screen every night of the week, in any city in America," Gregory said. "Her movies are on constant show."

Playfully, the reporters laughed at Gregory's retort. Then Earl MacInnes said, "When will we see her in a new picture?"

"Next year," Gregory said. "We are making plans to appear in a movie together."

"What's the movie about?" James Falk asked.

"I'm afraid I'm not at liberty to discuss that yet," Gregory said. "But you know what they say: watch this space."

"I understand that Miss Bowman is no longer a player for the Limelight Motion Picture Company," Dorothy Cooper said. "Can you confirm if that rumour is true?"

"I think you need to take up contract talk with Mr Vincetti," Gregory said. "I'm sure he'll be happy to enlighten you."

"Pardon my frankness," Earl MacInnes said, "but are you living as husband and wife, or is Miss Bowman staying as your guest?"

"Tula is my guest," Gregory said.

"Does Miss Bowman have a message for her fans?" Charlie Saddler asked.

"Indeed, she does," Gregory said. "Tula is very grateful for her fans' loyalty and well-wishes. The volume of correspondence means that she is unable to answer every letter personally, but I can assure you that she does read your letters and that she cherishes your words of encouragement and support."

"Do you plan to marry Tula?" Dorothy Cooper asked.

"I've popped the question," Gregory said, sounding sheepish, "but the answer is up to Tula."

"When will we hear her answer?" Earl MacInnes asked.

"I'm not sure," Gregory said. "I hope sometime soon."

I sat listening and thinking deeply about my past, present and future. I thought about my father, mother, Greta, and Finn. A lifetime is little more than the blink of an eye. When chances come along, they are often far apart and few in number. When a golden chance comes your way, you must take it.

Slowly but surely, I was coming to accept that I would never fully understand my father, his motivations and actions. I could spend the rest of my life thinking about him. Or I could live.

Something stirred within me. I wanted to live. I wanted to love. I wanted to act in motion pictures. Something compelled me to step on to the patio and join Gregory.

Before I could say a word, the cameras flashed and everyone applauded. I blinked and tried to get the flashbulbs out of my eyes. Then I raised my hands, in somewhat regal fashion, I must confess, to quieten the crowd.

"Thank you for your patience and attention," I said. "In regard to Dorothy Cooper's question about marriage, I feel that I can supply you with an answer. And that answer is 'yes'; I accept Gregory's proposal."

More cheers and flashbulbs greeted my announcement. Dorothy Cooper offered me a quiet smile. She placed her thumb and forefinger together in the shape of a circle and indicated her endorsement. However, I did hear one dissenting voice.

"Please reconsider," Earl MacInnes said, his

balding head glinting in the sunshine, mustard stains evident on his plaid shirt, odd socks visible on his large feet. "I'm still available."

At that, everyone roared with laughter. While they laughed, Gregory and I stepped quietly inside.

"Did you mean that?" Gregory asked, his eyes wide in wonder. "You'll marry me?"

"Yes," I said. "You've been very patient so far, and I ask for continued patience. If you can accept those terms, I'd be delighted to marry you."

Paris

Our wedding ceremony was a quiet affair. Gregory invited his closest friends and family while I invited Archie Bleeker, his wife, Lillian, plus Uwe Winter and his wife, Marlene.

For our honeymoon, we sailed to France, destination, Paris. I was still unsure about myself in regards to spending my nights with Gregory, so we slept in different beds.

I knew that I was trying Gregory's patience, but he offered a great deal of understanding, and the more understanding he offered, the more I fell in love.

The journey was a slow and luxurious one. That was deliberate on our part because it gave me more time to come to terms with my past, and with my new status as Mrs Gregory Powell. Of course, I would remain as Tula Bowman on the silver screen, but in all other aspects of my life, I would be Mrs Gregory Powell.

After three weeks at sea, we docked at Cherbourg and found a crowd waiting.

"Look," I said, my eyes wide in wonder, "all these people, all here to see you."

"These people are here to see you," Gregory said. I frowned and he explained. "Look at the pictures they are holding."

Indeed, on closer inspection I discovered that many members of the crowd were holding up my picture, images taken from studio publicity photographs or magazines. The level of support, the outpouring of goodwill, was overwhelming. My heart filled with joy.

Cameras flashed, reporters ran towards us brandishing microphones, fans swarmed around. Many people offered me flowers.

"They're treating you like a queen," Gregory said.

"But," I said, "but I'm jest a woikin goil from Brooklyn; I ain't nothing special."

"You're from Hollywood now," Gregory said, "and you're the 'Queen of Hollywood'."

With the help of the gendarmes, we made it through the crowd to a waiting taxi. After a long drive along straight roads, we arrived at our hotel in the centre of Paris.

The first week of our honeymoon was a whirlwind of sightseeing, delicious dinners, and theatre performances. We visited the Cathédrale Notre-Dame, the Eiffel Tower and the Louvre Museum. We dined on coq au vin, boeuf bourguignon and chocolate soufflés. We drank copious amounts of champagne. We enjoyed plays written by Jean-Paul Sartre, George Bernard Shaw and William Shakespeare.

I recognised that the style and discipline of theatre acting was totally different to the style and discipline of motion picture acting – the grand gestures of the theatre would look grotesque when magnified by the camera's intense gaze; furthermore, the projection of the voice was also different.

Despite the disparity, I wondered if I could try my hand at acting in a major play. Maybe. That was for the future. Now, along with Gregory, I had so much to enjoy.

On our fourth night, we saw Josephine Baker at the Folies Bergère. Her performance was sensational. Gregory was riveted. As I watched Josephine Baker perform, I felt a mixture of emotions – awe at her amazing talent, and jealousy because she totally captivated Gregory's attention.

Arm-in-arm, Gregory and I walked along the cobbled streets. Neon lights reflected in the puddles within the gutters, street entertainers doffed their caps and sought our patronage, men without legs or arms, victims of the Great War, begged for francs and centimes.

The discrepancy between my position in the world and that of the beggars disturbed me. I wondered if I could make use of my fame in a way that would do good. I resolved to look into that when we returned to Hollywood.

At night, Gregory and I kissed, then retired to our beds. As I placed my head on my pillow, I reflected that this was not right; we were on honeymoon; we should be together. Yet, I did not have the courage to accept Gregory's passionate embrace. If this continued, our marriage would be a disaster. I did not want that. I cried myself to sleep that night as I wondered what I could do to loosen my fear, to release the trauma.

Compared to the days spent in the asylum, I was feeling much better, much stronger, yet I realised that I still had some way to go before my recovery was complete.

After two weeks in Paris, we planned to fly back to Hollywood. I would have preferred a lazy cruise in an elegant ocean liner, but Gregory had business interests and movie projects to attend to; we could not afford another three weeks away.

I sensed that Gregory was becoming restless, and that made me feel agitated; I was beginning to think that our marriage, despite the love we felt for each other, was a mistake.

Gregory sensed my unease. One evening, after dinner, he said, "Why don't you telephone Dr Brooks?"

I considered the time difference between Paris and New York, and worked out that three o'clock in the afternoon, Paris time, would be a good time to contact my doctor. With sweat on my brow and perspiration on my fingers, I made the call.

"How are you, Tula?" Dr Brooks asked.

"Good," I said. "Except, our honeymoon isn't going as planned."

"You were hoping for an emotional miracle, a magic wand."

"Yes," I said. "I guess I was."

"The mind does not work like that," Dr Brooks said.

I nodded into the telephone and replied, "I realise that now."

"I cannot wave a magic wand."

"I know," I said.

"But you can banish this fear."

"How?" I asked. "Please tell me, I want to banish the fear."

"What do you fear?"

"I don't know," I said.

"Physical pain?"

"No," I said. "I know that Gregory would not be like my father; I know that my husband would not hurt me."

"Rejection?"

"No," I said. "I know that Gregory would not reject me."

"Shame?"

"There is no shame in sharing love," I said.

"So," Dr Brooks asked, "what do you fear?"

I thought about that and, even though it was irrational, the answer came to me. "My mother and father's disapproval."

"Your mother and father are no longer with us," Dr Brooks said.

"I know," I said. "I'm aware that my fear does not make sense."

"Your mother disapproved of your motion picture career," Dr Brooks said, "yet you embarked upon that path anyway. You made a great success of your career. You found happiness leading your life in your own way."

"Yes," I said, realisation dawning. "I must let go of the past. I must lead my life in my own way."

I pondered Dr Brooks' words for the remainder of our honeymoon. They became my mantra, morning, noon and night: *Your mother disapproved of your motion picture career, yet you embarked upon that path anyway. You made a great success of your career. You found happiness leading your life in your own way.*

On our final evening in Paris, Gregory said, "Shall we climb to the top of the Eiffel Tower one more time and take in the view of Paris?"

"Yes," I said. "Let's do that."

Atop the Eiffel Tower, we took in the

magnificent vista of the city and its sparkling lights one more time. As Gregory enjoyed the view, I took a step towards the edge of the platform and looked down.

"What are you doing?" Gregory asked, his voice rising in concern.

"Don't worry," I said. "I'm not going to jump."

I unfurled a piece of paper and allowed it to float down on the night breeze. I realised that this was a symbolic gesture, and that the healing process would develop from my own mind. Nevertheless, the action was cathartic and it helped to ease my mind.

"What's on that paper?" Gregory asked, arching an eyebrow.

"It's a letter," I said, "to my past." I stood on tiptoe and kissed Gregory. I hugged him and held him tight. "Now, let us make our way to our room."

"Are you sure?" Gregory asked.

"I'm certain," I said, watching as my letter disappeared from view. "I've let go of my troubled past. Let us embrace our future. Let us take one more special memory away from Paris."

Later that night, with Gregory in my arms, I cried, but my tears were tears of relief, of happiness. And, in the morning, I witnessed a rainbow; I witnessed sunshine after the rain.

Nine months later, I gave birth to our first child, Emrys. Gregory suggested the name, in honour of his grandfather.

I'm twenty-eight now. I've been married two and a half years and I'm pregnant again. My pregnancies have interrupted our filming schedule, but as independent producers, we can adjust the schedules to suit our needs.

The first feature in our light-hearted mystery series was a great critical and commercial success. Dorothy Cooper wrote, *"In 'Just the Facts, Ma'am', Gregory Powell is as solid, dependable and debonair as ever, while Tula Bowman displays a light comedic touch not seen from her before on the silver screen. Her timing is immaculate, her gestures a delight. Moreover, as for her fluttering eyelashes and flirtatious glances, they are enough to give the regulators apoplexy. With this performance, Tula Bowman will attract a new bevy of fans. It's a joy to see her again, acting in motion pictures."*

However, one male critic reckoned that I looked overweight and that during my break, 'I'd gone to seed'. Little did he realise that I was pregnant at the time carrying Emrys.

My favourite review came from James Falk,

because it placed the praise squarely where it belonged, on Gregory's shoulders.

"'Just the Facts, Ma'am' is capitol entertainment. The plot is sound, the dialogue crisp and the direction by Uwe Winter assured. Miss Tula Bowman has never looked better on the silver screen. Her performance was a delight and, in the comedic scenes, her delivery had people, literally, rolling in the aisles. I will reserve my laurels however for Gregory Powell. As the 'straight man' feeding Miss Bowman her comedic lines, he was pitch-perfect. In the past, Miss Bowman and Gregory Powell have demonstrated that they are a winning team, and with 'Just the Facts, Ma'am' they are certain to continue that success."

Over the past two and a half years, I've thought about my parents, a lot. I've come to understand who they were and why they behaved in the manner in which they did.

My mother was not a princess, not in Brooklyn and not in her ancestry. She was a sick woman who did not receive sufficient care, understanding or support. When I think of her now it's with sadness and sympathy.

My father was not an evil man. However, for a period after my mother's death, a demon possessed him and he carried out an act of gross barbarity.

At times, I wondered if I was responsible for provoking that act, but now my mind is settled on the matter and I have dismissed that thought.

In a moment of insanity, my father behaved appallingly. In time, I hope that I can forgive him. However, that moment has not arrived yet.

I trust that I'm a good wife to Gregory. Certainly, to date, he's not raised one word of objection or complaint. In our different ways, we've both suffered, therefore, we're fully aware of what's important in life and that, when you find love, you must cherish it.

I have a successful career, enough money to offer me luxury, a beautiful home, a wonderful husband, a handsome joyful son, and another baby on the way.

Occasionally, I still talk with Dr Brooks on the telephone. During our most recent conversation, he asked me if I was happy. I replied, "My mind is at peace. I am content. I am blissfully happy."

WEB LINKS

For details about Hannah Howe and her books, please visit https://hannah-howe.com

Hannah's Amazon page
https://amazon.com/author/hannah-howe

Hannah's iBooks page
https://itunes.apple.com/us/author/hannah-howe

Social Media https://toot.wales/@HannahHowe

THE SAM SMITH MYSTERY SERIES

The Sam Smith Mystery Series is a character-driven series about private investigator Samantha Smith. The series explores a number of adult themes in a psychological context. These themes include domestic violence, sexual abuse, rape, drug addiction, racism and alcoholism. The books do not contain graphic descriptions of violence. However, they may contain emotional triggers for some people.

The Sam Smith Mystery Series is a detective series centred on emotions, with a touch of humour and romance included to add balance and realism to the various plots. The series has featured in the top twenty book charts in ten countries, including seven separate spells as number one on the Amazon private detective chart. Audio book versions are available and translations are in progress.

EVE'S WAR

Set during 1942-44 and based on true events, *Eve's War* is a series of twelve novellas, approximately 20,000 words each. The series chronicles the life of Eve Beringar, the wife of a successful businessman, who initially is helping the French Resistance in Marseille. As the series progresses, Eve joins the Special Operations Executive. From there, she faces stark choices about love and war.

Audio book versions are available and translations are in progress.

THE ANN'S WAR MYSTERY SERIES

The Ann's War Mystery Series is a series of five novellas set in 1944-5. Each story contains approximately 15,000 words and a complete mystery. The stories are: *Betrayal, Invasion, Blackmail, Escape* and *Victory*. Ann's story arc will evolve over the series and reach its conclusion with book five, *Victory*.

The Ann's War Mystery Series has graced the top five of the historical mysteries chart in America, Australia, Britain and Canada. The series has reached #1 in Australia and #1 on the Amazon mystery, history and literature charts. Audio book versions are available and translations are in progress.

THE OLIVE TREE

Set between April 1937 and December 1938, The Olive Tree is a mini-series of five novellas based on true events.

The stories in The Olive Tree – *Roots, Branches, Leaves, Fruit* and *Flowers* chronicle the lives of Heini Hopkins, a young nurse from an impoverished part of South Wales, and Naomi Parker, a wealthy author from a privileged background.

Audio book versions are available and translations are in progress.

Saving Grace

A Victorian Mystery Based on a True Story

Who poisoned wealthy banker, Charles Petrie? Dr James Collymore, a man familiar with poisons, a man harbouring a dark secret that, if exposed, would ruin his career; Florrie, the maid who supplied Charles with his bedtime drink; Bert Kemp, a disgruntled groom who used poisons in his work, who four months previously had predicted Charles' dying day; Mrs Jennet Quinn, a lady's companion with a deep knowledge of poisons, and a deep fear of dismissal; or Grace Petrie, Charles' wife of four months, a woman with a scandalous past, a woman shunned by polite society.

With crowds flocking to the courtroom and the shadow of suspicion falling upon Grace in the shape of the hangman's noose, could dashing young advocate, Daniel Morgan, save her?

Saving Grace is an official Amazon #1 bestseller. Within the first month of publication, the book reached #1 in Australia and achieved top ten rankings in America, Britain and Canada. An audio book version is available and translations are in progress.

"Fabulous book by a fabulous author – I highly recommended this series!"

"I loved Hannah Howe's writing style — poignant one moment, terrifying the next, funny the next moment. I would be on the edge of my seat praying Sam wouldn't get hurt, and then she'd say a one-liner or think something funny, and I'd chuckle and catch my breath. Love it!"

"Sam's Song is no lightweight suspense book. Howe deals with drugs, spousal abuse, child abuse, and more. While the topics she writes about are heavy, Howe does a fantastic job of giving the reader the brutal truth while showing us there is still good in life and hope for better days to come."

"What's special about Sam's Song? It's well written: accomplished, witty, at times ironical, and economical. A lot of the impact comes from Hannah Howe's ability to achieve effects in a paragraph that many writers spend a page over."

"Sam's Song is more than a standard private detective novel. It has real characters, not stereotypes and it treats those characters with compassion and wit."

"I so enjoyed getting to know Sam Smith, a private investigator with an abundance of wit and compassion."

"In Dr Alan Storey, the author has created a strong male character that is willing to take a step back and support Sam in her career decisions because that's what she needs to grow stronger. I definitely recommend this series."

"I started the series and can't stop going from one book to the next..."

"Hannah Howe is a wizard with the way she creates suspense and intrigue."

"If you love empowered women sleuths, you must read the Sam Smith Mystery Series now."

ABOUT THE AUTHOR

Hannah Howe is the author of the Sam Smith Mystery Series, the Ann's War Mystery Series and various standalone novels. Hannah's books are published by Goylake Publishing and distributed through Gardners Books to over 300 outlets worldwide. Her books are available in print, as eBooks and audio books, and are being translated into numerous languages.

Hannah lives in Glamorgan, Wales with her family. Her interests include reading, music, genealogy, chess and classic black and white movies.

Through her genealogical research, which dates back to 880 AD and Hywel Dda (Howell the Good), Hannah has discovered that she is descended from the noble houses of Wales and Europe. She is also extremely proud of her working class ancestors, many of whom toiled in coal mines, limestone quarries and agricultural fields. She is the sum of all these parts, and all influence her writing.

COMING SOON

Sunshine, book two in the Golden Age of Hollywood Series, plus more Sam Smith mysteries including *Sugar Daddy*, and the latest additions to *Eve's War, Heroines of SOE*.

Further along the line please look out for *Colette, A Schoolteacher's War*, the first novel in a series about women and their involvement in the French Resistance.

You can keep up to date with Hannah's books and latest offers by following her on social media or by reading her weekly newsletter on her website https://hannah-howe.com